HUMAN WISHES / ENEMY COMBATANT

HUMAN
WISHES / ENEMY
COMBATANT

EDMOND CALDWELL

grand
IOTA

Published by
grand**IOTA**

2 Shoreline, St Margaret's Rd, St Leonards TN37 6FB
&
37 Downsway, North Woodingdean, Brighton BN2 6BD

www.grandiota.co.uk

Second edition 2022
First published by Say It With Stones (2012)

Cover photo courtesy of Lynn Bennett
Typesetting & book design by Reality Street
Thanks to David Rose for facilitating this

A catalogue record for this book is available from the British Library

ISBN: 978-1-874400-85-1

for Catherine

All are free to leave,
apart from those who will be detained.

– Orders from the general command
of the Israeli Defense Forces regarding
the townspeople of Lydda, Palestine.
July 12, 1948.

PART I

PART II

PART III

I

Apple Seized

They had just returned to the United States. He thought that the immigration official at the border-control booth had looked at him skeptically when running his passport, even though he was a citizen. Maybe he looked like a terrorist. Fortunately the line had been long and he was passed through with his wife. It helped that she looked more securely like an American, he thought. She had blond hair and an open face. Everything seemed to go easier when she was at his side. They went down the escalator to the baggage claim area. They had their item each of carry-on luggage but had checked their larger bags. Once in the baggage claim area, his wife said that she was tired and went to take a seat on a row of chairs against the nearest wall of the vast room. He hadn't slept well on this trip and should have been more tired than his wife, but he was filled with elation at the thought of being home, where he knew he would be able to sleep again and his bowels would return to normal. But at the far end of the baggage claim area he saw the customs gates and realized that home was still on the other side. They remained in one of those In-Between places that exist only in airports, he thought. It was a place where the use of cell phones and cameras was not permit-ted, a voice from a loudspeaker said. A screen hanging over one of the carousels was already lit up with the number of their flight, and passengers he recognized from the plane were taking up places around the sides of the carousel. The passengers were grouped the thickest where the conveyor belt emerged from the hump in the middle of the carousel and grew thinner and thinner around the sides of the carousel in a counter-clockwise direction up to the final stretch, which had no passengers at all until one returned to the original group. The conveyor belt in the middle and the sloped, interlocking metal plates on the sides were not moving but everyone seemed to know the counter-clockwise direction the luggage would travel, maybe from observing the passengers from other flights around their respective carousels, he reasoned. He inserted himself about halfway between the hole in the hump where the conveyor belt emerged and the nearest curve of the carousel itself, just a few yards after that end turned into the long straightaway before the opposite curve down at the far end. The only shortcoming was that the conveyor belt would convey the baggage over the opposite edge of the hump. He would be able to see their luggage items emerge on the belt from the hole in the middle but then they would disappear until the metal plates carried them around the curve. It wasn't a bad position but not a very good one either, he decided, but he immediately grew protective of it. There were still other passengers looking for places around the carousel, and many of these, instead of going down to the sparsely-populated end where they would have to wait longer for their luggage, loitered behind the front rank of passengers down at his end, poised to plunge in if they saw their bags and temporarily displace those in the front rank. But what if they misidentified a bag as their own – he'd seen this happen often enough – and after releasing it back onto the carousel they remained in the front rank, out of which they had displaced someone such as himself who had been there first? It might even be possible for someone to *pretend* to misidentify a bag in order to plunge into the front rank. He set his item of carry-on luggage down beside him, leaning it against his calf so that he could be reassured of its presence without having to take his eyes from the carousel. He propped the other foot up on the edge of carousel, then saw that nobody else was doing this and took his foot down. It seemed to be taking a long time for the bags to emerge. He squatted to take some stress off his legs, then stood up again. Nobody else had been squatting at that moment. Finally he noticed a woman further along the straightaway sit down on the carousel rim. Her back was to the central hump and her buttocks drooped over the rim. The woman was in the exact position that she would be in if she were going to take a dump on the carousel, he thought. He wondered if anybody else had the same thought. He felt briefly embarrassed at having had the thought himself, and imagined protesting, with a gesture at the woman's seated figure, that it had been inescapable. He turned away and looked for the attractive passenger he'd seen on the plane, hoping maybe to catch her eye. He knew he looked rumpled and unshaven, but he thought he might also look exotic and attractive in a world-weary way, at least for a man of his age. He had gotten some sun on the trip. Of course she would have to be into men of his age. But probably he looked like a Middle Eastern terrorist instead of a Mediterranean lover. It didn't matter because he couldn't locate the attractive passenger among those at the carousel. Perhaps, like his wife, she was resting somewhere while a male partner fetched the bags, although it had been his impression that she was traveling solo. He could see his wife, however, if he raised himself onto his toes. There she was with her Mac open on her lap. She had to be back at work early the next morning. He saw his wife set her laptop onto the vacant seat to her right and begin to take her sweater off. It had been cold on the plane when she'd put the sweater on. They had been in their seats – unfortunately the middle seats of the center aisle – so he'd had to help tug the sweater down her back, he remembered. Now his wife was on a different set of seats, against one wall of the baggage claim area instead of in the center aisle of the plane, and she wanted to take the sweater off. The seat on the other side of his wife was occupied by an older woman who leaned away so that she wouldn't be struck by flailing elbows as his wife struggled with the sweater over her head. As the sweater came up, the blouse beneath clung to it and his wife's midriff and even the cups of her brassiere were bared. He thought that the older woman in the next seat had an expression of disapproval on her face, although at this distance he couldn't tell for sure. Maybe she would have a better opinion of his wife when the blond hair and open face re-emerged. A high-pitched noise came from somewhere and went on for a long time. It was loud enough that a few people put their hands over their ears. He thought at first that it was the siren to announce the activation of their carousel, but the light which was supposed to accompany that siren did not light up and the conveyor belt did not move. Finally the high-pitched noise stopped. He thought of a joke he would have liked to make aloud: *They always unload the high-pitched noises first.* He wished his wife were at his side so that he could make the joke. She might have appreciated it, although more likely it would not have registered. The joke would not have registered because the high-pitched noise which had been the joke's occasion would not have registered, he understood. His wife had been concentrating for the last few days on updating the PowerPoint slides for her lectures, and even if the laptop had been closed and stowed away in her item of carry-on luggage the file would still have been open in her mind. Her powers of concentration were such that she could repel with an unconscious facial twitch a noise loud enough to make other people put their hands over their ears. But her presence would at least have provided a pretext for saying his joke aloud, so that other passengers nearby might overhear it and laugh. The man on his left or the couple on his right, for instance, he considered, might laugh. In his mind he tried out several variations of the wording of the joke, to get it just right. He glanced sidelong at the woman member of the couple on his right and wondered if to her he might look more foreign than American. If he opened his mouth for the joke he would clearly identify himself as American, but it was too late now for the joke to sound spontaneous. It had to sound spontaneous to be an example of actual wit. He ran his fingers over the stubble on his upper lip and around his chin. He found it more stimulating to stroke the stubble against the grain. Having stubble made him feel unwashed, or – since he always felt unwashed after a flight – extra-un-washed, and like people looked at him with suspicion. He was certain the passport-control agent had looked at him with suspicion. He was almost certain. There was a different noise, still loud but more like a honk than a whine, and the light over their carousel began to revolve. There was a shud-der and a jolt from somewhere underneath the central hump and the conveyor belt began moving, and the large interlocking metal plates which made up the surface of the carousel itself began moving. He was looking at the large interlocking metal plates and noticing the shearing sound they made as they moved together and apart but he had the ambient sense of a general reorganization of attitudes and postures among the group surrounding the carousel, of which he was a part. Down the hump to his right he could see the first bags emerge on the conveyor belt. He lost sight of the bags when they tumbled down on the other side of the hump, but the bags re-emerged eventually around the curve to his left and made their way on the large metal plates in his direction. It was just as he had visualized to himself some moments ago. He had the illusion that the carousel speeded up the closer the luggage got to him, going fastest right as the bags passed within reach. He remembered this illusion from past experiences at baggage-claim carousels, and he experienced it again on this occasion as his wife's bag approached. He had missed the bag coming out of the hump onto the conveyor belt but spotted it as soon as it appeared around the bend of the carousel, between several other luggage items. His wife's bag had a distinctive appearance, somewhat like a large athletic sneaker, he thought. He counted that it was the fourth bag out. As his wife's distinctive item of luggage approached it seemed to speed up, and he became acutely conscious not only of the accelerating luggage item but of his own physical separateness. Both feelings intensified with each second it took for the bag to get to him. Then there was a brief frenzy of motion and the task was achieved. He had grabbed the side-handle of the bag and lifted it out and set it behind him on the other side of the carousel rim. He was pleased that he had done it one-handed and without audible grunts. He looked around and spotted the attractive passenger he had been unable to locate earlier. She was the same woman who had been sitting on the edge of the carousel in the position of a person about to take a dump, he realized. He returned his attention to his wife's distinctive luggage item, pressing a button on a different handle and extending it to its full length until he felt it click. He could reach behind him to touch the handle and assure himself that his wife's bag was still there even as he continued to scout the carousel for his own item of checked luggage. His carry-on bag was no longer leaning against his calf, however. It must have been displaced in the brief frenzy of motion, he reasoned. But it was easy enough to confirm the bag's presence with a sideways motion of his toe. The successful and grunt-free extraction of his wife's luggage item from the carousel had left him feeling more secure about his mastery of the immediate terrain. Moreover nobody had tried to plunge into the front rank and displace him. He scouted for his luggage item among the bags that passed before him on the interlocking metal plates and from time to time craned for a better glimpse of the bags emerging on the conveyor belt from the hole in the hump. There was a high likelihood that his luggage item was imminent, because it had probably accompanied his wife's item into the plane, and his wife's item had already come out, he reasoned. The flat surface of the hump in the middle of the carousel was orange and one of the few things in the vast baggage claim area that had any color to it. Or one of the few things fixed permanently, he revised, unlike the passengers with their luggage items, who came and went and were occasionally colorful. Still his luggage item did not appear. No, he thought, reconsidering his earlier thought, if his wife's bag had been almost the first item out, his would surely be the last. For a while no new luggage emerged on the conveyor belt, and he wondered if anyone had misappropriated his item. It was black and rectangular; he could distinguish it from similar bags only by certain details of make and wear which to him were intimately recognizable but, he knew, subtle. But most of the passengers remained poised around the rim of the carousel, inspecting the same offerings of luggage and casting the same unrequited glances at the hole in the central hump. His bag no longer seemed imminent. He turned to look at a group of flight attendants passing between his carousel and the one behind him. He turned from the waist, keeping his feet planted so that his toes still faced the carousel, to maintain his spot. Each attendant pulled a compact bag on rollers behind her. They made up a larger contingent than would be needed for a single flight, he thought. Maybe they weren't flight attendants at all but a cadet corps of female pilots. They wore identical uniforms of white blouses and black skirts and jackets, with small black caps. They all had blond or lightish brown hair and spoke in high voices in a language he couldn't understand, and all of them were more or less pretty – probably prettier for being all together like that, he thought. He imagined them as a flock of birds swooping past. He turned back and was trying to think what kind of bird when he saw a woman in a different kind of uniform moving among the passengers on the other side of the carousel with a dog on a leash. The dog was sniffing at the luggage and sometimes it looked like the woman was leading the dog and sometimes it looked like the dog was leading the woman. Everyone was looking at the dog now. It looked like a beagle instead of a large dog like a German shepherd, which was the kind of dog he associated with police activities involving dogs. And yet he assumed that the dog was sniffing for signs of drugs or bombs. And yet everyone looked at the dog light-heartedly, because it was a small- or medium-sized dog like a beagle and because it was a woman on the other end of the leash. The woman was small- or medium-sized as well, light-boned and with light-brown hair cut in a bob, or something to his eyes a little longer than a bob but not yet shoulder-length. Her uniform was blue pants and white shirt. She and the dog moved in and out of the crowd and she spoke to the dog in low encouraging sounds. The dog's nose went right and left and the dog's tail went left and right. One or two sniffs was all the dog needed. Several children looked like they wanted to pet the dog; he wondered if the woman in the uniform had to warn them off, like a blind person if someone accosted their seeing-eye dog. He could see her lips move. *Working dog! Working dog!* she might be saying. Even small amounts of non-work interaction could weaken the training of a working dog, he thought. More luggage items were finally emerging on the conveyor belt and the passengers turned their attention to the new selection while the woman in the uniform and the dog moved off to the other carousels. Among the new items he still did not see his own. He reasoned that a transatlantic flight had many passengers, and therefore many items. He calculated that since only a third or so of the people had gotten their items it was too early to begin worrying. He propped a foot up on the edge of carousel, then saw that nobody else was doing this and took his foot down. He wondered who the items belonged to that just kept going around and around. He squatted to take some stress off his legs, then stood up again. Nobody else had been squatting at that moment. If he raised himself onto his toes he could still see his wife. There she was with her open face bent over her open laptop. It was not too early to feel irritated with her. He had her item of checked luggage already but still there was no sign of his item. They remained in one of those In-Between places that exist only in airports, he thought. But no, there were other, similar kinds of In-Between places, he revised. There were hotels, and especially airport hotels. There were highway rest stops. There were the spaces of shopping malls, including the food courts, and the more confined spaces of supermax prisons. He ran his fingers over the stubble on his upper lip and around his chin. He stroked the stubble against the grain and felt stimulated and unwashed and under suspicion. The carousels were like the rotors of a giant electric shaver, he thought. All he had to do was fall to his knees and place his breast on the rim of the carousel and lower his chin towards the large interlocking metal plates which made a shearing sound as they moved together and apart. He had an ambient sense of the people around him turning to look the other way and he turned to look, too. The woman in the blue and white uniform and the beagle-like dog were back, this time on his side of the carousel. The dog sniffed bags and shoes, nose going right and left, tail going left and right. One or two sniffs was all the dog needed. The leash went taut and slack, and taut and slack, as first the dog led, and then the woman. Everyone watched in a light-hearted way, although less light-hearted now that they were so close. The dog sniffed his wife's luggage item that resembled an athletic sneaker – one sniff, two sniffs. The dog sniffed his carry-on item that was by his feet – one sniff, two sniffs. Three sniffs, four sniffs. The woman with the leash said, What have you got there? He didn't know if the woman was addressing him or the dog. He said, Just magazines, a book. The woman gave a tug on the leash to see if the dog would be led away or come back. The dog came back. Five, six sniffs. He was looking at the dog sniffing his bag but he had the ambient sense of a general reorganization of attitudes and postures of the group around him, of which he was no longer a part. The woman said, Do you have anything in there that you did not declare on your customs form? Do you have any food or other items you purchased outside of the country? He shook his head and said no. Then he said, I don't think so. He was acutely conscious not only of the dog and his bag but of himself, and he became more acutely conscious the more the dog sniffed. He bowed and unzipped the front pocket of his bag to show inside. The dog and the woman were not interested in the magazines and the book. He unsealed the velcro strip of another pouch where there was a plastic water bottle, a poorly folded map, a rusted tin pastille case with a rubber-band around it, and an apple. The dog and the woman were interested in the apple. The dog sniffed and looked back and forth at the woman and twisted its rump and the woman said, There it is, that's it. The apple was yellowish-green with orange flecks and not very large. He handed out the apple to the woman. He rose and heard murmurs and possible laughter from the passengers around him at whom he did not look. The woman patted the dog and praised the dog in a sing-song that was higher pitched than the voice in which she had asked him about the items in his bag. The woman rose and said, Do you have the blue and white customs form you filled out on the plane? He fished the blue and white customs form he had filled out on the plane out of the front zipper pocket of his bag and handed it to the woman. She had the leash on her wrist and she lifted her knee to prop the form while she made a few quick strokes with a red felt-tipped marker. She had made the fruit item vanish. It was very difficult to concentrate on anything in particular. There was still a chance he might be taken to a separate room and asked questions, he thought. He wondered, Who would claim his bag? Who would alert his wife? Without looking he had a sense of everyone watching. The woman in the uniform gave him back the form and pointed to the far end of the room. She said, You have to show that to the man at the gate. He looked at what she had written on the form, a combination of red letters and numerals and then the red words: Apple Seized.

Return to the Chateau

The hill on which the hotel stood was like an island, except instead of the sea it was surrounded by tarmac. There was the little tarmac of the motorways and the big tarmac of the runways of the Charles de Gaulle Airport, and like the sea there was hissing and roaring, audible from this distance, among the hotels on the hill. If he shut the window he couldn't hear the hissing and roaring because the windows were treble-paned, probably for just this purpose, he reasoned. The small hotel room felt entirely self-contained, like a pressurized cabin. But the thought of a pressurized cabin caused him to experience anxiety, so he opened the window again and let in the sound of the tarmac-surf. Or rather, the thought had caused him to experience a spike in the anxiety that was already there, he revised. There was nothing to do now but relax for the next twenty-four hours but still he felt anxious, even restless. He was tired and characteristically he napped in the late afternoons, and his wife had discreetly left him alone in the hotel room for just this purpose, he reasoned. In part so that he could nap but also because there was rumored to be free wireless the next hotel over, he revised. From the window he watched his wife cross the looping driveway that looped in front of their hotel, the second of three hotels facing the loop, carrying the satchel that held her laptop. There was another hotel further up the hill and another hotel back down the hill, five hill-hotels in all by his count, connected by a system of looping and sloping driveways along which shuttle-buses appeared regularly to travel, many shuttle-buses and no automobiles. There were parking spaces available in lots behind the five hotels on the hill but he had seen almost no automobiles in the spaces, he recalled. A constituent of the hissing and roaring traffic-surf was from automobiles on the roadways, to his mind a distinct constituent, and yet only shuttle-buses washed ashore here, as the waves of the jets broke overhead. Thus there was something peculiar about this complex of hill hotels, this *insular* complex figuratively speaking, something to be gotten to the bottom of, the bottom of the peculiar thing not the bottom of the hill, making a total of two figurative expressions. With or without the window open the pressurized cabin-like quality of the small hotel room was having a dehydrating effect on his sinuses. He watched as his wife waited at the far curb of the grassy meridian in the middle of the loop for a shuttle-bus to pass, she had made it to the far curb of the meridian but not all the way across the loop before the bus had pulled out and now she had briefly to wait, her hand on the satchel that held her laptop, she held it against her canted hip even though the strap of the satchel was slung on her shoulder. Even from this distance he could see that she stood with her hip canted in that way she characteristically stood, a way that he liked, and the shadow of the hotel was at her feet on the trimmed lawn of the meridian, and the sun glinted off her sunglasses and gleamed on her bare shoulder next to the satchel strap, waiting for the shuttle-bus to rumble by she looked more relaxed than he felt, even from this distance relaxed yet poised there at the edge of the central meridian with her open-toed shoes in the shadow of the hotel. Another shuttle-bus had already pulled into the loop but it was stopping in front of the first hotel, whereas his wife was heading for the third hotel. With her laptop satchel she went into the entrance of the third hotel as the people from the shuttle-bus began moving with their luggage to the entrance of the first hotel. The shuttle-buses brought a steady stream of passengers from the Charles de Gaulle airport who had been bumped from their flights, along with the smaller number of those who had volunteered to take other flights, he reasoned. After his wife had disappeared with her laptop-satchel into the third hotel he had retreated from the window to the hotel bed, from window to bed in this small hotel room the hardly Napoleonic retreat of a single step, where he reclined on the bedspread and continued to reason. He reclined with his left forearm over his eyes and over the bridge of his nose beneath which the dehydrated chambers of his sinuses made him think of the shell of a dead nautilus, and his heels dangled off the end of the mattress. Even though he was not especially tall he felt his heels dangling off the end of the small bed, and behind his left forearm and closed eyes and the chambers of his dead nautilus he continued to reason about the people decanted from the shuttle-bus, as tired as he was he could not help continuing to reason, restlessly to reason. His reasoning was based on his own experience of having been bumped from his Air France flight that very morning. It was the first time he had ever been bumped from a flight but now he saw that it was a general practice, and that this island of hotels was specifically for the people who had been bumped, because many other people and not just he and his wife had been bumped. And were being bumped, and were to be bumped. He was part of a general condition of overbooking and bumping and thus should not take it personally, he reasoned. Various far-flung international destinations were waiting for all of these people being decanted from the shuttle-buses, and they would have to wait now a while longer, because they had all been bumped. People who had purchased tickets for their Air France flights to the United

States and to other destinations had been overbooked and bumped, as had people who had purchased tickets and who expected to take their reserved seats on Aer Lingus flights and Air Comet flights, and Aeroflot and Aeroméxico and Lufthansa flights, to say nothing of Blue 1 to Helsinki and Daallo Airlines to Djibouti and El Al to Tel Aviv and Royal Air Maroc to Casablanca, all of whose jets he had seen through the shuttle-bus window as it looped through the terminals of the Charles de Gaulle international airport, but chiefly the flights of Air France, which at the Charles de Gaulle international airport in Roissy-en-France, a mere ten kilometers from the capital Paris, had necessarily to be the chief offender hereabouts in this business of overbooking and bumping, it was Air France they had paid for the privilege of being herded into cramped and it now turned out only provisionally reserved seats, seats every year getting smaller and smaller and crammed closer together inside the narrow metal tubes which at any moment could drop out of the sky or burst into flames in midair or be plunged screaming into the hearts of tall buildings, like sheep they were herded into the metal tubes and there kenneled like dogs in the cramped hulls for hours, breathing recycled air full of virulent germs and waiting passively to plunge out of the sky after being forced to listen to the droll mandatory comedy routine of how to buckle and unbuckle the seatbelts and locate the emergency flotation devices. For this purpose and privilege he and his wife had long ago purchased their tickets and that very morning left their quaint hotel near the Gare de Lyon where the stairwell smelled of dog pee and the concierge had a large strawberry birthmark on her face and boarded the Roissy-bus to arrive at the Air France check-in counter in Terminal 2 E of the Charles de Gaulle airport in plenty of time to be greeted by the smiling Air France counter person who handed them boarding passes that said "Standby." At the gate they had the pleasure of mingling with the dozen or so other passengers who had also received boarding passes that said "Standby" and who were occupying themselves in the meantime by displaying the gamut of human disgruntlement from stoicism to sulking to tantrum, in which he took his place somewhere in the middle. His wife however was wholly off the scale, unaccountably delighted by the prospect of a twenty-four-hour extension of their holiday, a free night in a hotel, meal vouchers, guaranteed seats on a flight the next day, and six hundred Euros apiece for their troubles. Instead of being herded into the large metal tube of the Air France jet they had been herded into the smaller metal tube of the Air France shuttle-bus which shuttled them over a large number of looping roadways, unless it was a single roadway comprised of a large number of loops, going from one loop to another loop and from larger loops to smaller loops, and changing lanes within loops, until it had looped eventually up the side of a small hill crowned with five large hotels heralded by a large sign which he was able to read: Zone Hôtelière. In ascending order among the slopes and loops were the Novotel Roissy, the Suitehotel Roissy, the Château Roissy, the Kryiad Prestige Hotel Roissy-en-France, and the Millennium Hotel Roissy-Paris Charles de Gaulle, and although they all wore the appearance of generic airport hotels he thought, as he reasoned now in his room at the Château Roissy, that he had been able to distinguish in the subtle differences of name and situation and view and appointment among them the tokens of invidious distinction, such that where one was dumped for the night depended on whether one bore a coach class, a business class, or a first-class ticket, with special accommodations in addition perhaps for the Club 2000 and the Frequence Plus Rouge passengers, and thus while he was pleased that their shuttle-bus had not delivered them to the Novotel Roissy he was galled that it had not delivered them to the Millennium Hotel Roissy-Paris Charles de Gaulle. But such was life. They had been herded into the crowded lobby of the Château Roissy and after finally securing their small room they had taken their meal vouchers to wait in the crowded lobby until they could be herded into the crowded restaurant, which turned out to be a buffet-style cafeteria where he had gorged himself on the food items, in part compulsively because buffet-style cafeterias always made him anxious and in part deliberately in the hope of finding himself stunned into a post-prandial coma back in their room. And in spite of the variety the food items had all tasted the same, as if behind the scenes in the kitchen these items had all been prepared out of a single mix, bags of mix were delivered each morning to the hotel out which various shapes of foods were molded and dyed and sent out to the buffet-style cafeteria in the form of baguettes and mushroom and cheese omelets and melon wedges which as soon as one chewed and swallowed reverted heavily in one's stomach back to the original mix, there to wait in its original indigestible sameness for a slow peristalsis to transmit its bulk through one's intestinal loops to the hotel's plumbing, and from thence to the Seine. The hotel's so-called restaurant was really just a buffet-style cafeteria which did not appear set up even to handle regular paying customers but only bumped passengers with meal vouchers, which only went to prove definitively that this insular and generic Zone Hôtelière on the hill existed solely to service the overbooked and bumped, to process them in droves. Nobody, nobody would come to these hotels otherwise. Except for a stray motorist perhaps or someone on a layover nobody in their right minds would ever allow themselves to be brought to this island, save those who were bumped. It was cheaper to give everybody a hotel room and meal vouchers and transportation on the shuttles than to stop overbooking the flights, clearly. Or perhaps the over-booking and bumping was going on solely to service these hotels, to keep them fed with warm irate bodies, even though Air France had to pay for everything the airline exis-ted solely now and at a massive financial loss to keep this mechanism on the hill functioning. Nobody ever said such things had to be rational, he reasoned. Or rather, lots of people said they had to be rational, and even demonstrated in the newspapers and magazines and on news shows that they were indeed rational, but these were the apologists of a larger insanity. The small hotel room was aggressively clean and orderly and functional, in its aggressively minimal way. Every hotel room was a simulacrum of a real room, but the rooms in these special hotels for the routinely overbooked and bumped were clearly *the simulacra of hotel rooms*, i.e. the simulacra of simulacra. Everything in the room was sheathed in shininess, he observed when he removed his arm and blinked open his eyes. Everything was sheathed in shininess as if laminated, as if on their departure all that need be done to clean the room and prepare it for the next guests would be to hose it down. Nobody who was not insane would ever stay in such a place unless it was by acci-dent, he now understood, or unless they had been over-booked and bumped. Even as he shut his eyes and rested his left forearm over them again he had the feeling of lamina-tion, which the sound of the tarmac-surf through the open window did nothing to dispel, the insides of his sinuses now felt thoroughly laminated, and if he continued to breathe the insides of his lungs would become laminated too, he would die unless he held his breath, in which case he would die too and be left with the lump of food-mix in his intest-ines to be hosed down the drain the next morning. Beneath the laminated carpet on the floor of each room was a drain. To forestall a condition of complete lamination he decided to go for a walk. By the time he had crossed the grassy central meridian of the driveway loop in front of their hotel he could see his wife in the lobby of the next hotel along the loop, the Kryiad Prestige Hotel Roissy-en-France. Through the window of the lobby he could see her seated figure hunched over the computer on her lap, fingering the keyboard with one hand and sipping from a vending-machine cappuccino in the other. They had free wireless in the the the Kryiad Prestige Hotel Roissy-en-France but not in the Château Roissy, another proof of invidious distinction, as if one were needed, but at least they did not disturb his Château-Roissy wife in her use of the Kryiad Prestige Hotel Roissy-en-France free wireless. His wife had an open face and a large smile which were unmistakably American but which were so large and open that she generally got away with whatever she wanted to get away with, in the U.S. and elsewhere, whereas he possessed a large nose and a somewhat swarthy complexion and a heavy five-o'clock shadow even minutes after he'd shaved such that he was universally regarded with suspicion, he suspected. Shuttle-buses churned by in both directions as he hiked up the roadway past the invidiously-appointed Millennium Hotel Roissy-Paris Charles de Gaulle and turned on a gravel path which took him up to the top of the hill. On top of the hill was a park with gravel paths and benches amid level and gently sloping lawns of evenly green grass and groups of trees whose names he did not know and bordered plots of flowers he could not name, geometrically laid out in the style of French gardens and bathed in a laminated sunniness of June from a sky streaked here and there with clouds of that type which appear in streaks, unless of course they were rather the relaxing contrails of crisscrossing jets. And from the top of the hill and spread out around it in the form of a vista or a panorama, such that in relation to it the spot where he stood became a prospect, the viewer necessary to establish such a relation (linguistic as much as geographical) of prospect-and-panorama could behold in swatches of green and gold receding to the smudge of the horizon the broad fertile plain of the *Pays de France*. This prospect held the prospect of being an even better prospect if the viewer were to stray off the gravel path for some meters through the grass in the direction of a precipice at the edge of the hilltop. From the better prospect of the precipice he strained to catch a glimpse of the banlieues in the distance, he wanted to see the banlieues and he had not seen them from the Roissy-bus on the way out of Paris to the Charles de Gaulle airport, the notorious banlieues which the French youth of North African and Middle Eastern descent had so recently set aflame, the banlieues were deliberately kept out of the way and cordoned off from places that international tourists and right-thinking Europeans were likely to travel, perhaps in the smudge of the horizon he would just be able to descry these notorious banlieues, the smudge itself a sign they still smoldered. But from this better prospect he could also better perceive how the big tarmac of the runways of the Charles de Gaulle airport and the little tarmac of the roadways made of this hill an island of sorts, cutting him off and in fact stranding him from the alluring expanse of the *Pays de France*. This Zone Hôtelière turned out to be just another cordoned-off island like the banlieues, albeit for a higher-paying brand of castaway. He became aware again of the condition of lamination, of the almost complete lamination of his sinuses and the incipient but advancing lamination of his gorge, his windpipe, and his lungs, which threatened to bring him into a harmony with the external lamination of the Zone Hôtelière that would necessarily entail his complete annihilation by the time it reached his brain. Out in the green and gold swatches of the *Pays de France* or back in Paris it might have been possible to escape this condition of lamination, but here on the island of hill-hotels it was inescapable, this condition of lamination in which the park was implicated as much as the invidious hotels. He turned to make his way from the prospect back to the gravel path in the hope of finding perhaps something to combat or at least counter this advancing condition of total annihilation, of annihilation by lamination, the village of Roissy was supposed to be on the other side of the hill and perhaps it would offer something to combat or at least counter this condition, either antidote or talisman. But as he turned he stumbled, and when he regained his balance he stumbled again, twisting first one ankle and then the other. It appeared there were holes in the grass of the lawn, there were burrows of some kind in the soil beneath the grass, and now as he staggered carefully back to the gravel path he saw so many of these holes that he wondered how he had escaped twisting his ankles on his way out to the prospect. The holes beneath the grass were clearly not for sport or a game such as golf, he could never tell whether golf was a sport or a game, nor were they drains such as those concealed beneath the laminated carpets of the small rooms back in the Château Roissy, they were evidently burrows of some kind, a theory which received immediate and even decisive confirmation by the emergence of a rabbit some meters ahead, the rabbit whisked away across the lawn but its ears and the white flash of its tail had been unmistakable, as had the overall hopping gait produced by the motions of its large haunches and feet. Nor was this an isolated incident, for now he saw himself surrounded by rabbits just as he knew himself to be surrounded by ankle-twisting burrows. In fact there were so many rabbits nibbling or whisking about in the range of his vision that as soon as he thought he had counted them all he saw a new rabbit and lost his count, unless it was a previous rabbit which had shifted to a new location as he had been counting a different rabbit in a different location, it was too hard to tell, he concluded that there was an uncountable number of rabbits, certainly more rabbits than people because except for him and the rabbits the park was completely empty, they were all back in their rooms nursing their ankle sprains with complimentary ice from the hotel ice machines. And meanwhile the rabbits were burrowing away, hollowing out the hill underneath the loops of the roadways with the loops of their rabbit warren, the loops of the rabbit warren under the loops of the road-way under the criss-cross contrails of the Air France jets. The rabbits reproduced in a geometric progression, their population did not advance by addition but by explosion, a metastasizing of the rabbit-kind into a rabbit horde, wave upon wave of rabbits spilling out over the tarmac of the roadways and the Charles de Gaulle airport runways, and thence to the fertile farmlands of the *Pays de France*. His only hope of escaping the Zone Hôtelière island was by shuttle-bus, whereas the rabbit horde had simply to charge across the tarmac to make their escape, and even if they did not wish to make their escape in this manner they would be pushed to it by the exploding rabbit population behind them. There were seasons when the automobiles and the shuttle-buses on the roadways skidded and slid on the bod-ies of all the rabbits they ran over, so much rabbit blood on the tarmac that the automobiles and the shuttle-buses were in danger of hydroplaning, or in this case hemoplaning, multiple-car pile-ups were a real danger in the season of the rabbit horde, and worse was the appearance of the rabbits in droves on the runways of the Charles de Gaulle airport, at times an unbroken carpet of rabbits receding to the smudge of the horizon, like all of those birds surrounding the house in the final scene of Alfred Hitchcock's *The Birds*, except in this case rabbits. And even a far fewer number of rabbits could be a danger to the landing gear of the Air France flights such as the one he hoped to depart on tomorrow should he succeed in escaping the Zone Hôtelière, mowing down a few of these rabbits could completely gum up the works of an aircraft's landing gear, so that even if it managed to make it off the runway of the Charles de Gaulle airport in Roissy, France, it was still in grave danger of sliding off the short runways of Logan Airport and plunging into Boston Harbor, the aircraft would sink with everyone aboard trying to shriek their last words into their cell phones while clawing to be the first out of the emergency exits, the whole affair casting his dismissive attitude re: the location and operation of the plane's flotation devices in an ironic light. Therefore it was necessary at regular intervals to exterminate the rabbits, to visit upon the rabbits a mass extermination of some kind, in which the environs of the Charles de Gaulle airport and especially the grounds of the Zone Hôtelière had to be put under a temporary quarantine and divided into quadrants so that the mass extermination could proceed in an orderly fashion, a phalanx of exterminators in Charles de Gaulle Airport vests with the distinctive Frutiger sans serif typeface on the badges had to line up at one end of the quadrant and plug explosives into the burrows to blow the rabbits up and release weasels into the burrows to hunt them down and pump poison gas from hoses to choke the remaining rabbits and water from still other hoses to drown them in their burrows, and those who were flushed out at the other end were met by guns and dogs, at the other end of the quadrant an orgy of gunfire and ravening fangs awaited all the terrified rabbits who had managed to survive the flames, the gas, the water, and the weasels. It was a dreadful prospect, and he wished he could side with the rabbits, in the ordinary course of things his sympathies were all with the rabbits, but his fear of flying or more precisely of crashing was so great that in this instance he had to side with the victors, against his own better nature he identified with the exterminators, in fact he even felt a little of the victor's exultation at the extermination of the threat posed by the rabbit horde, which he knew and even exulted meant the extermination of the rabbits themselves, like blood in his mouth he could taste it, it even checked for a moment the feeling of the creeping lamination of his gorge brought on by the overall lamination of the Zone Hôtelière. He understood now why the French ate rabbit, it was the traditional ritual of the victor over the vanquished, the exultation of the victor's bloodlust, it was part of the French people's unceasing war with rabbit-kind for predominance over the rich lands of the *Pays de France*, and perhaps this also explained why the French people ate frogs, because frogs too could creep out en masse onto the runways of the Charles de Gaulle airport to clog the landing gear of jetliners and cause fiery crashes, it might even explain the taste for snails, which produce a dangerous slick when flattened en masse, although none of this explained why the French ate horses, it was simply impossible to imagine that such a danger existed from horses. Another theory would be required to explain why the French ate horses. He had not after all developed a Unified Field Theory of the peculiarities of the French diet. Nonetheless he felt an improvement in his condition as he crossed the park and headed downslope beneath the boughs of the trees whose names he did not know and past bordered plots of flowers he could not name in the direction of a village whose name he knew: Roissy. He knew the name of the village because he had seen it on the map in the guidebook and again on a small brochure they had given his wife at the hotel along with their programmed room key-cards, the key-cards tucked into a slit or pocket in the brochure, but he also knew it because of a literary association, it occurred to him only at that moment as the lamination receded somewhat in his gorge that the name Roissy possessed a literary resonance, and that it was in fact the purported location of the notorious chateau in Pauline Réage's notorious novel *Histoire d'O*, Pauline Réage aka Dominique Aury aka Anne Desclos the mousy bisexual Gallimard editor who wished desperately to secure the attentions of her wayward lover the *Academie Francaise* writer Jean Paulhan, a love-offering from a supplicant which managed to trump its object even as it secured his attention, with its international fame and impressive sales in the long run it trumped the reputation of Jean Paulhan, from the love-supplicant this palpable literary masterstroke. This came to him right as he stopped to urinate behind one of the trees he could not name but which was in fact a poplar, poplars and plane trees are two of the types of trees named in the novel *Histoire d'O*, he urinated behind a poplar into a flowerbed containing asters, a flower also named in the novel, stripping off purple petals with the stream of his urine while turning his head almost 180 degrees in each direction, first almost 180 degrees in the left direction and then almost 180 degrees in the right direction, like an owl he turned his head almost all the way around on the lookout for the local gendarmerie, in spite of the creeping lamination he was still able to rotate his head like someone impersonating an owl, blinking his eyes on the lookout for those enforcers of creeping lamination the gendarmerie, perhaps because the idea of punishment was in his mind at that moment he remembered the novel *Histoire d'O* and its literary association with the village of Roissy, and his penis tingled as he shook the last droplets off and secured it again in his trousers. Once his penis was secured and he was no longer in immediate danger from the local gendarmerie he was at liberty to speculate that he might be able to locate a house which had served as the prototype for the novel's notorious chateau, because the French were not prudes like the Anglo-Saxons perhaps they had seen fit to dignify this prototype with a commemorative plaque in several languages, perhaps after all there would be a point of interest here, a point of interest to redeem his stay in the Zone Hôtelière which was laminated inside and out and threatened to laminate him inside and out so that instead of escaping on the shuttle-bus the next morning to his ostensibly-reserved seat on an Air France jetliner to Logan Airport in Boston he would simply be hosed down the drain concealed under the laminated carpet of his small hotel room with the heavy bulk of the food-mix he had consumed the previous day still coiled in his intestinal loops, the bored harried Ukrainian housekeeper would roll back the laminated carpet to hose his thoroughly-laminated mass into the plumbing system, in the U.S. the hotel housekeepers were all Latinas whereas in Western Europe they were all Russian or Ukrainian or Byelorussian, the second world was becoming the third world, although in the U.S. and Western Europe alike the housekeepers were harried and bored, it was important to add that whatever their race or ethnicity or national origins the hotel housekeepers everywhere on the planet were harried and bored. Would the housekeepers be less harried and bored, he wondered, than the Slavic housekeepers of Western Europe and the Latina housekeepers of the United States, would they like it better if they were spirited off to an infamous chateau by their lovers where they could instead become the BDSM prostitutes of a secret male society, although if he remembered correctly the BDSM prostitutes in *Histoire d'O* still had domestic chores to fulfill at the chateau along with their BDSM duties, whereas the Slavic women who served as the maids in Western Europe and the Latinas who cleaned the hotels in the U.S. were routinely harassed for sex or sexually abused by their bosses and managers and were sometimes kidnapped and forced into sexual slavery, so that overall it was six of one half dozen of the other, life imitating art imitating life imitating art, it was really just a difference of emphasis, of emphasis and outfits, in one outfit or another half of the world always ends up with its ass in the air for the other half, fucked in the ass one minute and vacuuming under the bed the next. He tried to remember the distinguishing features of the chateau in the novel so that he would be able to identify the prototype if he happened to see it, it had a library with French doors facing west and an antechamber tiled in black marble and a red wing whatever that was and a refectory and a vaulted dungeon and a *porte-cochère* outside on the grounds, which were described as having a lawn and a park with gravel paths like the path on which he walked, but that park could not be this park because the park described in the novel had been a private park whereas the park he was leaving by one of its gravel paths was a public park, albeit one curiously bereft of a public. And now as he entered the streets of Roissy he found them as curiously bereft of the public as the paths of the park. At first glance however the village looked like an old-fashioned French village with quaint houses close to the narrow cobbled lanes so that he half expected to turn the corner and find himself in an old-fashioned square with old men playing *boules* in the dirt under the plane trees or having retired from *boules* because the afternoon was warm to sit around a table at a sidewalk café drinking a robust local wine or Pernod or whatever the French equivalent was for Cinzano in Italy and retsina in Greece, but around the corner there was no old-fashioned square and no old men just some shops which were closed. There were no cars in the street, no moving cars and few parked cars, he saw almost no cars, and on closer inspection he could see that the village was not a real village, everything was new although it had been built to look old-fashioned and quaint, it was shiny and clean and laminated and new, all new subdivisions built in the kitschy style of a retro French village, from a distance and if you blurred your eyes it might appear for a moment like that village lane in Arles in that Van Gogh painting but only for a moment, he began to grow anxious and feel the lamination descending again from his already-laminated sinuses into his incipiently-laminated windpipe and gorge, and there was now in addition a feeling of lamination over his eyes, over the balls of his eyes a feeling as if strips of acetate had been placed over them, the eyes too needed to breathe in order to function just like the nose and the mouth and his eyes could not breathe, his eyes looked at the fake streets and the fake houses as if through a film of acetate. The so-called village of Roissy was of a piece with the rest of the Twilight Zone Hôtelière, it was all of a piece on both sides of the whole laminated hill-hotel complex, they were two sides of the same Zone Hôtelière coin, the only people who lived in this kitsch village of so-called Roissy were the employees of the Charles de Gaulle airport, he now understood, there were no cars because they took the shuttle-buses to work, that very morning they had loaded onto the shuttle-buses en masse to go to work at the Charles de Gaulle international airport, the employees of the airport and especially the employees of Air France busy at that moment at the ticketing counters overbooking and bumping passengers to feed them back into the Zone Hôtelière loop. The so-called Roissy village was a company town as they used to call them in the old days, it was all part of the same arterial system, he hadn't realized until that moment that he had a horror of arterial systems and especially of the arterial system known as the company town, the whole planet was soon to become a company town. He began to look at the municipal signage to see if it used the same typeface that the Charles de Gaulle airport used for all of its signage, the distinctive sans serif typeface created by Adrian Frutiger and named for Adrian Frutiger, the Frutiger typeface that the Charles de Gaulle airport commissioned from Adrian Frutiger in 1968, when the students were tearing up the paving stones of the Paris boulevards to build barricades and tipping over cars and torching the tipped-over cars, and the fire from the torched cars lit up posters on the walls with the most utopian slogans imaginable telling us for instance that beneath the paving stones of the boulevards we might find the beach, and the workers wanted to go to the beach so they went on the hugest general strike in the history of France, the students occupied the universities and the workers all left for the beach and the fate of Europe hung in the balance as they might put it in a schoolbook or a documentary, in the midst of which President General Charles de Gaulle had a brainwave and commissioned Adrian Frutiger to create the distinctive Frutiger typeface for the signage of the airport that is named after the President General, a clean and modern sans serif typeface whose prominent ascenders and descenders and spacious apertures make it easy to read at all angles and sizes, a quintessentially modern typeface whose distinguishing qualities are cleanliness and proportionality and rationality, and all the workers and students started reading the signage with the new Frutiger typeface instead of the notoriously utopian slogans of the posters burning in the boulevards, they were captivated by the ultramodern Frutiger typeface whose sleek easy-to-read lines told them that the best way to the beach was to call off the strike and go back to work, right as the extermination squads in their Charles de Gaulle airport vests were lined up waiting for them at the end of the burrows with the guns and the dogs they went back to work. He looked at the fake laminated paving stones of the street and then up ahead for any possible signage with the distinctive Frutiger sans serif typeface, at which point the well-known literary mechanism of association made available to his conscious recollection the lettering style used on all the signage in that old Patrick McGoohan TV series *The Prisoner*, the Village in that TV series reminded him of this ersatz village of Roissy, except that the former had more character and even a beach instead of being surrounded by tarmac but he wondered if perhaps the lettering was the same, if they had used the distinctive Frutiger typeface for the ubiquitous signage of the sinister ultra-conformist dystopian Village it would have made a nice joke, but he remembered that the typeface of the Village had not been so sleek and modern as the Frutiger sans serif typeface, there were still serifs in the older-style Albertus typeface of the Village, the Albertus typeface still had serifs very minimal serifs it is true but serifs nonetheless, the Frutiger typeface was sans serif whereas the Albertus typeface was avec serif. And probably even if he did manage to locate the house which had served as the prototype for the notorious chateau of *Histoire d'O* it would turn out to be some monstrosity that the French heritage industry had subcontracted to Disneyworld France and it was now The Story of O World, after paying for tickets you stood in a long queue to be herded onto miniature shuttle-buses which looped on tracks through a series of animatronic tableaux reenacting the travails of O, which if he remembered correctly had more to do with clothing and fabrics than sex, the novel was really just a high-end adult clothing catalog for haberdashers and outfit-fetishists, excruciatingly tiresome and moreover excruciatingly Catholic, O like a nun with her wrists chained to her collar at night to keep her in an attitude of prayer and the chateau run according to the most restrictive rules that even the men of the secret society had to obey, to his mind it didn't sound like much fun for the men at all, so many rules and timetables like some sort of monastic order, it was a religious tract enjoining service and submission, sex the last refuge of the sacred in a secular age blah blah blah, the Catholic Church in France had given the Disney corporation its blessing and even sent out a priest to the Story of O World to bless it with holy water and incense at the grand opening, with plenty of politicians from the conservative and Gaullist and so-called socialist parties and the National Front on hand to have their pictures taken and speak of the French tradition of art and commerce. He was just about to quit and return to the hotel-zone when he saw a man ahead, from around the corner an actual person of the public walking in his direction on the same public sidewalk about thirty paces ahead, he was surprised to see an actual live person, there were so few other persons on the streets that this one had to be an official of the Charles de Gaulle airport or a representative of Air France out on official business, unless he was just another addled tourist who had been overbooked and bumped, although as the stranger approached he gave off distinctly the air of a French person, somehow it was clear right away that the stranger approaching him was French, perhaps because his attire looked stylish in that subdued way of the French who as a people love stylish vestments more than sex, including Italian shoes, to be a properly dressed French person requires Italian shoes, but more especially because of his prominent nose, a truly impressive Gallic honker worn no doubt in honor and emulation of the victorious commander of the Free French forces and later President of the Fourth or is it the Fifth French Republic the late General Charles de Gaulle. And he worried that he would be in trouble with this distinctly French person wearing Italian shoes and a nose in honor of Charles de Gaulle because his own appearance inspired suspicion and maybe he had strayed into some kind of forbidden zone, unwittingly he had strayed into a zone that was off limits at certain times of the day, or off limits at least to suspicious-looking characters such as he had always suspected himself to be. He and the approaching French stranger shared the trait of wearing large noses but the French stranger wore the large nose of a Gallic person and whereas he wore the large nose of a Semitic person, or so the mirrors had always communicated to him, mirrors and other reflective surfaces which he gazed into anxiously had communicated to him this idea that he wore a nose of the Semitic type, even spoons and the surface of his watch could communicate to him this idea that he wore a Semitic-type nose, to say nothing of his wife's sunglasses, he wore the nose of a Jew or an Arab in spite of the fact that to his knowledge he was neither Arab nor Jew, the old problem of appearance versus essence. To his mind neither Jews nor Arabs were especially popular in France right then but he thought that on the whole the Arabs were less popular than the Jews, which was unfortunate because he believed that on balance he looked more like an Arab than a Jew, in the context of his complexion and hair and five o'clock shadow and the *je ne sais quoi* of his overall demeanor his Semitic-type nose came off more like an Arab's than a Jew's, at least to people in the United States and Europe, in the United States and Europe everyone took him automatically for an Arab, in fact everyone everywhere took him for an Arab except for the Arabs who took him for a Jew. He did not wish to be classed as an

Arab by this French person, possibly an official of some kind although in no uniform save that of the well-attired French person, in principle his sympathies were all with the Arabs but at that particular moment he did not wish to be classed among things such as rabbits, frogs, snails, and Arabs, things which the French people and Western Europeans in general fear are going to overrun their tarmacs in hordes and thus need at regular intervals to be exterminated en masse, he and the French stranger were heading right towards each other but it would have looked even more suspicious for him as a suspicious possibly Arab-looking person to cross to the other side of the street even definitively suspicious an open and shut case of suspiciousness, he wished his wife were at his side she had blond hair and an open face, he needed to get the Frenchman's mind off his appearance right away, now that they had drawn near to each other he would speak first in such a way as to demonstrate the harmlessness of his presence in the zone – *Excusez-moi, monsieur, et bonjour, eh . . . je suis ein tourist, eh, er . . . un tourist Canadien, oui, et je suis tres interessant dans le literature, n'est-ce-pas? Et je . . . je . . . et*, to, to look for, I'm looking for . . . um, *parlez-vous anglais?* As he spoke the French stranger lifted his nose, throughout this demonstration of his harmlessness the French stranger slowly but steadily lifted his nose, pausing only at the interrogative to roll its Gallic impressiveness from side to side like the dorsal fin of a sea mammal and expel from the pucker beneath it a brief *Non*. Oh, that's alright, I mean, *c'est ça, oui, mais . . . je, je voudrais aller a la musée, oui, je voudrais aller a la musée de la chateau de le roman* Histoire d'O, *oui? Eh, eh, le roman de Pauline Réage, n'est-ce-pas?* To make his meaning perfectly clear he supplemented his speech with gestures, indicating first himself, then making walking fingers in the air, then pointing to the nearest house, then making a waving motion as if to erase the house and bringing his hands together and apart as if opening a book, and finally lifting and lowering his fist in the air to suggest flogging. Yet the French person only continued to lift his great Gallic nose skyward by worrisome increments as if sampling the air in order to determine if there might be an Arab on the tarmac, or else he was farsighted and had to rear back his head in order to bring the importuning questioner's nose into focus in order to determine if it was a nose belonging to an Arab. And so the questioner found himself steadily lowering his chin, dipping his chin downwards in increments in the hope of foreshortening his nose in the French person's perspective, the French person lifted his nose while the questioner dipped his chin until at last it was difficult for him to question let alone breathe, with his chin tucked into his breastbone his last question came out in a wheeze while the French person's nose had positively taken off and now soared like the Concorde over the *Pays de France*. At last in exasperation *S'il vous plaît, monsieur, le château!* he cried, raising his chin again but making up for this insolence by cringing deeply and flailing his arms in several directions, *Le château, s'il vous plaît! Où est le château, n'est ce pas, le château? Où est le château?* at which point the Concorde returned to earth and the light of a successful communication circuit came on in the French person's control panel. *Ah, le château!* cried the French person. *Oui, le château!* the questioner cried. Suddenly they were friends. The French person turned and pointed. *Le château est là!* All the questioner had to do, it turned out, was to continue in the direction he had been traveling and he would without question find himself at the chateau. He and the French person parted in high spirits and each bore their noses buoyantly in opposite directions. Buoyantly he bore his after all perhaps

not so Semitic-looking nose in the direction he had originally been traveling through the village of Roissy, for the
moment no longer the "so-called" village, it might not be so
bad a village as all that with such a literary point of interest
as the prototype of the notorious chateau of Pauline Réage's
notorious novel *Histoire d'O,* a serious literary investigation
into erotic clothing as the last refuge of the sacred in a secular age. He left the buildings of the village of Roissy behind
him as the road climbed and curved up the hill, there was a
curving bank of trees of a type he could not name on the left
side of the road and on his right he could see over the last
houses of the village the green and gold swatches of the
Pays de France receding to the smudge of the horizon,
there were no other streets so he had to be going the right
way to the chateau, of course the chateau itself had to be
located at some small distance from the village, there had to
be room for the grounds and the park and the *porte cochère*
and you wouldn't want the villagers to hear the screams so
it had to be located at least some small distance out of town.
And just as he was beginning to feel his breath, from the
climb and perhaps a little from anticipation to feel his
breath which was reviving from the condition of lamination
he surmounted the crest of the hill and rounded the curve
and saw before him the chateau to which the French person
had directed him, obviously and clearly this was the very
chateau the French person had meant, the Château-Roissy
hotel on the driveway loop between the invidiously-appointed Suitehotel Roissy and the Kyriad Prestige Hotel Roissy-
en-France, with the Novotel Roissy and the Millennium
Hotel Roissy-Paris Charles de Gaulle on their respective
sub-loops below and above them on the hillside. Shuttle-
buses churned by along the tarmac loops in both directions
as he tried to catch his breath, he had felt his breath not
because of the climb or because of anticipation but because

of the lamination, it had not been revivification but con-
striction, the whole time the lamination had been advancing, insidiously and inexorably the lamination had
advanced. Everything on the hill-island worked in such a
way that even if you walked in what you thought was a
straight line you went in a circle and ended up back at your
hotel in the Zone Hôtelière, or rather especially if you went
in a straight line you ended up back in the Zone Hôtelière.
The gravel paths of the park and the tarmac of the loops all
led to the same place, subtly and deceptively they were laid
out in the triskelion pattern which had been the symbol of
the secret society in Pauline Réage's notorious novel *Histoire d'O*, the triskelion pattern of three interlocking spirals
on the secret-decoder rings which everyone in the society
had to wear and by which they made themselves known to
each other when not at the chateau, because everywhere
you were really at the chateau, coming or going you were
always returning to the chateau. He had won his talisman
after all, not an antidote but the poison itself. There was a
sort of fatalism to it, it was a Gallic fatalism. It was the
degree-zero of traveling, it was the essence of modern
travel, with a kind of continental fatalism the Grand Tour
led only to this. The future of Europe was this shrinking
compass, in which everything went in loops and came back,
and so time must too, and he would always be returning to
the chateau, in one way or another he would always be coming back, he would never get out. He might as well be living
in the departure lounge of Terminal 1 in the Charles de
Gaulle airport along with Mehran Karimi Nasseri, it would
be better to live in the departure lounge of Terminal 1 alongside Mehran Karimi Nasseri than in the Zone Hôtelière,
from 1988 on Mehran Karimi Nasseri had been sleeping on
benches with his head on his suitcase in the departure
lounge of Terminal 1, a degree-zero man *sans-papiers* liv-

ing in an airport terminal even after they made a movie about him, a Middle Eastern man at the zero-degree. In the movie of course they had had to make him into a European, into a white European of some kind or else who would have gone to see it, in the movie a Slav of some kind and thus sufficiently exotic and foreign while still white and European and still Tom Hanks, above all still Tom Hanks, from a Middle-Eastern prototype Tom Hanks with a Polish-sounding accent. If by chance he should escape the Zone Hôtelière tomorrow on one of the shuttle-buses and the plane didn't crash on take-off because of the rabbit blood on the tarmac no doubt the in-flight movie would be *The Terminal* starring Tom Hanks as the displaced white European who wants nothing more than to live and breathe free in the United States of America, while Mehran Karimi Nasseri or probably by this time only his ghost remained in the terminal, terminally in the terminal, in the In-Between, at the margin itself, in the center of Europe a margin. As he passed the Kyriad Prestige Hotel Roissy-en-France he saw his wife through the lobby window staring into her laptop with a look of ferocity, hunched and staring like a lion about to strike, she must be getting very good wireless reception, she must have had many vending-machine cappuccinos. She had willed and caffeinated herself into a crazed state of concentration in order to resist the condition of lamination, it took a leonine concentration which he did not possess. Some would survive and others would not. He returned to their room, passing the dour Ukrainian housekeeper on the way. He lay down on the small bed, put his left forearm over his eyes and listened to the sound of the tarmac-surf through the open treble-paned window. He felt the lamination in the chambers of his sinuses and in his gorge, his windpipe, and his lungs. He felt the food-mix he had consumed that morning still heavily coiled in his intestinal loops and thought of the quick dour look the Ukranian housekeeper had pretended not to give him. His only hope was in the banlieues, among the young French persons who wore North African and Middle Eastern noses in the decaying council flats of the endless cités, he reasoned. They had made the banlieues burn last fall and they would make them burn again, they would finally burst out of their insular banlieue prisons, join forces with the rabbits and flood all the tarmacs, the rabbits by themselves were no match for the exterminators in their Charles de Gaulle airport vests and their extermination equipment including dogs and weasels but together with the youth of Algerian and Moroccan and Tunisian descent and suspicious appearance they could make a go of it, burning the banlieues and flooding the tarmacs. His only hope of escape from the creeping condition of lamination and loops was to ally himself with them, with the banlieue youth of suspicious appearance who had never been overbooked and bumped and washed ashore at the Zone Hôtelière because they could not afford the luxury of being overbooked and bumped, and the rabbits who wanted the tarmacs for themselves. His sympathies were all with the banlieue youth and the rabbits but he was torn, torn. His only hope of escape was to ally himself with the banlieue youth and the rabbits, but a final showdown would leave the tarmac flooded with blood and cause the Air France jetliner to hemoplane on take-off and kill him in a fiery crash.

The Four Horsemen Bridge

He had come to a crossroads, the bridge riddled him its riddle, much would depend on how he answered, he knew. Midway through his life's journey, but in St. Petersburg on a White Night not an umbrous wood, no shadows on a White Night, and no Virgil to guide him, over the Anichkov Bridge flowed the Nevsky throng (he had not thought death had undone so many), plenty of Russians and literary associations but no Virgil. Midway through life's journey (by medieval reckoning that is, his mid-thirties), but instead of a wood on the outskirts of hell the strange and estranging vista of the unreal city from Nevsky Prospekt and the Fontanka Embankment, a garage sale of outmoded architectural styles baroque neoclassical art nouveau Soviet all dancing now to the tune of the Crazy Fruits! slot-machine casino's neon marquee. It was like a handful of somebody's European vacation slides grabbed up at random by the uninvited but inevitable guest and viewed simultaneously, superimposed. Or palimpsest, literary word, always reminded him of palmistry for some reason. His fortune. By what collisions of agency and contingency had he come to this crossroads, that he thought it might portend a fate? Let's back up, rewind the frames. There he goes herky-jerk in reverse. He had wandered, our little wayfarer, had come upon the bridge by long wandering, without checking his map, without consulting the guidebook, without a plan or a destination in mind, wandering at will, at whim, at whiff even, just submitting himself to an autohypnotic *dérive* in a strange somewhat men-

acing city, shambolic wayfarer with a literary bent autohyp-
notizing himself until he was labyrinthinely lost, literarily
bent and now lost in the labyrinth, and thus when he found
himself again it should of necessity be momentous, he
reasoned. Might be murdered, for instance, might get his
skull kicked in by skinheads, he looked enough like a *kachi*
for it, a *kachi* at least if not a *chernozhopyi*, he suspected he
looked to these Slavs very much like an Azeri or worse yet a
Chechen, if any militia were on hand they would just laugh,
maybe even put in a boot or two themselves, laughing and
sharing smokes with the skinheads while scraping his
brains off their boots on the curb, he'd seen the way they
looked at him. He'd seen plenty of militia but not many
skinheads to speak of, word was that Putin had had them all
combed out, along with the street drunks, to make the town
more presentable for the G8 Summit next week or was it the
week after, one-way bus tickets to Kamchatka or the Russian Army, little thugs combed out to make way for the big
thugs. And his wife off doing science at her conference at
the university across the Neva while he wandered lost in the
labyrinth, his Penelope presenting her findings in Power-
Point which she had prepared by staring at length into the
same all-purpose laptop on which she had analyzed her
data and booked their flight and hotel, by twitching her fingers on a tiny mouse pad but mostly by staring, by dint of
very intent staring and feral powers of concentration she
could bend data sets to her will until they confessed patterns of significance, and by now she had finished her
presentation and even finished listening to the other scient-
ists taking their turns with their PowerPoints on their
laptops, they were all sitting down to that banquet to which
he was invited too because others were "bringing their
spouses," if he wanted he could be sitting there beside his
wife at the long table but it would have been too excruciat-

ing, that allegory they would have made over the little plates of *zakuski* and vodka shots, like a frieze: Art trailing in the wake of Science. She had almost insisted: Did he want to be alone on his birthday? But it was their last night in St. Petersburg and still the city had not yielded up its secret to him, and so all day he had worn down the treads of his Converse All Stars after it, unless of course it was after him, through streets parks palaces arcades courtyards alleyways squares and still more streets, streets narrow and streets crooked and the broad thoroughfares of death-dealing traffic, over the bridges and along the embankments of unreal St. Petersburg, into the evening which was not an evening because it was a White Night, of the famous St. Petersburg White Nights. No maps this time, no guidebook, no camera, and no little writer's notebook, nothing but the naked encounter, except for his clothes he was entirely naked. It had been hot all day and it was still a warm evening, a hot St. Petersburg summer day in which the Russian men some of them anyway from among those not rich enough to want to be showing off their tailored Western European vestments these other Russian men had slipped off their T-shirts or the tops of their tracksuits to warm their pale thin hard torsos in the sun, wearing tight jeans or the bottoms of their tracksuits but no T-shirts or tops and never shorts, most definitely never shorts, he had stupidly worn shorts what a way to scream I'm a foreigner but he kept his T-shirt on because his torso was flabby, his foreigner's torso was hairy and flabby unlike the invidious Russian male torsos which were pinky-pale hairless and hard, he had blinked at stabs of sunlight glancing off the shiny hard torsos while he spat away pollen tufts stuck to his lips. They were countless, these tufts of poplar pollen, drifting down everywhere from nowhere unless they were rather the torn-off shreds of high clouds from over the Gulf of Finland, according to science they were tufts of pollen from poplar trees but according to poetry they were the torn-off shreds of high clouds from over the Gulf of Finland, on balance he favored this second explanation because it conformed to and even ratified something he was coming to suspect about the so-called summer weather generally here in St. Pete, which was that the warmth was not really warm at all it was fake warmth, even a fake-out warmth. Long before the afternoon's slide into dusk he had fallen for the fake-out, lifting his grateful face to the sun, but each time he stepped into the shade of a high-walled garden or beneath the sagging balconies of dilapidated communal apartments he'd found his perspiration turning to cold sweat, and out of the gentle breeze that fluttered up his T-shirt and the blowsy legs of his cargo shorts had come sharp ice fingers to play arpeggios on his ribcage and osculate his scrotum. Was it fever oh no had he let some of the St. Petersburg water into his mouth in the shower that morning was it cholera like Tchaikovsky or no that giardia germ, from the dregs of the Neva this germ found also in the Nile? But the torn-off cloud-tufts from the Gulf of Finland helped him finally to a positive ID: it was the cold dead fingers of the Arctic that had him by the balls. The very warmth of the summer's day had been infiltrated from within, out of the reaches of the Arctic these stealth ice fingers in a fake-warm glove. Not content with having infiltrated the summer breeze they wanted his warmth too, they were feeling for a way in, prying, seeking the marrow and the seed. The Arctic Circle just a few hundred kilometers away and even on the warmest summer day – a heatwave they were calling this! – it wouldn't let anyone forget who was really in charge here. No wonder the Russians were pro-global warming. And no way to shake it, that Arctic chill knew the St. Petersburg streets better than he did and always thought five moves ahead, no way to tell which direction it would come from next, you go one way it goes the other, you fake left cut right down Stolyarny Lane, cross the Kammeny Bridge at a running crouch, feint another left but turn right on Sadovaya Street, try to lose yourself in the crowd until you see the Griboedova Canal, then disappear into the darkest dankest courtyard you can find and pop out again through the back passage onto Srednaya Podyacheskaya Lane thinking you had just pulled off the perfect crime only to feel the chill tap on your shoulder of this super-adhesive hyperborean Porfiry Petrovich. No, nothing to do but submit, one way or another the despotic Arctic was going to cop its feel, maybe it had even steered him to the Haymarket by its cunning ticklish byways, letting him think it was his doing, to arrive here in the Haymarket where Raskolnikov had abased himself to kiss the cowshit and beg its forgiveness, where during the terrible privations of the Siege of Leningrad it was rumored you could buy strange meat, if you got tired of soup made of shoe leather sawdust and wallpaper paste and that was on a good day you could always go to the Haymarket for strange meat, it was said of those darkest of hours that when you met someone with a sanguine glow to their cheeks instead of the usual pallor you knew they had dined on strange meat. A people's northernmost outpost last stop before the land of the dead. But that would be Murmansk or Norilsk or smaller villages if those counted. And yet thronged with people as these streets were, this Haymarket today all market and no hay, he could not help feeling that he wandered a ghost city, an abandoned city, a city built by a race of giants and then abandoned, among whose colossal decaying monuments now scrambled a lesser race, the bed lice of its former occupants, reeling, dwarfed. And even these were a ghost race, as the day lengthened into White Night he was nagged by the suspicion that these vermin were ghost vermin, and he a ghost among ghosts, in this unreal city of spectral inhabitants he began to suspect his own unreality strongly, and faint with the strength of this suspicion he wandered through the Haymarket thinking that he too might be unreal. A number of the ghosts appeared to be shopping. Could he warm himself by following girls? Sheer profusion of beautiful girls on these streets, from his first day they'd been turning him like a turnstile. Just a St. Petersburg phenomenon? Certainly urban to a degree, our anthropologist reasoned, in their efforts at metropolitan sophistication (clumsy in fact even cheap in a manner at once poignant and piquant to his condescending discernment or discerning condescension): the lowest-slung, hip-huggingest jeans ever seen, the tiniest tops, slender scapulae revealed beneath negligible wisps of spaghetti strap, by comparison the late-spring quad scene of his wife's U.S. campus looked like a Quaker village. And the accoutrements: troweled-on make-up and raccoon eyes, sparkle and sequin arabesques on the rump pockets of designer jeans knock-offs, halters and shorts with tarty unidiomatic slogans clinging to curves of breast and buttock, and everywhere the highest of high heels, on which the willowy sylphs teetered like Tatlin's tower. But the raw material, those slender bodies thus attired and accoutered, those waists no thicker than the neck of a bottle, those cat eyes and broad high cheekbones, this was what was really superb! Where had such profusion come from? By one of those chances too coincidental for fiction but which happen now and then in the so-called real world a Russian taxi driver who spoke some English caught our besotted wayfarer looking: *It is product of the mix of bloods*, he began, but in such a way that it seemed he had never left off. *First the Finns then the Slavs then the Tartars, the how-you-say raping hordes, and quite a heady genetic cocktail it is mak-*

ing, yes? I know, he added, *because before I had great fortune to drive the taxi I was geneticist for Soviet State.* Our
little wayfarer mouthed *spasiba* and wandered on. Maybe
this explained the astonishing eyes, blue or brown just
didn't cut it. Opal? Azure? Jade? Strange eyes like his, green
eyes admixed with mother-of-pearl. Where had his own
strange eyes come from? He was American of Portuguese
descent, our hero ("he" being short for hero, besides in his
case just being short), or so he had been led to believe, or
rather to never fully believe, for he had always suspected
that he'd been adopted, picked out at the Little Wayfarers
Orphanage before his parents discovered they could make
their own (hence the ambivalence of birthdays), one
brother two sisters but they all had brown eyes (only his
were mother-of-pearl), they all had wavy dark hair (only his
a wire brush), and they all had noses (only his was large and
Arab-looking). A cowbird chick in the nest? A Semite in the
woodpile? He trained his strange opalescent eyes on the
green-eyed girls and continued to trail, selecting from the
profusion a pair of them (girls, not eyes, although they came
with eyes) who had just come from the Yusupov Gardens,
hand in hand as if to balance each other on those precarious
heels, licking the ice creams in their free hands, poking out
their chests and bare tummies where navel piercings
flashed briefly in the last ray of sun like twin fishes jumping
out of the Fontanka canal. *Dyevushki*, explained the taxi
driver. Somehow now he was back, leaning in the crook of
the open passenger-side door, one foot on the curb,
smoking a cigarette, for all the world like he'd been there
the whole time. Had the girl-pair led our wayfarer in a circle
and he hadn't noticed, hypnotized as he'd been by the twin
rise and fall of alternate buttocks in shiny nylon shorts?
They had finished their ice creams and were now queuing
up to buy something to chase them with at another kiosk

(always another kiosk, everywhere another kiosk, punctuated here and there by *blini* stands). *Dyevushki* (helpfully
continued the taxi-driving erstwhile Lysenko-school geneticist in our wayfarer's ear), *it is plural of* dyevushka, *our
word for the woman of childbearing age who has not yet
had the child. Who gets to be this word is wide* (and here
the cab driver spread out his hands). *A* dyevushka *can be
twelve, thirteen years if she has had her period yet, or she
can be* her— (he pointed to a college student necking with
her *modniki* boyfriend on a bench next to the kiosk), *or she
can be twenty-nine! The word in your language that is the
closest is, is outdated, the archaism, yes: it is the word*
maiden. *But—* (the cab driver threw up his hands in a shrug
of fatalism) *the word is not so wide that it is everyone! You
see, it is like this—* (And now, in a gesture that seemed to
sum up in its definitive abracadabra all the trompe l'oeil of
our hero's day, all the baffles and blinds, the sudden fore-
shortenings of only apparently receding perspectives, the
taxi driver reached out and plucked a young girl right off the
street, not one of our hero's beer-buying girl-pair but
younger, a veritable youngster, pinched her up by the neck
and placed her in the palm of his hand where she nested like
a doll, so that, even though the only things like PowerPoint
bullets were her ingenuous eyes in a wide frozen stare, dis-
sertation became demonstration): *When she is younger
than twelve years, like this, she is girl-child*, devochka. *But
as soon as she is able to bear the child, she become this—*
(with the lightest of two-handed twists the taxi driver separated the girl into halves and decanted from inside her a sister, smaller but older) —*the* dyevushka *like those you are
enjoying here, the desire of your eyes and maybe of your
heart too – or at least this is what the romantic like you
think! Because really it is like big farm, what is going on.
Her eggs, your seeds, yes? Like on research farm at agro-*

nomical institute where I was twenty years a geneticist. But when your dyevushka *grows to be, of certain other age*— (here the cab-driver's speech became as tentative and delicate as his shucking away of the shell of the beloved was decisive and brutal) —*she becomes* tyotya, *which is auntie. Inside there*— (the taxi driver held out this third, diminished iteration of the original *devochka* in the direction of a cafeteria-style eatery through whose broad front window our wayfarer could see customers bearing trays to their tables) —*where is the women who dish out the food, those are* tyotya. *We would say, if we do not know her name,* 'Tyotya, *please, give me more meatball', and it would not be impolite to say this. And then, if the toilet in the back is not making the flush, we say,* 'Tyotya, *please clean out the toilet, I need to shit out your meatballs!' The auntie is not for making babies any more, she is for work!* (The taxi driver snapped his fingers, all it took for the husks of the *tyotya* to go flying away and leave cradled in the hollow of his hand when he opened it again the smallest and oldest of the sisters yet, with a few scratched lines where the *devochka's* wide eyes and cupid's-bow lips had been.) *And then everyone in the world, even the not Russian, knows the famous* babushka, *grandmother. Here she is, the little grandmother, see? This is whether or not she has the real grandchildren, it is just any old woman. I have a couple of years before my wife will be* babushka! The taxi driver cupped his hands in front his face to cover a fit of coughing and when he took them away the *babushka* was gone and a lit cigarette dangled from his lips. Or maybe that was all that had been inside the *babushka* that had been inside the *tyotya* that had been inside the *dyevushka* that had been inside the *devochka* all along: one frail tendril of smoke which made a feeble clutch at the taxi driver's nose hairs before giving up the ghost. Our little wayfarer turned in time to see his pair of caryatids totter off with huge cans of beer in their tiny hands. He took the first step of renewed pursuit and felt fingers on his elbow. *I can take you to the place where it will be girls just like those, the whole night for 3,000 rubles.* Our hero shook his head and tried to move away. The fingers on his elbow were joined by an opposing thumb, noble hallmark of our species. *Or if it must be those two, for I see you have set your heart, this too can be arranged. Only 15,000 rubles but I will have to make the phone call first. Then we follow in my cab to keep the eyes on them while we wait for the van.* Pleading a maxed-out credit card our hero politely disengaged himself from the taxi-driver's grip and set off solo towards the corner where the girls had disappeared, wind at his back carrying the helpful cabby's closing argument: *Try it with verses then and see what you will get, Pushkin. Welcome to capitalist Russia!* Our little wayfarer tried to think about Pushkin instead of capitalism while he watched the twin rise and fall of alternate buttocks in nylon shorts less shiny now that the sun had finally gone down. The Arctic ice-fingers had followed him around the corner even if the taxi driver hadn't and he tried to rekindle the warmth of his original pursuit, but now even Pushkin couldn't help. The Russian men loafing on the benches had their T-shirts and the tops of the tracksuits back on. Hadn't Pushkin been part black? The tsar's moor and all that? Any minute now the girls would turn and notice and start screaming that a dusky-skinned moor was stalking them, or a part-moor, or worse yet a Chechen, an evil Chechen was going to snatch and make a meal of them unless the Russian men and the militia came to save the day by kicking his *kachi* skull in and squashing his green eyes like grapes under their boots for the reckless eyeballing of Russian *dyevushka*-hood with intent to eat. They were ghosts but his blood in the gutter would make them feel real for a while, all of them, the men the militia the onlookers even the girls. When here all he'd wanted to do was play horsey and offer the girls a lift, drop to the pavement on all fours and ferry them to their destination, even if it meant taking them to other boys, maybe especially if it meant taking them to other boys, come ride the harmless Chechen pony, feeling their warm buttocks on his back and warm thighs on his ribs even let them slap his haunches and cry giddy-up, innocent enough, eat a cube of sugar from their sticky little palms, then back to the hotel to jack off, nice warm and alive and real to himself, man of simple pleasures, free gratis save himself 15,000 rubles, wouldn't have laid a finger even though the age of consent in Russia was fourteen. He dropped back another ten paces and felt less warm than ever. Over the tops of the poplar trees and apartment blocks, over the domes that reminded him less of onions than of stylized ice-cream cones and, in dun silhouette now, cartoon dog turds, the sky was undergoing a subtle transformation, as imperceptible to the naked eye as it was unsettling to an imagination in which the figure of speech "bleeding out" had made itself all at once so appallingly at home, while bells near and far announced the commencement of the White Night. This was brightness without the source of brightness, whose departure had left in its attenuated wake only the frostily technical denotation of the word "blue," from which had been subtracted – leached, bleached – all the rich spirits of its connotations, and for which he now discovered (even though his little writer's notebook was back at the hotel) a lyricism in equal measure angular and crepuscular: White Night hours of dusk and White Night hours of dawn, the In-Between of dusk and dawn unnaturally extended, the limen of night and the limen of day yawning open a crevasse of blue-grey ice-wide sky. Been here a week and couldn't get used to it, something strange, unsettling, always a little unsettled at dusk anyway and to have dusk stretched out like this, and stretched and stretched, to become a state, not a threshold any longer but a state, maybe that was it. But when he looked back down from the sky to his girl-pair ahead of him on the sidewalk he began to suspect that it was an altogether more serious condition than just a distended limen: Those girls cast no shadows. None of the other strollers were casting shadows either. The trees and the kiosks had simply dispensed with shadows. The Pushkin sculpture in the little colonnade had washed its hands of the columns and the wrought-iron railings following suit. Finally in horror he looked at his own feet: *He* cast no shadow. A few more steps and he was reduced to weaving figure-eights on the sidewalk, patting himself and scanning the ground as if he had lost something, although this was less like a missing billfold than a mass amputation featuring him as the only amputee to find it alarming. The shadows were all gone. The shadows had flown. It was still light out, but the shadows had flown back to wherever shadows fly when it's dark, when it is utter dark. But it was still light out. He staggered around a corner to where it was brighter still, a river-broad boulevard where the trees were supplanted by street lamps and the statues by pulsing neon marquees, all the lights redoubled in the expanses of shop windows, and to see the flare of big-city nightlife underneath such a bone-white sky was a migraine's worth of cognitive dissonance. He joined the crowds on the big avenue and continued threading after his girls, but he sensed that his term in their company was reaching its end given his new preoccupation with this startling absence, between the multitude of propulsive hindlimbs and the sidewalk, of the usual complement of shadowy integument, including most crucially his own. At least now he knew the function of shadows: they kept you from being ghostly to yourself. They kept your ghost separate from you. You stroll along thoughtlessly real to yourself as long as you've got your shadow with you, la de da, me and my shadow, the primrose path. Plain as day. But now it's light and he has no shadow. Because *he* was a shadow, a void. His shadow had flown back to him and taken him over. He wandered the Nevsky Prospekt like a ghost, just another ghost in a ghost town, a shade among the shades. He had lost his way in the limen, in the ashen In-Between, forever now In-Between. He would never get out. Even here where the buildings appeared finally to drop away – he thought he could glimpse the embankment of a canal ahead – the ghost-crowd was thicker than ever. He was brought up short at a stoplight while his ghost-*dyevushki* disappeared in the current on the other side, swallowed in the shadow-less flow. With the feeling that they had somehow accomplished their task he relinquished them and backed out of the throng to brace himself against the corner building and take a few swallows of intensely-brackish mineral water out of the bottle that he carried in a pocket of his cargo shorts. Over his head an inscribed metal plaque was bolted into the salmon-colored stucco of the wall. Since he'd managed to learn only a few letters of the Russian alphabet his sally at reading it was half-hearted, yet when he lifted his head for another swallow his second look at the plaque was already redundant – he understood it all. He didn't know how, a foreign tongue in a foreign alphabet, but hey presto there it was, off the plaque and into his mind, not letter by letter or word by word but in one leap, full-blown and worth every shiver: It was the Belinsky House. Here to this crossroads over a century and a half ago a young Fyodor Mikhailovich had been summoned, roused from sleep in the middle of the night by his pals the poet Nekrasov and Somebody-or-other-else and summoned to an audience with the great critic Belinsky, man of enthusiasms and discernment, after the latter had devoured the manuscript of *Poor Folk* at a sitting and demanded to meet this future of Russian letters this successor of Gogol, the sleepy-eyed mussy-haired and socially maladroit at any hour of the day or night young Fyodor Mikhailovich. He (our third-person hero, not Fyodor Mikhailovich) had been able to decipher the commemorative plaque with enough of an assist from grace to know that his fate as a writer was to be decided there and then, or rather here and now, but only to the extent that he could decipher the larger riddle of this crossroads, and for this task he would be on his own. With the next pack of pedestrians he crossed the street from the Belinsky House to the embankment where he at last got a look at the challenge he had accepted. On tall pediments at each of the bridge's four corners stood large bronze statues of individual horsemen alongside their steeds; they appeared to anchor the bridge's broad, triple-arched span, beneath which flowed the Fontanka canal, over which flowed the crowd of ghosts and literary associations (he had not thought death had undone so many). See, we're back where we started, we're done with the foreplay, now the "story" can commence. We have assembled here the three parts essential to story: The Beginning (of the story), Middle (midway through life's journey), and End (death). He had come to a crossroads, the bridge riddled him its riddle, much would depend on his answer, he knew. Over our little wayfarer loomed (without casting a shadow) the nearest horse-and-horseman pair, first figure of a four-part rebus, a slender youth whose stripped supple torso and narrowly muscled arms appeared no match for his sinewy steed, whose thighs billowed like thunderclouds. It wasn't easy getting a good look jostled by all these sharp-elbowed Petersburg ghosts, or to concentrate with the megaphoned barkers on each side of the bridge dinning his ears with offers of midnight Neva cruises, but he was quickly able to perceive that this horseman and his three fellows were too young and beautiful to be harbingers of an apocalypse. No, their message was personal: to each crosser of the bridge, no matter in what ghostly conglomerate, they bespoke a singular fate. What did these bronzes signify – a historical episode, legend, or myth? What story, if story at all, was told here over the heads of the flowing crowd? Were they four individual horse tamers, each frozen in separate struggles to break and mount their respective beasts? Or was it a single horseman depicted at four distinct moments of one agon with a single steed? Our wayfarer thought the latter, because youth and horse looked like the same pair on each of the corner pediments. But then which was the correct sequence? For read in one direction the figures presented a narrative, in four successive tableaux, of triumph. First: the almost supine youth's desperate one-handed clutch at the reins, the rearing horse poised to bolt out of his grasp, the young man would be dragged down the Nevsky Prospekt if he didn't let go! Next: a more braced footing, a new tautness in the strong thighs, the youth still on the defensive but both hands now on the reins and tugging the beast's muzzle back. Then: the youth has risen onto two feet, his grip on the bridle is secure enough that his other hand is free to place on the horse's loin in a gesture that is no longer desperate but *quieting* (one thing was clear to our hero now, it was the fleetness of the youth's mind that had gained this edge on mere brute strength). Finally: the youth stands triumphant, fully upright, beside the tamed steed; the horse still rears, but now it so much dressage, as if it were merely toasting, horsey-fashion, its vanquisher. The horse tamer and not the horse is now the center of gravity, the fulcrum that bears the tensile stress and shear of all that frozen bronze energy and makes it appear weightless. But wait: reverse the sequence and they tell a different tale, not triumph but failure, disaster: the youth stands by the steed, caught in a moment of complacency, easy victory, hubris, and just then the horse rears, and the victory unravels. The youth reaches futilely for the horse's flank where there's nothing to hold onto; he slips, tries to plant his feet to regain the initiative, but it's too late, he spills and swerves as the horse prepares to spring away, and we last see the youth at the moment he is confronted with two flavors of public humiliation: to relinquish the reins or be dragged down the thoroughfare by the victorious beast. An apt metaphor for this equivocal city itself, reared on a swamp and plagued by epidemic and flood. Which would win, nature or culture? Apocalypse harbinged after all? Solve the riddle right and your fortune will be made, wrong and you will be trampled. Summoned to this crossroads over a century and a half ago, had Fyodor Mikhailovich chosen right? Certainly his fortune had been made that night: fame, yes – followed in quick succession by derision and mockery, insult and injury, from the very circle into which he had been summoned, fêted for *Poor Folk* then derided for *The Double*, for the better novel they had made him the goat, Fyodor Mikhailovich Goat in comic laurels. But ridicule and ostracism turned out to be just appetizers – there remained arrest, mock execution, Siberia, and exile. Quite a detour for one's literary fortune, and enough to render the whole question of chancing victory or defeat at one throw a tad ambiguous. By this time our hero had crossed the bridge, and he removed himself a few yards further down the embankment on that side to try to take in all four statues at each of their corners in a single comprehensive view. But now every time he squinted and refocused his eyes he felt the sense of waxing insight wane. How could he have missed it before? For all at once it appeared to him as if, in order to construct either plot of the horse-tamer's story, heroic victory or humiliating defeat, one couldn't simply proceed by compass points in either direction. No, for to do so, from this new vantage at least, produced a sequence in which the struggling youth simply went up and down, up and back down, or the reverse: down up, down up. In fact, unless our hero's sight deceived him (light-headed, blood sugar plummeting, how many hours since those *blinis*?), to come up with a sequence that made any kind of story one had to leap kitty-corner across the bridge in a series of x's. How to decode the meaning of that? It made no sense. It was neither clockwise nor counter-clockwise, it was . . . Cyrillic. His narrative arc crumbled into a *mise en abyme*. Well, fine, let that be the answer! No story, then. So be it. Story was a trap, a false friend, an unreliable prosthetic, a delusion. He would go without story to make his fortune, without story his literary fortune would be made. He crossed over the Four Horsemen Bridge. He would keep on the way he had chosen, or that had been chosen for him. The taxi driver waited on the other side. Leaning in the crook of the open passenger-side door, one foot on the curb, smoke curling from his cigarette, smoke the blue-grey of the White Night, for all the world like he'd been there the whole grey time. Our wayfarer says, It's not girls I'm looking for. The taxi driver smiles. Our wayfarer adds, It's not boys either. The driver shrugs, flicks his butt into the Fontanka. *Whatever you say, Fyodor Mikhailovich, whatever you say. Get in.*

The Cruiser

Figure, seated, at rest, arms bent, elbows on horizontal surface, at rest, buttocks at rest on lower horizontal parallel to upper horizontal, inner edge of lower horizontal almost flush with outer edge of upper horizontal, knees open and bent, feet flat on concrete surface parallel to upper horizontals, at rest. Look closer, one foot not at rest, heel rises and falls, rapid, toes planted, heel hammers, sock bags. Revise: nominally at rest, then. Mostly at rest. Ambience: wafts of petrol, susurrus of traffic. Coughs, a coughing susurrus, rising to cacophony, as when the truck churns into the driveway on the figure's right, figure at rest, let the resting figure be the ordinal point, at rest. Resting to rest, continuous and infinitive, rest to be rested, active and passive. Cars and trucks downshift to rest, decelerate to rest, driveway splits, trucks to left cars to right, long rows of angled allotments, painted in stripes, parallel, on tarmac, get out, legs stretch, arms lift, rest. Up the curb, concrete plaza, two larger structures, block-built, concrete blocks, restroom building and snack kiosk, smaller structures include signboard under sloping eaves with map in glass case, trash barrels in concrete housings, and picnic tables, three. Behind: woods, rising, sheltering, breakwater, figure of speech, from the traffic susurrus coughing to cacophony, susurrus subsiding to rise again, a cove, a figure, a rest stop, full stop. Summer day, mid-morning, cloudless sky, truncated shadow. The figure has been seen at this rest stop before, was spotted in the company of his wife here some months ago, has returned alone now with digital camera and notebook, seated at rest at picnic table with camera in a scrotal pouch and spiral-bound notebook open, college-ruled leaves over which his hand holds, poised, a pen. Poised is still, a different stillness from at rest. The pen a fluted column with ergonomic grip, must have appropriated it from among his wife's pens. Can of soda open must have purchased it from the snack-kiosk vending machine, pen appropriated and poised, soda purchased and at rest. Head poised at angle, as if waiting for inspiration, that internal susurrus. As if waiting for his muse (most definitely the angle of the head), but a chin dip and bob of the Adam's apple suggest instead the silent burp of carbonation from the duodenum and esophagus. Ruminatively the figure burps while giving off the air of a Chatterton, admittedly a swarthy Chatterton, in self-conceit if not completely in fact a somewhat swarthy somewhat Semitic-looking Chatterton a Chatterton who needs a shave and is moreover getting a little long in the tooth, a thirty-something Chatterton if such a thing is not the complete negation of the whole idea of a Chatterton, of a Chatterton or a Werther or a Keats, if we can manage to set aside what might after all be such a fig-ure's very essence, were he holding a quill pen poised over a piece of parchment he would be a dead ringer for an Arab Chatterton approaching middle age while waiting for his muse. The plan: Note the appearance and activities of the rest stop, hence the notebook and the ergonomic pen but also digital photographs to jog the memory later on, note first the rest stop's major features then the rest stop's finer points, note macrostructure of the rest stop first and fill in details afterwards, fill in and flesh out. Among the major features note what is fixed and invariable including the major structures and the routes then note what is unfixed and variable e.g. the visitors and their comings and goings, not at rest and at rest. Not at rest: the state police patrol cruiser which had cruised through the rest stop twenty minutes ago and continues to cruise through the seated figure's mind, his mind an extension of the parking lot and driveways and features variable and invariable of the rest stop through which the patrol cruiser cruises yet, keeping an eye out for the seated figure. In the figure's notebook and mind he has already noted what he considers the most salient features of the rest stop and it is time for the enumeration of the finer points, some of which he has already noted, viz. the contents of the vending machines in the snack kiosk (coffee sodas energy drinks snacks salty and sweet) where he stopped on his way to the picnic table after visiting the restroom, and the contents of the concrete-housed trash barrels (coffee cups soda cans energy-drink bottles salty and sweet snack wrappers newspapers and a diaper), although a finer point re: finer points suggests that something as prefab and generic as a highway rest stop could be said to be inherently bereft of finer points, the generic rest stop is the staging of a basic existential situation like the staging of a Samuel Beckett drama, only different, it is a different existential situation which requires a prefab restroom building and snack kiosk and a picnic bench on a concrete plaza instead of say for example a single denuded tree or a row of jars with figures in them or a wheelchair. Although the rest stop facilities are wheelchair accessible, note that down. But with burp-relief comes a further consideration in fact the chief consideration, from the duodenum and esophagus rises and pops a salutary reminder of what has brought the figure back to this resting place in the first place, a story or more precisely a text embodying the essence of the rest stop, essence embodied in the main features and finer points of the rest stop to be embodied again in the main features and finer points of a text, the embodied essence of the rest stop which is restfulness, repose, and relief. To capture what is the embodiment of rest, to communicate it in the body of a text, that which he has experienced at rest stops and which is embodied rest, a consonance or alignment of body and mind and place and text such that we credit again the old ideas of Arcadia, Elysium, the Happy Hunting Ground, Eden, in their modern or perhaps postmodern or to be less loaded and problematic and put off for now the vexed question of periodization let's choose as our adjective contemporary their contemporary incarnation as the In-Between. To the figure's left a sedan drives into the rest stop and being a sedan and not a truck pulls right not left where the driveway divides, it is the state police cruiser cruising, keeping an eye out, it is the cruiser decelerating and drawing near, surely it is the cruiser cruising. Pen again poised the seated figure waits for the cruiser and watches as the cruiser draws near, senses poised a different stillness than at rest, suspecting himself to be suspicious-looking he watches and waits, to have been spotted here once wasn't ipso facto suspicious even though he was suspicious looking he was only suspicious-looking enough for a question mark, the cruiser had cruised away with a question mark but to be spotted at the same rest stop half an hour later was to court an exclamation point. And hadn't he been spotted taking photos of the snack kiosk? Why had he gone and done a thing like that nobody would believe it was for his text who did he think he was W.G. Sebald? A suspicious-looking character had been spotted casing the joint, a suspicious- even Arab-looking character casing the joint for an Al-Qaeda operation, press F9 for your tasty vending-machine treat and BOOM! a nasty Al-Qaeda trick instead, bloody teeth shoot out like shrapnel taking down everyone standing near, collateral damage. Yes of course folks on vacation stop at rest stops and yes folks on vacation take snapshots with their cameras but of their families and scenic vistas and family members standing in front of scenic vistas but what kind of person takes snapshots of a rest-stop snack kiosk especially this particular person who sure as shit doesn't fit anyone's description of "folks," a single somewhat swarthy somewhat kinky-haired man taking digital snaps of snack-kiosk vending machines is obviously highly suspicious, might be a professional photographer but professional photographers have professional cameras with all kinds of fancy lenses not dinky digital cameras one evolutionary bump up from disposable. Surely by this time the suspicious behavior of this suspicious character has been phoned in, an alert vacationer a right-thinking citizen has no doubt phoned in a report to prompt the police cruiser's return, this cruiser cruising now nearer and nearer. And he thinks he knows who phoned in the report it had to have been that family doesn't it just figure it was a family. A lone person of any kind is always suspicious next to a family, a family trumps a lone person every time, if you are alone and not one of a family you might as well not go out of your house if there are any families about, next to a family you have no rights, families own the place whereas your solitary ass is merely suffered when it is not actively resented or regarded as highly suspicious, your solitary ass is barely tolerated if there is a family on the premises and it was most definitely a family which had ambushed him on the snack-kiosk premises when he had been taking his snaps, move aside pal a family's here, step away, get back, amscray, you can always tell when a unit of intergenerational people is a family unit even if there's no immediate biological resemblance, such a unit immediately identifies itself as a family unit by a set of unmistakable unifying signs, for instance bullying and humiliation and lack of respect for boundaries and presumption and put-downs masquerading as compliments and character assassination and gratuitous churlish-ness and self-pity and all the rest of the refined repertoire of torture techniques, performed moreover with an utterly groundless self-congratulation and fatuous complacency and high-fiving esprit de corps like they'd just won the Super Bowl or something What are you going to do now We're going to Disneyland!!! It's like a kind of radiation that family units give off, he had a built-in Geiger counter for this sort of family radiation and it had been crackling like crazy when this particular unit had shoved its way into the snack kiosk, they'd given off all the signs and had all the roles filled the big boss the appeaser the kapo the double agent and of course the goat, every family has to have a des-ignated goat, where there's a family it is de rigueur to have a human sacrifice. In this case it was the middle child or at least the middle girl, there were four kids a boy and three girls and the middle girl heavy and sullen and obviously the goat, everybody was getting an ice-cream sandwich except the goat who was getting her arm wrenched out of her socket could have been wearing a sandwich sign designat-ing Goat. And he had given a what-can-you-do shrug of sympathy when Mom the designated goatherd looked up at him while wrenching the young goat's limb out of its socket, he had wanted to fit in and not rock the boat and not be taken for an Arab terrorist casing the joint for an Al-Qaeda surprise snack-attack so he had made himself a collaborator in the family system, to his shame the rankest of collaborat-ors, he always had to pitch in and please everybody and authority figures most of all not because he identified with them or held them in anything but contempt but because he wanted to escape punishment himself and the best way to escape punishment was to deflect punishment in fact it was the only way, there was always going to be punishment it couldn't be escaped it could only be deflected, the hammer was always falling it's only a question of on whom so he had smiled his sympathetic smile and mimed a sympathetic what-can-you-do shrug of collaboration and deflection and it hadn't done any good at all, plenty of room under the hammer for him too, in fact he had only drawn attention to himself, he had helped to fix his image in the Goatherd's mind for her subsequent report to the state police on her cellphone afterward and now the state police cruiser was cruising by again to investigate the suspect, to investigate and interrogate, he should prepare for the interrogation because the cruiser was coming, having taken the right not the left fork of the driveway the state police sedan was cruising right at him, petrified is a different stillness from at rest, it is the cruiser cruising, it is the cruiser, oh wait it is not the cruiser, it is not even *a* cruiser, unless it is an undercover cruiser. A man in sunglasses gets out and steers his body to the larger block-structure containing the restrooms instead of the slightly smaller block-structure containing the snacks. It is not even an undercover cruiser it is simply the cruiser-shaped sedan of a driver who has to pee, something the seated figure sympathizes with. His relief at not being investigated and interrogated mingles with the sympathetic relief summoned forth by imagining peeing. He could use a pee-break himself but it is not yet time, relief from anxiety takes his mind off his bladder and steers it back towards his theme, in this interval of grace from the incessant urge to pee courtesy of the ambience of the rest stop the seated figure is prompted to recur to his theme, that temporary abeyance of the anxiety-always-present which he had experienced the last time he was spotted at this rest stop, that time in the company of his wife, and which he has experienced at other times at other highway rest stops, with or without his wife, and which he believes to be embodied rest. This temporary abeyance of the anxiety-always-present which he attributes to some essence of rest stops is really the result of three factors extrinsic to rest stops, three factors he transports with him into rest stops much as he transports the contents of his trunk, less a case of essence than of transportation. First that he is afraid of crashes, to drive or be in a moving vehicle of any kind is to experience fear of crashes, whether driving or a passenger he experiences a defining fear of crashes, of being injured severely or dying horribly in crashes, crashes brought on by his own negligence or other driver's negligence or by sheer chance, the injurious or fatal collision of agency and contingency, the definition of motion is the fear of motion's injurious or fatal cessation. Second that he is afraid of being pulled over by the cops, of being pulled over for some trifling or not so trifling traffic violation and the encounter escalating, the rules of the road are set up in such a way that to drive entails violating the rules of the road, you have to drive over the speed limit and if you don't you are driving too slow, suspiciously slow, the definition is driving is the violation of the rules of the road, but this driver in particular tends to inspire suspicion by his very being, he is an inherently suspicious character and behind the wheel of an automobile necessarily violating the rules of the road his inherent suspiciousness becomes suspiciousness squared, a suspicious character behind the wheel of a deadly weapon, even if it were just a broken taillight the encounter would no doubt escalate and instead of rest he would experience arrest. Third that he always has to pee. The bladder he ferries about in his trunk is an inherently weak bladder, it was a bad day at the bladder factory when they made the bladder he was assigned, the least volume of pee in this bladder produces the maximum of pressure in the lower quadrant of his trunk so that he always has to be up and peeing, he can't sit through a movie without having to ferry this bladder to a restroom every fifteen minutes, on a road trip he must stop at every rest stop to empty this bladder, the first thing he does at a rest stop is make a beeline for the restroom to empty this bladder, by now he has been spotted at every rest stop in the continental United States and Alaska ferrying and emptying this bladder. Given these three factors it is only natural that he experiences an exquisite sense of relief at rest stops, a well-nigh metaphysical sense of rest and relief, it is a hiatus in his anguish of crashes and cops and pee, it is a holiday, a holy day, it is not too much to say he is graced with a glimpse of the sacred in the secular round. The man in the sunglasses transports his body back to his sedan without visiting the snack kiosk. To the seated figure the man in the sunglasses transports his body with a lighter step, something the seated figure understands. He has chosen a weekday so that he will be able to note the features of the rest stop without the incursions of too many variable and unfixed rest-stop denizens at their temporary rests, just a representative sample to be sure such as the non-cop now driving away but not the weekend horde, the rest stop he has selected is on the main route to the Lakes region of New Hampshire because it was here he had his epiphany, every weekend in summer hordes of people pour up the highway in the direction of the Lakes region and pull into this Granite State rest stop, on their way to buy fireworks and stock up on tax-free alcohol and visit the Lakes to swim and boat and relax with a drink and some exploding fireworks, that is unless they're pouring south in the direction of the Cape, in summer hordes of people from Massachusetts pour north to the Lakes region or south to the Cape, it was on such a weekend a few weeks ago that this perhaps Semitic-looking definitely thirty-something Chatterton figure in shorts now scratching a mosquito bite on his hairy shin while one sock bags down around his black Converse All Star was spotted here with his wife, this figure who has returned to this Live

Free or Die rest stop and taken a seat at one of its three picnic tables on the concrete plaza between the restrooms and the snack kiosk because it was on this very spot that he had experienced the culmination of all his rest-stop experiences, he who narrates to himself his epiphany of the rest stop that is embodied rest, he who wishes now to embody this in a story or setting aside for the moment the vexed question of story a text. Because the paradise of the rest stop was only ever transitory in his experience, and because that experience was always so paradisal, for the briefest of moments the lid of paradise winking open winking shut, blinking his eyes in the summer sun he was heard to wonder aloud what it would be like to live at a rest stop, full stop. And his wife after a sip of her highly-sweetened vending-machine cappuccino was heard to respond, Yes, why don't you write a story about it, a gentle encouragement perhaps to the ostensible writer she supported that there might be more to life than twenty-four hour cable-TV news and twenty-four hour internet pornography. And so by this gentle collision of agency and contingency he has come to imagine the text of a man who lives at a rest stop. His plan being only one of preliminary research and investigation he had not a more precise idea before his return to the rest stop but even as he sketches his description of the fixed invariables of the rest stop and its unfixed variable denizens and proceeds from thence to the enumeration of finer points as the preliminary ground or basis for his text he can't help but begin to project the permanent denizen himself, to describe this man nondescript in every way, the features of this featureless figure for whom the portal will open and stay open, whose very featurelessness perhaps will be the open sesame, he can't help but project. Our projector projects a figure almost entirely featureless returning from a gambling casino after experiencing that collision of agency and contingency known as hitting the jackpot. He projects a figure seated in a car at night returning from a casino with buckets and buckets of quarters who pulls into a rest stop, a million dollars in quarters in the back seat and trunk but instead of feeling weighed down he feels light, as light as a bubble with a million dollars in quarters in plastic casino buckets, he had tipped so liberally on his way out they let him keep the plastic buckets, too astonished to cash out and exchange the quarters for a check and tipping so liberally handfuls of quarters to left and right they let him keep the plastic buckets and even helped ferry the buckets over the tarmac of the parking lot, his suspension groaned and the frame of his car sagged lower and lower on the tires as they loaded the buckets into the trunk on the first trip and the backseat the second trip and the passenger-side front seat the third and off he drove with the chassis sagging and groaning, weighed down with all these quarters on the freeway returning light as a bubble, with nothing in his mind nothing at all except a vacant bubble of astonishment, a mind for years weighed down by worry, for decades a heavy freight of worries, every thought a worry such that without them he doesn't know how to think, his mind now empty of thought and light as a bubble, after a lifetime of heavy worry this single floating bubble of wonder. Without thought he pulls into the deserted rest stop and without thought he ferries the buckets of quarters into the dark woods behind the rest stop, bucket by bucket a one-man bucket brigade into the woods behind the rest stop with no one else around until all the buckets are in the woods, at the bottom of his trunk he finds an old army-surplus blanket and a small army-surplus shovel and ferries these into the woods too, without thought he uses the shovel to bury the quarters, a squirrel with its cache of nuts would have given more thought to what it was doing, then tired from his labors he rolls himself into the old army-surplus blanket on top of the buried buckets and rests. Wink and it's morning. Light as a bubble. Nothing in mind but a need to pee communicated from the bladder and a need to eat communicated from the gut, he takes quarters from the cache and goes to the restroom to wash up, shaving kit with him, taking his empty-minded time. Sleight of hand transforms quarters into coffee bottled water peanut butter cheese crackers trail mix, he retires to the picnic bench abracadabra these too vanish empty-minded sunrise over trees and susurrus-rise over highway shine and sing. Turn your face to the grateful sun, turn your cheek to the lifting earth. Wink: it's days. Look, they're towing that car. Not one of the cars that come and go but the one that's been there the whole empty-minded time, how many days now, something familiar about it. But only with its absence does he realize its presence had kept his lightness from its fullest emptiness, that the time had not been fully empty after all, time after all and mind after all, only a little time and a little mind the weight of a single word, a word had been on the tip of his tongue, this whole time a word, asking to be uttered. Until now: pop, it's gone. At last now inside mind and outside mind are the same three picnic benches some trees a wordless round of relief refreshment and rest, instead of thoughts the comings and goings of relieved occupants of automobiles and the darker-skinned visitors at intervals mowing and mopping and taking away trash and a lighter-skinned visitor restocking vending machines and taking away quarters including his quarters, theme and variation but no inside no outside, all of our troubles come from inside outside, the minute you have inside outside you have weight attracting more weight until you are weighed down, so weightless is he inside outside nobody at the rest stop notices him any more not even the patrolman in his state police patrol cruiser so perfectly is he a piece of the peace at rest at the rest stop, technically everybody still sees him of course but his invariable thereness goes as unremarked as the picnic benches, he the familiar of the place its presiding spirit, feeding quarters into the food and beverage meters the sole cost of keeping himself alive. A jangle, that fall, a discordant note. The projector cannot convincingly make the quarters fall without sound, the quarters are not feathers or bubbles, the sound of those falling quarters keeps jangling his ears as he again holds the ergonomic pen poised over the college-ruled page of the spiral-bound notebook on the higher of the picnic bench's two horizontals. Poised is still a different stillness than at rest. Literary allusion: Coins also fall significantly onto the significant salver in James Joyce's short story, "Araby." Discuss. Epiphany, irony. Bane of undergraduates. Funny how money— Crack in the teacup fly in the ointment snake in the grass that jangle clanking through guts of the vending machines so that high-cal high-carb sat-fat goodies can clog one's guts and keep mind worry-free, the old problem of base and superstructure. And anyway there was too much story in his text, even if there was not much story it was still too much story, the text was getting weighed down by story, plot theme character symbol hogging the limelight when the rest stop should be the star of the show. *Rest stop? You get to be the setting, now set down and shut up!* Instead it was irony, ugh, irony, centerstage with sharp elbows for everyone else, as usual, irony. And epiphany! How could he have been so naïve? Epiphany the worst offender of all, the lynchpin of the whole conventional "story" con, plot and character's cumshot consummation, ratifying the spurious "interiority" of the character in the temporal schema of "character development," all for the purpose of flattering readers with their puny reflections in its little hand mirror, flattering and ratifying, those flattifying little hand mirrors of epiphany! No, what was needed was *anti*-epiphany, which dissolves deconstructs and otherwise breaks down "character" into the ensemble of its constituents, in this case chiefly the constituents of the rest stop. He should return to his original plan get up and tour the rest of the rest stop enumerating finer points, he had listed the main features of the rest stop but had allowed himself to be sidetracked into story, story had come and hijacked everything as it is wont to do, you have constantly to be on your guard against the spirit of story, that inimical spirit bullying everything with its beginnings and middles and ends its ironical ends, he had determined to list the main features of the rest stop and then and only then proceed to the enumeration of finer points it was a good plan but he had allowed himself to be sidetracked and even hijacked by story, it might even be too late to go back to the original plan which was contaminated with story but he had to try because it was a good plan. He wanted to produce a text about grace, embodied grace, grace embodied in a rest stop embodied in a text, he realized. Not a "story" with grace the "theme" and the rest stop the "setting" how banal is that. With story there is no grace and there can never be grace, where there is story there is no grace and where there is grace there is no story, in story is no abatement of contingency, in story is always death, finitude and infinite death, even the happiest ending is an ending a plunge into the infinite gulf between words such as for instance the article The and the noun End. Story: four quarters, banal wrapper, sugar coating, chewy death center, rest in peace. Bury me under the picnic bench. He has to pee. Has had to pee for some time now, the soda has made its presence felt as both liquid and diuretic, in his weak bladder the double whammy of caffeinated beverages. Now's a good time no one about, he trails a shadow slightly less truncated than on his several earlier trips to the john, the lengthening day. There are two stalls and three urinals one lower on the wall for children cripples and dwarves and in the air between him and these evacuation stations hangs the fecal funk and ammoniac skunk of public men's rooms a miasma on warm afternoons like this of human waste products and industrial-strength cleansing products, he moves to the furthest or leftmost of the three urinals the first or rightmost being the lower one for children cripples and dwarves and the centermost well he simply never takes the centermost don't want two flanks exposed bad enough having your back to the door. Prick out, he pricks up his ears for any sound of car or scrape of footfall or rearrangement of light and shadow on the yellow wall in front of him, and hearing and seeing no change sighs himself into an out-of-the-body experience remote viewing they call it five hundred feet overhead gazing weightless down at the two rest stops one on each side of the highway floating like kidneys, maybe his double was easing his bladder at that southbound-side rest stop at that very moment. Going to wash his hands he jumps at a siren. A siren song, anyway – it's just the digital camera in its scrotal pouch on top of his spiral-bound notebook on the corner of the other sink, beeping its siren ditty: Change my batteries! Almost gave him a heart attack, but now it gives him an idea: Here's the chance to complete his research of the rest-stop restroom, a golden opportunity as the saying goes to note the main features and enumerate the finer points of the restroom for his text, which is embodied rest, he can return to his original plan it is not too late, later even a little later it would be too late, and besides the well-known phenomenon of olfactory fatigue was setting in, the well-known operation of the olfactory system by which offensive odors are attenuated, pleasant odors too, admittedly, in the olfactory system as in every system there is cost along with benefit, there always has to be a cost along with the benefit, always a zero-sum game, in a bakery instead of a men's room he would grow as numb to the olfactory charms of freshly baked bread, the olfactory tending to its steady state, at rest. He exchanges the exhausted batteries for a new pair from the pouch and hey presto: digital camera now surrogate eye and memory, held over one meat-eye with the other squinched shut he roves the men's room snapping features and fixtures, storing them up for later, why waste meat-memory, the wetware, the fallible meat. Urinals sinks empty soap dispensers inoperative hand dryer trash can cracked malarial tiles flies iron grate crust of dried waste paper and scunge over drain in stained concrete snapping them all up into digital memory, the term snapping a vestige from pre-digital dark ages of film cameras, like "rolling down" car windows by the one-fingered caress of an automated button. And now for the stalls, the stalls from the outside and then from the inside, in stall one a retchworthy shitspatter of wall-to-wall extra chunky he snaps it anyway and in stall two behold: The Man. Too late, his flash goes off in the same instant The Man flashes a badge – Officer Wood. That's it, busted, gig's up, end of story, he can see it now, tomorrow's headlines, Terror Plot Foiled in Granite State Rest Stop, photo of grinning cop posing next to perp dangling from the yardarm, his big Arab nose upended like a prize marlin's.

OFFICER WOOD
You're under arrest.

HE
[*Cringing.*] I, er, no, this isn't what it looks like.

OFFICER WOOD
[*Smiling.*] Oh yeah? What does it look like?

HE
I'm writing a story.

OFFICER WOOD
With a camera?

HE
It's set in a rest stop, the story. A man who lives at a rest
stop. I have handwritten notes, too, in that notebook, I can
show you. It's all . . . research.

OFFICER WOOD
Research.

HE
Not that kind, uh, not— It's for the story, to get the all the
details right [*smaller and smaller voice*] . . . you know,
verisimilitude . . .

OFFICER WOOD
Are you kidding me? That kind of stuff went out with Emile
Zola.

HE
What about the thirties?

OFFICER WOOD
OK, fine, Depression-era documentary realism, a hiccup,
still proves my point. And I know what you're going to say
next – Tom Wolfe. Big deal, another exception that proves
the rule. I mean, a lot of people had fun with *Bonfire*, it was
funny, but please. *A Man in Full*? *My Name is Charlotte*?
That's not art, that's . . . information.

HE

No, I, see, I, this is all a big misunderstanding. I completely agree with you. I don't even like Tom Wolfe. It's just, my plan, er, approach, I was going to use the "facts" to abolish the whole notion of fact, the tyranny, wrong word— I mean, use what usually takes the place of "setting" in a conventional story to blow up story from in— Or *not*, not blow up! Very wrong word! I don't really want to write a story at all, but a text! A text!

OFFICER WOOD

[*Deadpanning.*] You just told me you were going to write a story. You can't even keep your own story straight. [*Holds for laugh, doesn't get one*]. Alright, let's go.

HE

So, wait, I'm under arrest for researching a rest stop with the intent to commit literary naturalism?

OFFICER WOOD

We can't arrest anyone for that yet. You're under arrest for Solicitation of a Lewd Act in a Public Place. And [*pointing*] Indecent Exposure.

HE

[*Drops camera onto concrete, zips up fly.*] I, no, that's an accident! Lewd act? This whole thing is absurd!

OFFICER WOOD

Tell it to the judge. This is a family place, pervert. [*Points to cracked-open camera.*] And no good trying to destroy the evidence. We can retrieve whatever we need from the chip. Now turn around for your bracelets, Cinderella. How's that for cop patter.

HE
Aren't you going to read me my wri—, er, rights?

OFFICER WOOD
[*Smirks, scratching head.*] And what are those, again?

HE
What do you mean? You're supposed to be telling me!

[OFFICER WOOD, *still smirking, waits.*]

HE
[*A child reciting its lesson.*] I have the right to remain silent,
anything I say or do can be held against me in a court of law,
I have the right to an attorney, if I can't afford one the court
will appoint one to me blah blah blah . . .

OFFICER WOOD
Voilà, there are your rights.

HE
But you didn't read them to me.

OFFICER WOOD
[*Martyred sigh.*] Everyone wants a bedtime story. Look,
your 'rights' are being read to you all the time. We've set it
up that way. Where did you learn to recite them like that
anyway? And don't tell me it was civics class.

[*Pause.*]

HE
From TV.

OFFICER WOOD
Exactly. Cop shows, detective dramas, police procedurals . . .
In fact – I'm sure you'll notice from now on if you haven't
already – if you surf through the five hundred channels on
your TV you'll see that on at least one channel at any given
time, on one show or another, someone is being read their
rights. Why do you think there are so many Law and
Orders? Back at the big mainframe it's set up that way and
it's timed perfectly. When they finish reading somebody's
rights on one show they start reading somebody else's rights
on some other show, and so on. Twenty-four hours a day,
three-hundred and sixty-five days a year, year in and year
out, in a continuous loop, viewers everywhere are being
read their rights. So don't go whining you haven't been read
your rights. The judge will explain this to you again at your
arraignment but I'm in a good mood this afternoon, an
expansive mood. Discursive, even. It's a really nice afternoon.

HE
Yes, but not everyone has five hundred channels.

OFFICER WOOD
That's just illegal aliens. [*Cinches cuffs.*] Those too tight?

HE
They're fine.

OFFICER WOOD
Compliant. I like that.

HE
What about my car?

OFFICER WOOD
You can pick it up at the tow yard tomorrow after your arraignment, should you make bail. Otherwise your wife can pick it up.

HE
How do you know I'm married?

OFFICER WOOD
The ring, Watson. But it's always the married fags out cruising like you.

HE
Look, officer, I'm telling you, this is all a big mis—

OFFICER WOOD
Is this really so bad, though? Isn't it even kind of erotic? The realization of a fantasy? Don't all you faggots dream about sucking a cop's dick? Big Bad Daddy like me?

[*Lengthy pause.*]

HE
Would that help?

OFFICER WOOD
Wouldn't hurt.

HE
Ah.

Figure, kneeling, at rest, arms behind back, wrists at kidney level, kidneys floating like mirrored islands on each side of a central column, elbows crooked, knees on horizontal surface, bare, bare knees, bare concrete, at rest. Look closer, head not at rest, head bobs, back and forth, each bob forward a collision with a vertical that depresses the tip of the figure's nose, lips parted around fluted cylinder, cylinder horizontal, parallel to horizontal on which the kneeling figure kneels, mouth open, gorge gags. Revise: Nominally at rest then. Mostly at rest. Let the resting figure be the ordinal point. Under arrest or at rest, a cost for every benefit, a benefit for every cost, the collision of agency and contingency, each system tending to its steady state, at rest. Full stop.

American Rabbit

Why must he always read the plaques first? It is a weakness, or else it is a compulsion. If the former a moral condition if the latter a medical condition not his fault possibly treatable drugs. Museum after museum he reads the plaque first then addresses himself to the work, he leans in stretching his neck before he stands back, settling his shoulders. What will the words tell him that the picture won't? Or box, in this case, boxes mostly, and collages. What if the plaque-words even obscure the picture, or in this case the box, serve to obscure rather than illuminate, foreclose rather than disclose, the picture or in this case the box, attenuate the encounter? Do the words forestall an anxiety, remediate a vertigo, as if the frame were not enough to keep him from falling in? Keep the encounter in the key of analysis rather than, what? Ecstasy? Aesthesis as ex-stasis, find yourself standing next to yourself, art the last holdout of the sacred in a secular age blah blah blah. Too crowded anyway, onlookers, extra guards, a weekend, kids even, mistake, too crowded. If the latter not his fault medical condition possibly treatable pills. He imagines a Joseph Cornell box with one of those bygone phrenological profile-maps of the brain-bumps each characterological county the repository of differently colored pills, bring old Cornell up to date with neuroscience. Write that down. If he's not staring at the plaques he's scribbling in his little pocket notebook, must have the cranial bump of a word nut, eighty-plus milligrams of fluoxetine and a beta-blocker indicated. Wants to remember the joke spring it on his wife at their debrief over coffee like he'd made it up it on the spot, appearance of spontaneity. She's already sped through the exhibition rooms and homed in on the touch-screen computers, in the final room a little circle of uncomfortable couches around a coffee table stacked with Joseph Cornell books and catalogues for your perusal and a bank of touch-screen computers against the wall and there sat his wife on a tall stool hunched over a touch-screen touching away, happy as a clam. At the next touch-screen two kids on two stools, brother and sister by the looks of them, sis reading the words on the screen to kid brother and pushing his chubby fingers away he wants to touch to the next screen, cute, annoying, it would annoy him if he were on the other stool in place of his wife but his wife's powers of concentration are positively feral. His wife also reads the plaques first before giving the pictures or in this case the boxes the once-over then it's on to the next plaque, it's information she wants not aesthesis, she has an excuse, no time for outworn religion in any form it's all science now, buster, unless of course science turns out to be the last out-post of the sacred in a secular age blah blah blah. He's almost done himself, done with the exhibition and maybe even with Art, tagged the bases in all the rooms except the room he will return to presently, the room he'd had to short-shrift on the first go-round because of that annoying guard, even though it was the room with some of his favor-ite pieces the Soap Bubble series and the Medici Slot Machines and Penny Arcades, ruined by that especially annoying guard. The other guards the normal ones just stood against the walls, one normal guard per room, this wall or that, changing walls occasionally different angle unobtrusive standing like Wooden Indians but no not this guard with the refulgent mustachios, obviously very proud of his refulgent mustachios, this guard had to be marching around peacocking his refulgent mustachios, this guard stepping or rather marching in such a way that he led with his refulgent mustachios, the rest of him bringing up the rear, not happy being a Wooden Indian he had to be Natty Bumpo, a Natty Bumpo with refulgent mustachios. These mustachios functioned as antennae which tingled every time the guard invaded the personal space of potential museum malefactors the art thieves and vandals and thus their wearer had to rove in order for the mustachios to work, had to rove the room thrusting the mustachios into everyone's personal space if their sensitive whiskers were to tingle out the malefactors, and on clomping boots no less, on those leatherstockings he didn't rove so much as clomp, hear him clomping up behind you when you're trying to concentrate on having an aesthetic experience or at least on seeing how the art illustrated the words on the plaque, the Cornell boxes safe in glass cases guarded by the words on the plaques so why did the guard have to clomp so close, clomping up behind until you saw the glint of his refulgent mustachios in the glass, making you conscious of the glass instead of the Cornell box inside, it made you conscious of the reflections on the glass and therefore conscious of your-self too, the dim outline of your head with its pronounced cranial word-nut bump and its large nose glinting, oily, not much light in the room don't want to fade the Cornell colors but enough to make an oily gigantic nose glint suspiciously, luring the mustachioed guard like a spinner lures a bass in the depths of a lake, a simile. Impossible to concentrate, he'd had to move on, Soap Bubble Set notwithstanding. By now he has made it through the whole exhibition so of course he has to pee, urgently to pee, has made sure his wife is occupied at the touch-screens happy as a clam picking up information and germs of the other visitors' kids before having to trot all the way back through the exhibition halls and down to the restrooms, out and down all those stairs to the restrooms, trotting and also because of the weekend throng threading, he trots and he threads, but the men's room is empty a miracle he addresses himself to the urinal. And while he's getting his dick out he thinks about how tiresome this novelistic job of moving characters about in space is for writers and readers alike, and how when he becomes Commissar of Culture his first decree will be that henceforth and henceforward all characters in fiction be granted the power to transport themselves through space, like on Star Trek but instantly without all those fizzy effects. And as he sighs himself into his pee and his bladder drains he notices that the mounted gleaming urinal the plumbing fixtures and the wall-tiles appear to him like charmed items in a Cornell box, the Cornell boxes now frame how he sees, how he sees as he pees. He might be having an aesthetic experience after all. You go to museums and look at the pictures or in this case the boxes so that you can have an aesthetic experience in the restroom, everyone emptying their bladders into Marcel Duchamp's fountains, *nota bene* Duchamp a friend of Cornell. He (not Duchamp or Cornell but our protagonist) feels restored by his aesthetic experience, his aesthetic palette had been cleansed, he no longer suffers from museum fatigue, his default setting for museum fatigue by the way is quite low, he thinks he loves museums a culture vulture as well as a word-nut but museums fatigue him after only a short time, after an hour or even forty minutes all the exhibits start to look the same, every piece different and yet the same, every piece a museum piece the common denominator, he ends up after the shortest of times seeing only this common denominator and he blames himself, he doesn't recognize that it is the function of museums to emphasize this common denominator, if the function of art is defamiliarization the function of the museum is refamiliarization yet he blames himself, what art unmakes through defamiliarization the museum reinstates and even institutionalizes as the familiar yet he blames himself, the pall of museum-habit is draped over the works and nailed down by plaques, keeps the visitors nailed down too no ex-stasis in a museum wouldn't be decorous yet he blames himself, insight overridden yet again by guilt in the face of authority, his habitual posture and automatic attitude of guilt in relation to all authority including natur-ally the authority of the museum, the structure of the museum which is embodied authority, his default setting to blame himself. But right now he thinks he's got a reprieve, with the relief of peeing which he mistakes for aesthetic experience although who's to say maybe it is, is that too, whatever it is it is a little bit of grace and a lighter step, so light in fact that instead of threading through weekend throngs up the stairs he transports himself instantly no fizz-ing back up to the heart of the exhibition, from the bladder and bowels of the museum to its very heart, the room with the Soap Bubble Set and the Medici Slot Machines which he'd had to short-shrift on the first go-round because of the annoying guard with the refulgent antennae, and instantly he remarks that his luck is holding out, it is a lucky day, he is lucky after all: the annoying guard is no longer there, either roving or at rest. Another guard has taken his place, Natty Bumpo has been replaced, a changing of the guard has taken place, this guard a conventional Wooden Indian or better yet head down writing something in a little note-book a Writing Indian not even looking at the onlookers. Crowd of onlookers a little thinner too by lucky chance, now is your chance, address, address yourself to the works! Not the plaques but the works! He imagines that a deeply authentic encounter with these Cornell works unmediated by their plaques will inspire him to compose (too Romantic!

revise!) will motivate him to construct a series of prose-poems commemorating his deeply authentic aesthetic experience, a series of whaddaya-call-'ems, word for it, tip of his tongue, for poems about paintings, such as for instance Auden's *Musée des Beaux Arts* (this citation his ego's consolation prize for failing to remember the term of which the Auden poem represents one well-known example, and which by the way is *ekphrasis*, as he himself will remember about a hour later, in the coffee shop with his wife during their exhibition debrief, he will remember the term at around the same time that he springs on his wife with all the appearance of spontaneity his joke about the Cornell box with the phrenologist's chart whose different cranial regions are the repositories of various brain drugs and to his abiding chagrin, abiding for hours afterwards and even into the next day and from time to time also the next weeks and months, his wife with the photographic memory will helpfully respond, Wasn't that a *New Yorker* cover?), except he didn't believe in poems so they would be prose-poems, or more properly texts, texts that would deconstruct and indeed explode the conventions of the whaddaya-call-'em poem from inside out, his whole aesthetic being an anti-aesthetic, a blowing up from inside, gelignite strapped to his midriff draped in bohemian (and slimming) black. They, these, these boxes, they . . . are windows, that's it, keep going, they are little windows opening onto big worlds, but big dream worlds, always so wistful and dreamy that they are little worlds too, because the distance was always acknowledged, the desideratum and the dream-distance at the same time, like a travel brochure or looking out a train window at something passing, something fleetingly glimpsed by the traveler going home, when you travel there's always something you miss and it's what you've missed that you think you glimpse for a instant outside of

your train window, or your plane window, or the porthole of
the ship. Not the trip itself but the torn ticket, the romance
of the torn ticket and the souvenir and that thing lying
always just outside the border of the snapshot, thing intim-
ated rather than disclosed in postcards, not France itself but
the romance of French names, Cornell in love with French
names but never going to France, or did he, no, no biography, no plaque, our constructor of texts no longer sees
the box but rather again his dim reflection in the glass, his
big nose, the temptation to look at a plaque has made him
conscious of his reflected honker, or was it the other way
round doesn't matter no stealing a look at the plaque for
Christ's sake, no poking your giant beak at the plaque, look
at the boxes, look at the damn box and have a goddamn aesthetic experience for a change. The plan is first to have an
aesthetic experience and proceed from thence to the decon-
struction even detonation of the aesthetic experience, of the
whole idea of aesthetic experiences. He looks at the Cornell
boxes and looks and looks and after a while he hears music,
that's it keep going, he hears a music like chimes, minor
music, chamber music for these little chambers. *Synaes-
thesia* another Greek term but this one borne to mind
instantly on the chimes, looking at colors he hears effortless
chimes. The blues especially, Cornell had a way with blues,
with a shudder of the well-known literary phenomenon of
involuntary memory summoned forth effortlessly by the
blue chimes he remembers no revise re-experiences how
colors appeared to him as a boy, how color lived for him
when he was but a boy, a mere lad, a wee bairn even, every
day a circus day of color and blues always in the center ring,
the mystery of color in his uncle's marble collection so cool
in the hand such wealth to the eye and the blues always best,
and here this cobalt, this midnight, these thousand-and-one
shades of firmament, would have swapped eyes for them

back in the day. And once in a blue moon these moments of grace still, little still moments of grace, little grace notes, little chamber music notes of grace. He notes the thimbles and corks and chemist's bottles and Dutch clay pipes and wine glasses with marbles hung in them like planets and movie-star glamour shots cut out of magazines and toy plastic lobsters lined up like ballerinas and the coiled springs out of clocks, products of mass production side by side with the harvest of the older craft ethic arranged in Cornell's craftsman-like boxes, nostalgia in the age of mass machine manufacture, the craft ethic and mass mechanical production reconciled in these boxes, out of time and at rest, fantasy reconciliation of the historically residual and the historically emergent, the aura and the loss of the aura, the craft ethic and machine mass-production, mechanical production breaking down craftsmen into machines themselves, from agents to adjuncts mass-producing these knick-knacks for Cornell to pop into his boxes, workshop of the artist the last holdout of the craft ethic in the age of mechanical reproduction blah blah blah, the oft-cited "magic" of Cornell really this reconciliation's hey presto, art the imaginary reconciliation of real social contradictions. Too analytical! Intellectual not spiritual! He ignores the plaques only to scribble academic exegeses in his pocket notebook! Have an authentic aesthesis already before you go exploding aestheses from inside out! And speaking of aestheses, that girl standing next to him has got a nice one, must be an art student, art-girls always up for a good time, scribbling away in his notebook trying to look all important and serious, can't look past his own nose unless it's at some girl's aesthesis. Focus! Try, try again . . . Depth and the illusion of depth, that's it keep going, great depth of the sky blue in the day dark at night and azure in-between, intimate foregrounds and vast backgrounds with no middle ground at all, distillations of longing which admit no middle ground yet by this very omission admit longing's confinement and doom, suspended for a moment in these boxes before it dissipates between foreground and background longing's distillation and doom. And Joseph Cornell himself confined, doomed decades with his ageing mother in that same house on Utopia Parkway, days collecting gewgaws and bric-a-brac from the shops on Fourth Avenue insomniac nights in the basement workshop and never a date in his whole life, plenty of days but never a date and the art-girls down in the Village always up for a good time, Cornell afraid of women and obviously hung up on mom, dying a virgin after a life spent compulsively crafting these little windows for his autistic prison cell and decorating his emotional stuntedness with the ephemera of doomed longings, they were guillotines these boxes, they were all about castration, they were apertures of vagina dentata, the sharp teeth sublimated into playthings but gnashers nonetheless, gaze out the window all you want but step through and be severed, he was a grown man who played with dolls. Cornell's dolls including his cast of paste-up film-fantasy girlfriends, Lauren Bacall Hedy Lamarr Jennifer Jones, if he (our little wayfarer not Joseph Cornell) had been an autistic paste-up artist of the same era he would have picked Veronica Lake, a life spent worshipping Veronica Lake with her peekaboo bangs and bedroom eyes was almost worth becoming an autistic romantically-challenged paste-up artist for, or better yet Gloria Graham, he'd always had a thing for Gloria Graham, Gloria Graham who'd always played the tramp, back in the day when they could only imply such things in movies Gloria Graham was always implied to be a total tramp, Gloria Graham typecast as the gum-crackin' chippie, Gloria Graham always reminded him of the words Game and Gamesome, Gloria Graham would have been Game and

Gamesome in the sack, like the art-girls those B-list chippies were always up for anything, he wanted to be teased and tortured by Game and Gamesome blonde shiksas, especially ass games, especially games of hovering that sexy sphincter just inches from his tongue, stretching his tongue until its root becomes a ring of ache, a constricted ring of ache straining for a constricted ring of anus, Gloria Graham always second- or third-tier never Hollywood's idea of big Game but for that very reason the top of his list, an A-list actress never lets you play ass-games but his A was for Ass Games, if he were an autistic paste-up artist he would project his doomed dreams through the frame of Gloria Graham's sphincter, a sphincter-dentata through which one may look long and longingly but venture through and your tongue or whatever gets cut off, like Lucy tempting Charlie Brown with the football in the old Peanuts cartoon strip except it is Gloria Graham instead of Lucy or if he wants someone not dead then it is porn star Annette Schwartz instead of Lucy and it is our suspicious possibly Semitic-looking little wayfarer instead of Charlie Brown and it is an anus instead of a football and it is castration instead of landing thump on your back but otherwise it is exactly the same. He is getting a hard on. The art-girl with the nice aesthesis is gone he steals a look at the guard sidelong glance nothing obvious don't go drawing attention to yourself but the guard's still scribbling away in his little pocket notebook, quite a scribbler that guard, something familiar about him too, a bit of a strutter by the looks of him just like the guard with the refulgent mustachios but this guard channeling the strutting into his scribbling, this guard's scribbling gives off a strutting air what a jerk. Ignore him since he is ignoring you or rather pretending to ignore you because his scribbling may just be a clever ruse, this guard doesn't have mustache-antennae so he uses a different snare to catch the museum malefactors a fake-out like he's got better things to do. The previous guard got on his nerves for being too obtrusive whereas this guard is getting on his nerves for being too unobtrusive. He should just smash the glass case one smash right in his reflected mug and make off with the Joseph Cornell box inside, he would make off with this *American Rabbit c. 1945-46* box under his arm and hop right out of the Peabody-Essex Museum if only on principle, if only for the principle of the thing. Radiating his most museum-malefactorish vibe he looks back and forth from *American Rabbit c. 1945-46* to the guard but the guard only continues struttingly to scribble and obtrusively to not obtrude, our protagonist performs a broad pantomime worthy of a silent film actor of an art thief sizing up the joint while the guard only continues to obtrude his scribbling with a strutting air what a jerk. It is getting personal now, it is beyond personal. He (our protagonist, he being short for hero, it bears repeating, besides just being short) bends again to his own pocket notebook and starts making notes about the *American Rabbit c. 1945-46* box even though it is not an especially interesting box, it is just the box that happens to be on hand but it will do, we'll just see who can make notes here, buddy, we will compare notes and we will see whose notes are best. And your mother wears Army boots. He can even identify what kind of notebook the guard holds in his hand, the brand that's advertised as having been Hemingway's Notebook of Choice, a "writer's notebook" how pretentious is that, what a show off, look at me I'm like all a Writer and stuff, you're all yahoos and philistines but I am a Writer. Whoa, everybody – Writer At Work! Our hero identifies the notebook instantly, he knows it very well, because it happens to be identical to the notebook he holds in his own hand that very moment. With the appearance of absorption he notes the features of the Joseph Cornell box

American Rabbit c. 1945-46 in his identical notebook, just to emphasize and as it were underline the depth of his absorption he tries to make the scratching of his pen audible and he succeeds, with the point of his pen in his identical notebook he succeeds in making an audible scratching noise and an even more audible tearing noise. He casts another sidelong glance at the guard trying to catch the guard casting sidelong glances at him, he knows the guard is casting him sidelong glances, it is transparently obvious that the guard is casting him sidelong glances, even though he is not able to catch the guard actually casting any sidelong glances it is transparent that the guard is doing it. It is only because of the subdued lighting that he is unable to catch any of the guard's many sidelong glances, clearly it is the result of the subdued lighting, the lighting which has to be subdued so as not to fade the colors of the Joseph Cornell boxes and collages, even though the particular box before which he stands tearing the pages of his notebook and casting sidelong glances is not especially colorful and contains none of the madeleine-flavored blues so prominent in the other Cornell boxes in the room, doesn't it just figure *American Rabbit c. 1945-46* is not one of Joseph Cornell's more colorful boxes, a little reddish-brown here a little brownish-red there, some off-white and shades of rust. What is clear however is that the guard is now mocking him, even in the subdued lighting it is glaringly obvious it is plain as day that he is being mocked by this scribbling guard. Our hero had taken out his pocket notebook for the sole purpose of writing up his impressions of the boxes but this had been intentionally even maliciously misconstrued by the side-long-glancing guard as our hero's attempt to impress the art-girl with the nice aesthesis, to impress her with a show of art-seriousness just in case the girl happened to be one of those art-girls who as a rule are up for anything, and now even though the art-girl had taken her nice aesthesis with her into another room the guard continues to mock him and to mimic him, our protagonist is the prototype and his antagonist is the mimic, our protagonist the original and his antagonist the copy, unless of course it is the other way round. Admittedly the guard had had his notebook out first, this has to be taken into account, maybe the guard believes that it is our hero who is mocking him. Fortunately there is a formula for figuring such things out. This guard this Wooden Indian or rather Writing Indian also happens to be a White Indian, even a WASP Indian, whereas our protagonist is swarthy and Semitic-looking probably more Arab-than Jew-looking although in Palestine or the so-called Holy Land it can be tough to tell the difference sometimes just a matter of which side of the bulldozer or big wall you happen to be on, one in a series of swell historical ironies which I'm sure they're all savoring together over their tea in the West Bank or Gaza as we speak, but it's the Way of the World that when you see two people doing more or less the same thing but especially anything to do with Writing anything to do with Language or with Culture and one of them is lighter skinned and the other one is darker skinned the lighter-skinned one is always the original and the darker-skinned one is always the copy, as night follows day the lighter one is always primary the darker one always secondary, just to clear up this dispute, this dispute in the subdued lighting, the lighter one is the prototype and the darker one is the mimic, the Way of the World a bitter pill. And to make it go down easier or is it to stick in his craw more exquisitely our protagonist realizes at that moment where he has seen this familiar-looking WASP Writing Indian guard before. He is an actor, this guard, a performer, our protagonist has even seen him perform on the stage, in a college production of Samuel Beckett's famous and influential play *Waiting for*

Godot two or three months ago in the company of his wife our hero had seen this very museum guard as it were treading the boards for the greater glory of Thespia, or whoops no it's Thespis got it mixed up with Lesbia, and not in the costume of a museum guard but rather in the guise of Pozzo, in make-up and silver wig and stuffed tunic to give him a big rich bastard's swagger-belly no wonder our hero hadn't recognized him right away in his new role as Museum Guard 2 at this afternoon's matinee performance of The Joseph Cornell Exhibition now playing at the Peabody-Essex Museum, sort of actor who disappears into a role, he reasoned. Even remembers his name, our hero won't remember *ekphrasis* for another seventy-three minutes but go figure he remembers this actor's name, this actor's name is Jim Wood, out of the woodwork as it were, the actor and this guard one and the same Jim Wood. Jim Wood's performance as Pozzo had been the best performance of the cast, the other actors' portrayals of the other Beckett characters had been of student quality whereas Jim Wood's portrayal of the character Pozzo had been of professional quality, in their debrief of the performance in the coffee shop after the production our hero had gone so far as to single out the actor playing Pozzo as the best actor of the bunch and his wife with the photographic memory had agreed saying, Yes of the five actors *Jim Wood* was certainly the best actor. Our protagonist wasn't good with names but his wife with the photographic memory tended to be good with names go figure and she had given the program a summary glance and could even tell you who had done the lighting if you'd asked, how annoying is that. Yes, she went on, it was a good performance it was very funny, that Jim Wood was especially funny. And now to himself our protagonist quips If you thought he was funny as Pozzo you should see him as Museum Guard 2 he's a fucking riot. But it is true they had both laughed at that production of *Waiting for Godot*, it is the unfortunate and lamentable truth that both our hero and his wife along with everybody else in the theater that evening had been made to laugh very heartily indeed, they had laughed and had laughed because Jim Wood and the rest of the cast had played their production of *Waiting for Godot* for laughs, already a funny play but they had played it especially and even solely for laughs because they had played it exactly like a Monty Python sketch, had deliberately and consciously modeled their performance after the famous and influential Monty Python's Flying Circus sketch-comedy TV series complete with the silly voices and silly walks, it had been an extended Pythonesque "take" on Samuel Beckett's tired old tragicomedy *Waiting for Godot*, it had been a two-hour dead parrot sketch. (Our hero gives a nod at the Joseph Cornell box *Habitat Group for a Shooting Gallery c. 1943*, which like many Cornell boxes features parrots. It all hangs together, doesn't it.) But afterwards even as his wife had lauded the production he realized that it had been a terrible production, not a terribly funny production just a terrible production, he had started out the debrief saying nice things about the production but the more his wife lauded the production to the skies the more deeply the production sank in our protagonist's esteem, the more deeply it sank and it stank, even within the strict guidelines mandated by the Beckett Estate for any and all productions of all Beckett plays they had managed to botch this *Godot* by doing a Monty Python schtick with twitty British accents and silly walks and Jim Wood turning in a John Cleese impersonation as Pozzo, like John Cleese in Monty Python or whenever Pozzo went apoplectic in the play then like John Cleese going apoplectic as Basil Fawlty in *Fawlty Towers*, not a performance but an impersonation, the actors had pandered to the audience with their impersonations and they had played to the lowest common denominator and the audience had pandered back, laughing like cretins, complacent and self-satisfied laughter the easy laughter of familiarity and recognition the laughter of satisfied philistines the cretinous laughter of sitcom laugh-tracks, and like a cretin and satisfied philistine he had laughed with the rest of them and found it good. Somehow they had gotten this appalling production past the Beckett Estate, the Beckett Estate which demanded that each and every production of every Beckett play be performed according to the strictest of guidelines, the Beckett Estate which had almost total control over all productions of all Beckett plays everywhere in the world, even if you didn't contact the Beckett Estate they seemed to know instantly where any production of a Beckett play was being launched anywhere in the world, through a network of spies and informers and sophisticated electronic surveillance the Beckett Estate kept watch on every drama troupe in the world, professional and amateur, and knew instantly when any one of them anywhere was even considering launching a Beckett production, and in addition to the vast and soph-isticated intelligence network they had Black Ops units and Special Forces teams that could swoop down instantly on any production whose director was for example contem-plating cutting or changing a line even a word of the Beckett text or having a female actor play a male role or vice-versa or in which too much emoting typical of the Stanislavsky method were being employed in rehearsals, as soon as the chopper was heard overhead it was too late the masked Spe-cial Ops forces of the Beckett Estate were already rapelling down ropes and sealing off the exits while the theater filled up with a paralyzing gas, the production would be made to disappear as if it had never been and the director and the stage manager and some of the actors would be made to disappear as if they had never been also, and if they ever reappeared it was in a completely broken-down state, immobilized and interminably mumbling like Beckett characters themselves, as if they had been transported to a special drama school for the proper techniques of Beckettian acting and had graduated as the master class, poetic justice courtesy of the all-powerful Beckett Estate. And yet this terrible performance of *Waiting for Python* starring Jim Wood as John Cleese in a Pozzo wig had been allowed to pass, to pass and to go forward and be met by the chorus of laughing cretins and applauding philistines among whom to his shame our hero had turned in a more-than-creditable performance of his own. In retrospect the whole spectacle bespoke the existence of a mind-boggling flaw if not an encroaching senility somewhere in the vast and sophisticated network of the Beckett Estate, a chink in the armor which the clever might exploit for their own purposes, perhaps this Jim Wood who looked too old to be a student actor hair thinning on top maybe a grad student or else just make-up part of his museum-guard costume maybe this Jim Wood was privy himself to this flaw or senile oversight in the Beckett Estate network. Jim Wood had thumbed his nose at the Beckett Estate and lived to act another day, he had mocked the Beckett Estate and yet here he stood in the role of Museum Guard 2 mocking our hero, unless of course it is the other way round. And still our hero could not catch this clever actor in the act of a single sidelong glance, how infuriating is that. Speak to him, say something, say that his secret stands revealed, his ploys and guises do not work with you, ask for his autograph. Jim Wood could scratch it right there in your little notebook or on a page of his own identical little notebook and tear out the page for you although it would be more polite to offer him a page of your own. But then of course our hero would crumple the autographed page and hurl it back into the actor's face saying, Ha! Two can play at this acting game! He would throw the crumpled autograph back, or like a gauntlet down. And he is just about to do it, our hero, to approach this actor and do something heroic, or do something at least, anything, to, to, well, to act. He screws his courage to the sticking place so as not to let the native hue of resolution become sicklied o'er by the pale cast of thought, turning his back on the actor Jim Wood to scowl and rub his chin in the manner of one resolving, as soon as his metaphors are all properly mixed he will no doubt act. And at that moment a serendipitous entrance: The girl with the nice aesthesis returns! His luck is holding out, he is lucky after all, must have impressed the art-girl with his show of genuine art-seriousness after all. She is only pretending that she has returned for another gander at the Soap Bubble sets and the Medici Slot Machine and the Penny Arcade for Lauren Bacall, flipping her curly red hair from her alabaster brow and obtruding her nice aesthesis in the manner of an up-for-anything art-girl while casting him sidelong glances, no doubt in the subdued lighting she casts him sidelong glances, he will try to catch her eye he will catch her in the act, this art-girl with the nice aesthesis and curly red hair. He will ignore Jim Wood just as Jim Wood pretends to ignore him and he will speak to the art-girl, he will approach and hold converse with the art-girl and make her laugh, that's it keep going, make her laugh loud and long, he will be artful and "on" and the art-girl will applaud the performance and laugh in the manner of being up for anything and Jim green-with-jealousy Wood will eat his black heart out. And there, he's done it, caught her eye, hasn't he? Now is your chance, address, address yourself to the art-girl! Whereupon from behind him moving across the gallery floor like a thunderhead over still seas (a Homeric simile) rolls the unmistakable scent of a great fart, the cloud of a great gaseous fart from behind our hero rolling and wafting, a wall of fart so strong that in its midst the temperature and humidity rise by measurable degrees and the feathers on the dead parrots in *Habitat Group for a Shooting Gallery c. 1943* start to curl, from behind our hero but not from our hero's behind and rolling in the direction of the girl with the nice aesthesis this tropical weather-system of a fart. It is a rich fart, too, were he not so mortified our hero would perhaps be able to savor the richness of this fart, if it were his own fart he would no doubt savor its textures, its body, its bouquet of peat bog and garlic and hint of mustard and not a little mushroom, a fart at once playful and profound, silent in its origin only because it so patently speaks for itself, a fart full worthy of its setting, in fact a masterpiece – an Art Fart. But still a fart. The girl's pert alabaster nostrils flutter and scrunch. Our hero makes a broad show of turning behind him, practically bows and sweeps his arms as if to direct the art-girl's attention to the fart's true indubitable source, Jim Wood in the role of Museum Guard 2, Jim Wood who let a great fart of a performance in his role as John Cleese in a Pozzo wig in *Waiting for Python* has let an even greater fart in his role of Museum Guard 2, return engagement, credit where credit is due. But Jim Wood is not there to take the bow. Jim Wood has exited stage-left as silently as he had let his great fart, and no one else stands near. Unmistakably now the art-girl meets our hero's gaze and scrunches her adorable alabaster brow into a frown before exiting stage-right with her nice aesthesis bringing up the rear, evidently some ass-games she's not up for. Footfalls echo, a dying fall, a pause. And it is no good now going back to try to have an aesthetic experience he has already started to find the Cornell boxes cloying, as the well-known phenomenon of olfactory fatigue numbs our hero's sinuses to the layered if dissipating charms of Jim Wood's

fart he grows more acutely conscious than ever of the cloying sticky-sweetness of the Cornell boxes, Cornell's work
inferior and minor and precious and cloying he (our hero
not Cornell) had been a fool to allow himself to be seduced
by its minor magic, a major exhibition of a minor magic,
just right for a town like Salem Massachusetts which otherwise specializes in kitsch shops full of crystals and penta-
grams and witch costumes, instead of heading south to New
York to see a major artist he had headed north to Salem to
see a minor artist the story of his life, Cornell was perfect for
this town whose major holiday was Halloween, a major
exhibition of a minor artist for a minor museum in a toy
town. Reviewing his notes he finds that he has a Marxist
analysis of the boxes (the imaginary resolution of the real
social contradiction of residual craft ethic and emergent
machine mass-production) and a psychoanalytic analysis of
the boxes (vaginas with fangs) but has he had an aesthetic
experience yet? Is aesthetic experience even possible anymore? Is the idea of aesthetic experience itself a nostalgia?
Perhaps any aesthetic experience we have today is not an
aesthetic experience but rather a simulation of an aesthetic
experience, a reproduction of an aesthetic experience, a
reproduction of a reproduction, he reasons. And anyway the
exhibition galleries are getting too crowded again, there had
been a lull in the crowds a lucky lull and he had let himself
be lulled by the lull but the room is filling up with more visitors now, seniors especially, bald gents and blue-haired
ladies, somebody must have bussed in a bunch of senior citizens for the afternoon, can't they come on the free day in
the middle of week a fixed income and all that unless of
course these are the well-heeled elderly shuttled in from
some well-heeled invidiously-appointed holding pen in
which the well-heeled elderly wait to die. Earlier the exhibition rooms had been crowded with young people whereas

now the exhibition rooms were crowded with old people, earlier the exhibition rooms had been too crowded with families with annoying children who brings children to an art exhibit anyway children who ignore the art and dash instantly to the touch-screen computers and smear germs on the touch-screens in the last room of the exhibition hall where even now his wife sat happy as a clam touching a screen and picking up the germs, his wife with the photographic memory and the powerful immune system picking up the germs she will communicate to her husband without getting sick herself, over their coffee debrief in the coming hour she will communicate her information and an upper-respiratory infection courtesy of the morning museum rush when there had been a lot of families with children in the rooms whereas the afternoon museum rush appears to be comprised of the aged and the infirm, aged and infirm senior citizens blinking and wheezing and shuffling from box to box like they're on a field trip down memory lane, it's not aesthetic experience they're after but sheer indulgence in nostalgia, nostalgia which plays so great a part in the Cornell boxes and which is in fact pandered to in the Cornell boxes, remembering the good old days of the Zippo Waterproof Lighter and the Long Island Railroad Company ticket to nowhere, beachfront boardwalk pink palace holiday hotel postcards and shave and a haircut, two bits. Museum Guard 3 has taken up her post this one's a woman with a mortuary smile for all the old folks any one of whom could have been responsible for the lingering aftermath of the fart, what was once a vigorous and youthful fart now a dying fart unless it is rather just the usual stink of the dying elderly in their filthy adult sanitary undergarments, from Museum Guard 3 a pitying smile such as one puts on for cripples and retards and the dying incontinent old. One pair of dying oldsters draws our hero's particular attention, something familiar about this pair, must be drawing everyone's attention because you can't help hearing them even if you're not looking at them, the male half of the couple is obviously half deaf as well as half blind so his wife has to read every plaque to him aloud, she reads the plaques and then she describes the boxes, in a loud voice a voice trembling and cracking with age but still loud enough to be audible to the half or even three-quarters deaf she has to shout every word of every plaque while he sags on her arm and blinks through his useless bifocals and drags around after him a little wheeled cart with an oxygen tank and a clear plastic tube running up to the clamps in his nostrils, he's wheezing and she's shouting as they recall their life together in the bygone days of the Zippo Waterproof Lighter which lit all those emphysema-producing Chesterfields the good ol' days cup of coffee two bits so that they won't have to think about how they're going to be dead soon, how tomorrow or the day after tomorrow at the latest they're going to die and be lowered in boxes of their own into that big exhibition hall in the dirt where the lighting is very subdued indeed. And it is a little-known fact that in his last years Cornell's own boxes took on the appearance of coffins, intimating mortality but perhaps also acknowledging and commemorating the boxed-in living-death that had been his life Cornell produced his final box series the Coffin series, in one way or another Cornell had always been building his own coffin decorated with sublimated vagina teeth but in his final years he made it explicit, instead of precious gewgaws and cloying bric-a-brac he filled his final coffin-boxes with macabre shit, disturbing even, no longer the faces of Hollywood pin-ups but rather their arms and legs and torsos torn out of magazines, and strange primitive medical implements, unless of course they were torture implements, implements from back in the day when modern medicine was only beginning its long emergence out of the practice of torture, its long well-documented struggle to emerge, science emerging from alchemy and medical science from torture, centuries of ambivalent struggle with the compulsion to torture, origins which even today medicine still hasn't entirely shaken off, maybe after all really just a series of refinements and sublimations to keep the victim alive and suffering longer, Cornell placed the primitive medical-torture implements in his coffin-boxes along with actress parts and prostheses and two-headed fetuses in formaldehyde jars and rabbit carcasses and many-pronged dildos and plenty of tacky plastic Halloween crap from Salem tourist joints until each was a little charnel house or serial-killer torture basement, but after his death the Cornell Estate suppressed the final Coffin series, they suppressed the series and they destroyed the coffins, Cornell's reputation would have been damaged by this series they reasoned, irreparably damaged they had to save him from himself, senile dementia in his final years, from autism to senile dementia in diapers why let it spot his reputation, Cornell's spotless reputation for snow globes and wistful longing and softcore surrealism and other precious cloying kitsch. Found dead in his home of a heart attack they probably put him out of his misery, or rather to put themselves out of misery fretting about the coffin boxes they gave the old fart a shot of something and made a bonfire of all those coffins. The lost coffin-boxes just a rumor now, the apocryphal Coffin Series a whisper, unless of course the Cornell Estate saved the boxes, they put the coffin-boxes in cold storage and subdued lighting and saved them there, waiting for the inevitable day when Cornell's reputation would flag, inevitably the Cornell reputation would flag and the Cornell industry wane to a footnote, waiting for that day to spring the coffin-box series on the public, occasion for revisionary biographies and monographs and new retrospectives and coffee-table books and touch-screen documentaries and dollars, most of all the dollars, keep the industry coughing along a while yet, spotted reputation better than no reputation at all, art the news that stays new, or is it news. And now as our hero watches the ancient couple and thinks his mortuary thoughts and can't help hearing the old woman cawing the words on the plaques to the wheezing old man who sags on her arm and drags behind him the little wheeled oxygen tank with the tube running up to the nostril-clamp he (our hero not the old man) realizes where he has seen this couple before, not husband and wife after all but brother and sister, they are siblings, in fact the very brother-and-sister siblings our hero had seen on their stools next to his wife at the touchscreens in the final exhibition room, they were very young siblings in that room whereas in this room they are very old siblings but they are definitely the same siblings, in that room the female sibling was reading to the male sibling because he was too young to read the words whereas in this room the female sibling is reading to the male sibling because he is too old to read the words. And now our hero realizes that in fact all of the people he sees in the room are older versions of the same museum-goers he had seen earlier in these same rooms, all equally familiar he has seen them all before, their younger incarnations threading these same galleries, even the art-girl is back but no longer up for much of anything, hobbling on her walker go ahead and get an eyeful of that withered aesthesis, older now but the same they're all here, not one of them has left the exhibition hall, they have never left the exhibition hall, they circle through the cool dark rooms again and again, each circuit an age, and now in his dim reflection over the shades-of-rust and off-white forms of *American Rabbit c. 1945-46* our hero can see that he too has aged, in dim outline sagging features and a sagging frame, he's lost his hair and his snout is positively pendulous, nose and ears only stop growing when you're dead and his bigger than ever, very bad case of museum fatigue indeed. Never quite living and never quite dying they are all stuck inside this Cornell exhibition, no windows but the windows of the Cornell boxes, they circle around and around looking into the boxes for a way out and longing for a way out only to be brought up short by their own reflections, in dim outline over the Cornell boxes the ghost-boxes of their own lives reflecting back their paltry passages, in each box faring their way and circling back and no way out, the common denominator stuck in a box. There are nine such boxes devoted to our hero, nine boxes in three glass cases, three boxes in each glass case. The hero stands before the fifth box in the middle of the second glass case, he's in the very middle of this sequence of nine boxes devoted to his nine lives, to his left are the four previous boxes and to his right the four further boxes. In the first box of the first glass case the hero never leaves the baggage-claim area of Logan Airport, in the second box of the first glass case the hero always keeps returning to the Hotel Château-Roissy in the Zone Hôtelière, and in the third box of the first glass case the hero stands forever at the threshold of an equine unriddling which my witty spell-check insists on correcting to "unbridling." That is the end of the boxes in the first glass case. In the second glass case and still proceeding from left to right we have the fourth box, in which again and again the hero sees a New Hampshire state patrol cruiser cruise through a rest-stop parking lot, then the fifth box, in which the hero stands looking into a box in which he stands looking into a box in which he stands looking into a box, you get the idea, and then the sixth box, of which more anon, quite anon. That is the end of the boxes in the second glass case. This leaves only the third glass case, containing the last of the hero's boxes, boxes seven eight nine the remaining lives of the hero, nine boxes in all nine lives and no more, nowhere else on earth does the hero exist except in these nine boxes and even in these he can barely be said to exist, can he, in the subdued lighting nine boxes radiating each their little radiance and bearing the titles *Apple Seized, Return to the Chateau, The Four Horseman Bridge, The Cruiser, American Rabbit, Time and Motion, The Little Wayfarer, Human Wishes,* and *Enemy Combatant.*

Time and Motion

Simon says, Closed circuit cameras are in use to help provide you with the lowest possible prices. In some places Simon says it in English and in other places in English and Spanish. Bilingual Simon says, Criminal activity of any kind will be prosecuted and *La actividad criminal de la clase será procesada*. Simon used to just say Shoplifters will be prosecuted and *Shoplifters será procesado* but then 9/11 came along and it was important for Simon to find a term that covered acts of terror as well as petty theft and employee pilfering, since 9/11 you never knew if the guy pocketing electronics components in Radio Shack was going to use them to blow up the food court and then instead of bringing everybody low prices Simon would have to wait for the Department of Homeland Security to separate the charred shopper parts from the remains of Burger King Whopper patties. But Simon is shy, Simon prefers to work behind the scenes, Simon wants to keep his eye on you but doesn't want you keeping an eye on Simon, so Simon says, Photography and videotaping on the premises is forbidden without the permission of the management, meaning the permission of Simon, if you wanted for instance to take a picture of the old Boston Garden scoreboard now hanging in the food court or of your kids with ketchup smears on their T-shirts standing under the old Boston Garden scoreboard now hanging in the food court you wouldn't be allowed to unless you had Simon's say-so first, Simon being the Simon Property Group, Inc., the incorporated entity named Simon who from his Indianapolis headquarters (like corn a pure product of America) has a say-so in bringing you low prices at 380 shopping malls and related properties in the United States including regional malls in the New England area such as the Burlington Mall, the South Shore Plaza Mall, and the Arsenal Mall in Watertown Massachusetts where our hero now stands in a B. Dalton's Bookseller flipping through a copy of Claire Messud's acclaimed work of literary fiction *The Emperor's Children* ("Entrancing!" *The San Francisco Chronicle*). The Arsenal Mall built in 1983 on the site of the old Watertown Arsenal and even incorporating two of the original factory's large red-brick buildings (complete with crossed-cannons seal under the peaked eaves) houses over 65 stores including five anchor stores, got to have the anchor stores to keep the smaller stores from floating away to Mexico or Asia, where Simon also has properties. Inside there is an up-escalator at the west end by the anchor stores Filene's Basement and Marshalls feeding shoppers who enter the ground-floor main plaza via the north parking-lot entrance up to the second-storey concourse and the food court with the restaurants Burger King Sbarro Bourbon Street Cajun Grill Master Wok and Trini's Mexican Grill on one side and the other side taken up by a mega-sized Foot Locker and Lady Foot Locker and there is a down-escalator at the east end of the second-story concourse to feed shoppers into the mall's central corridor and towards the east-end anchor stores Linens-N-Things Old Navy and Home Despot I mean Depot. The speed of the up-escalator and the speed of the down-escalator are precisely calibrated to feed shoppers up to the food court and down from the food court at a set rate, so many units in foot-pounds per minute, it is a matter of finely-calibrated speed and feed and necessarily therefore of surveillance, of ever-vigilant surveillance via closed-circuit cameras to ensure the regular and unimpeded speed and feed of shoppers in search of the lowest possible prices. Our species' ceaseless quest for the lowest possible prices. In 2007 it's closed-circuit surveillance cameras and speed and feed courtesy of Simon's say-so at the Arsenal Mall on the banks of the Charles River in Watertown Massachusetts whereas a hundred years ago it was speed and feed and it was surveillance at the Watertown Arsenal armaments factory, at this level of generality you might say that nothing has changed in the last one hundred years, speed and feed and surveillance in the first decade of the twentieth century and speed and feed and surveillance in the first decade of the twenty-first century the same then as now, *plus ça change*. But if you were to look more closely at the history which is there in strata, if you were to do a little picking and digging like an archeologist say or a geologist at the strata you might find that it was different too, it was different and it was the same. For instance a hundred years ago instead of a mall named the Arsenal there was a real arsenal the Watertown federal arsenal and armaments factory and it was men with stopwatches and slide rules instead of surveillance cameras and it was Frederick Winslow Taylor instead of Simon giving the say-so and helping to bring everyone the lowest possible prices and it was skilled craftsmen patterning molding forging pouring cutting grinding and polishing machine parts and weapons parts over their lathes and planers and grinders and drills instead of unskilled mostly female retail cashiers and shelf-stockers but then as now it is Scientific Management, at the Watertown Arsenal whether a mall or an armaments factory it is one hundred years of Scientific Management, so-called. Even as our hero stands flipping through Claire Messud's acclaimed work of literary fiction the *The Emperor's Children* ("Sheer Genius!" *The Boston Globe*) in the B. Dalton's Bookseller just off the connector concourse between the west buildings and the east buildings of the mall he can feel it beneath his feet like a kind of tectonic unconscious, these strata of history in which there are fault lines, the faintest tremor of one jagged plate attesting to the otherwise buried fact that he stands on the site of the first labor strike in U.S. history against the Taylor system of so-called Scientific Management. The molders called it a spy-system and went out on strike, the first strike against the Taylor spy-system and therefore against Taylor himself, Taylor who used to boast that the introduction of his spy-system of so-called Scientific Management had never been met with a strike, a dubious boast at best because actually he had never before tried to introduce it into a place where the workers were as strongly organized as at the Watertown Arsenal, at Midvale Steel in Pennsylvania for example where it all started when the workers objected and the workers had definitely objected (where there is oppression there is always resistance) they just quit or were fired individually, but at Watertown Arsenal the molders of the molders' union wrote up a petition and walked out in a body an act of solidarity against Taylor and Taylorism and against the federal government itself, from Colonel C.B. Wheeler in charge of the Arsenal up the chain of command to General William Crozier the chief of Army Ordnance who used his trophy scalps from the Sioux Wars to paper the walls of his D.C. office up to the Commander in Chief President William Howard Taft himself, the molders defied them all because they didn't care to be spied on. So the federal government made up a special Congressional committee to hold hearings and consider the pros and cons of introducing the Taylor system (so-called) into government manufactories, to smooth the way for the introduction of the Taylor system by putting on a show of impartial hearings, even though then as now the purpose of Congress is to maintain and to further the interests of the capitalist ruling class and to adjudicate between competing factions of the capitalist ruling class they still felt they had to hold hearings and take the workers' voices into some kind of account, imagine that, because the power of labor was strong and the level of class struggle was high the capitalist politicians felt they had to put up a pretense of giving the workers' voices some kind of hearing imagine that, imagine that happening nowadays where were the hearings on NAFTA, where were the Congressional representatives pretending to be interested in the workers' voices when NAFTA was breezing towards approval under a Democratic (so-called) president, but one hundred years ago labor was stronger and more organized in some sectors anyway certainly the skilled craftsmen of the foundries and machine-shops of the federal arsenals organized in the AFL craft unions so Congress had to act like the fix wasn't already in, at least it was something today it is nothing, today when the fix is in the fix is in, period, full stop, shut up and get back to work or whoops your work isn't there anymore is it, tough shit look there are still plenty of service jobs around, the Watertown Arsenal used to make things but now it is the Arsenal Mall and it sells things you can always get a job selling things, at the Arsenal they molded and forged the side-frames of the twelve-inch mortar carriages and the other components of the seacoast gun carriages the fixed artillery and the gun forgings for the smaller mobile artillery and the projectiles for the seacoast guns, the raw pig-iron and the copper ingots and the steel was ferried into the Arsenal grounds and there was molding casting grinding and polishing, there were years of experience in the estimations of speed and feed, always speed and feed, experience and knowledge in the workers' heads expressed by the rule of thumb their highly skilled and experienced thumbs and their knowledgeable heads, in went the pig-iron and the copper and steel and out came the Fifteen Pounder Barbette Carriages and the Fourteen-inch Disappearing Gun Carriages and the Castor Wheels and the Drain Plugs and Cylinder Plugs for the Recoil Cylinders of the Gun Carriages, there was speed and feed and today there is still speed and feed but it means something different, there are still jobs at the Arsenal plenty of jobs but now this means selling stuff made in China at Circuit City and Dollar Days and Ritz Camera and Hallmark Cards and Bath and Body Works and B. Dalton's Bookseller where our hero stands flipping through a copy of Claire Messud's *The Emperor's Children* ("Mesmerizing!" *San Antonio Gazette*) and Pearle Vision Center and Victoria's Secret and Home Despot I mean Depot, back then when labor was stronger the workers didn't want reduced prices if it also meant being reduced to demeaning unskilled labor this was not a deal they were interested in, they didn't want to be spied on by the snotty Taylor college boys with their stopwatches and slide rules calculating speed and feed when they could calculate speed and feed just fine themselves thank you, at the hearings of the Special Committee to Investigate the Taylor and Other Systems (so-called) of Shop Management the molder Ed Sherman testified, *Every time I turn I find a man with a watch watching me, if I go after anything he is watching me, when I come back he is watching me, and if it is any kind of half-decent job at all that man would get me so nervous that I really would not know what I would be doing*, over thirty years a molder a skilled craftsman proud of his work, Ed Sherman his testimony. And machinist Richard Stackhouse agreed saying, *I think a man's nerves cannot stand it I know mine cannot*, Richard Stackhouse his testimony. And John Hendry at his bench trying to make molds for a pommel couldn't work with Taylor's man standing over him clicking away at his watch and pestering him with questions about his every single movement, demanding to know if every single movement of Hendry's every single muscle as he pounded the sand into the frame around the pattern was a necessary movement or an unnecessary movement, *I could not do my work right*, John Hendry his testimony. And Joseph Cooney over a decade and a half a skilled molder said, *any man on whom the stopwatch was pulled should refuse to continue to work,* Joseph Cooney his testimony, and that is what they did, the watch was pulled and Joseph Cooney refused and he was fired on the spot, and in that moment they all went out, without even alerting their union leadership it was a wildcat action, the workers themselves taking charge or trying to take charge of their destinies. And the molders wrote up a petition saying *The very unsatisfactory conditions which have prevailed in the foundry among the molders for the past week or more reached an acute stage this afternoon when a man was seen to use a stopwatch on one of the molders, This we believe to be the limit of our endurance, It is humiliating to us, who have always tried to give the Government the best that was in us, This method is un-American in principle, and we most respectfully request that you have it discontinued at once,* thus Joseph Hicklin, Isaac Goostray, Martin Roach, John Hendry, G.E. Lawson, John Weir, J.J. Flynn, J.F. Murphy, E.L. Sherman, L. Katz, Thomas Kane, A.P. Doherty, B. Hall, John Wilson, James T. Fraser, A.F. Perkins, E.A. Joyce, J.R. Cooney, John T. Sullivan, George V. Miller, and John F. Gatte, once upon a time real live human individuals who wanted to continue being human individuals not nameless cogs, these humans their testament. And when the molders returned to work at the urging of their union's president with the agreement that their voices were to be given a hearing by the U.S. Congress they saw that the soldiers guarding the Arsenal with their guns were now guarding the Arsenal against them, the molders who molded guns for the U.S. Army were now potential enemies of the state and persons to be regarded with suspicion, with well-armed suspicion, just one in a series of escalating insults courtesy of the Taylor system, a series of insults the speed and feed of whose introduction and escalation was finely calibrated in the new Planning Office from whence issued the Taylor men with their slide rules and stopwatches, the molders and the machinists who used to be trusted to put in a day's work now had to punch a time-clock to prove when they started and finished their day (an insult), who used to be able to walk into the bolt and strap room or open the tool cabinets to get whatever they needed now had to submit a chit for someone to fetch out the item from the locked storerooms and the locked tool-cage as if they were nothing but a bunch of thieves and bunglers (an insult), and you weren't even allowed to sharpen your own tools anymore the Taylor men had equipped all the grinding wheels with pre-set mounts and templates so that even a boy could sharpen the tools (an insult), and then the names of all the parts and tools were changed, you wanted to submit your chit for a tool but you didn't know what the tool was called anymore, the customary names of all the tools and the parts were changed into symbols for which management possessed the key (another insult), it was all about keys now and management possessed all of them, all of the keys, the key to the bolt and strap room and the key the new symbol system of number-and-letter combinations of the renamed bolts and straps in the bolt and strap room and the renamed tools in the locked tool-cage, everything written now, turned into print, for every task an Instruction Card for every machine a Utilization Record for every specific job a Job Card and all in the new language of the new managers and all geared to speed, to faster and faster speed (insult upon insult upon insult). Finally instead of being paid for a day's work the machinists and molders were put on piece rate as if all they had ever wanted to do before was loaf around the shop and shoot the breeze with their mates, piece rates set by the Taylor men who knew nothing about the skills of molding and machining but knew plenty about stopwatches and slide rules, Taylor men specifying the speed and feed and the angle of the renamed tools they knew nothing about. And to establish the speeds and therefore the pay rates the Taylor men used rate-busters, brought in from the outside some goddamn arse-kissing out-for-himself rate-buster no better than a scab, for instance one Edgecomb brought in from outside to bust the rates a traitor to his class, the Taylor men said look Edgecomb can do it in less than half the time if Edgecomb can you can too, John Hendry said you could make nine pommels a day if you were making them right but the Taylor man pointed to Edgecomb brought in from outside who could make twenty four pommels a day, this Edgecomb who worked like a nigger instead of a white man did nigger work, if you wanted a nigger you got nigger work his pommels were nigger-shoddy, the way he skipped steps didn't set the right reinforcements didn't put on a proper finish anyone a woman a child even a nigger could do it like that, this rate-busting Edgecomb who hogged the crane instead of sharing it with his mates and stole the sand for his molds that other molders had prepared for theirs all for a few more cents a day turning out shoddy nigger-work pommels should have been ashamed of himself instead of preening for the Taylor men, Edgecomb the brown-nosed coxcomb. But the Taylor men weren't interested in quality they just wanted more speed, told Lawson to lay off nailing his castings, he didn't need to do so much nailing on the cope of the top-carriage even though it meant leaving blemishes and

weak spots it was not a good cope, not by his standards anyway, not by Lawson's standards but standard was coming to
mean something different, the word standard was given a
different meaning by the Taylor men not good or high anymore but the same, everything fast and shoddy and the
same. For the molders and the machinists this was the
worst insult of all this was worse than being spied on, for the
molders and machinists the quality of their work was of the
greatest possible importance, the source of their pride as
working men was the quality of their work, their reputa-
tions and self-esteem and their very sense of themselves as
men were all based on producing good work, *I won't stop
nailing* Lawson told the Taylor man *That is going to hurt
my character*, G.E. Lawson his testimony. The piece rate
made not only the work but the workman inferior, that is
what the molders testified, *And that will be the case for me
if I have to be speeded up, I don't think I will stand for it, I
value my reputation yet*, a Watertown molder his testimony. They weren't complaining that the work was difficult
but that it demeaned and dehumanized them, at the end of
the piece rate day they went home to their wives tired and
ashamed of being turned into niggers, they wanted to be
treated like men and not like animals and niggers and
machines. And it is true that the workers were being treated
like objects and turned into objects, Taylor freely admitted
that what he and his men were doing with the workers was
an experiment, his method was scientific and science
requires experiments, from Newton and Bacon to Tuskegee
and Nagasaki such is the Scientific Method, but today for a
researcher to perform an experiment on a human subject
the experiment has to be approved by an Institutional
Review Board to ensure that the subject is not exploited or
traumatized that the subject is not turned into an object,
since the sixties at least in research institutions such as uni-

versities all human-subject experiments have had to pass institutional review although not in private enterprises such as workplaces, come to think of it even today at their workplaces the workers remain the subjects or rather the objects of countless experiments, ceaseless experiments because capitalism needs constantly to revolutionize the means of production in order to make more profits and bring us the lowest possible prices, capitalism and its handmaiden science, revolution always a bad idea of course someone might get hurt but what is capitalism itself other than a ceaseless and relentless revolutionary process enlisting so-called science and performing countless and never-ending experiments on human objects without any kind of review at all other than the quarterly review of the bottom line, the permanent revolution that is Capital. After a day of piece rate at the Watertown Arsenal the workers the machinists and molders would go home wrecked, to their wives and their families drained and dispirited and wrecked, in the words of experienced molder Edward Joyce so *tired out* that he *would not feel like going anywhere, whereas by working by the day I feel as though there was something to live for, and feel like going out for a walk evenings*, Edward Joyce his testimony in the days before television had solved this problem for exhausted workers everywhere. And one of Joyce's fellow-molders testified that his wife was now threatening to leave him, he had changed so much had become so irritable, makes you wonder what was going on there, behind the scenes, what happens when people are treated like objects do they pass the buck, do they pass the incredible savings along to those waiting for them on down the line in the form say of a broken tooth or a black eye? Come to think of it what of the women, what of the wives and the mothers and the daughters of these Arsenal craftsmen, these craftsmen who were men, were males, we have the record of their crafts-male voices but we do not have the record of the voices of their wives and their mothers and daughters, maybe we are on to something here, what are the voices of these women saying today for it is mostly women who work at the Watertown Arsenal now that it is a shopping mall what for example do these women's voices say? Maybe as he listens to Claire Messud's voice in her acclaimed work of literary fiction *The Emperor's Children* he can hear the voice of these women? ("A masterly comedy of manners – an astute and poignant evocation of the hobnobbing glitterati," *The New York Time Book Review*). Or maybe not. But still it seems that we're on to something here, a fly in the ointment crack in the teacup another faultline maybe even the fatal flaw. Maybe the craftsmen of the molders' union and the other craft unions of the AFL were only interested in defending their craft privileges, at the Watertown Arsenal as elsewhere they operated a closed shop more like a medieval guild than an industrial union they didn't let in women and they didn't let in black people, when the white male molders compared the Taylor method to the slave-driver's whip maybe this was all they meant, how dare you treat us like the niggers and women and other beasts of burden, they identified with their rulers and bosses on the basis of their so-called whiteness and their penises, they had sold their souls as working people to wear the white penis and to identify with the white penis, the shoddy privilege of being so-called white men, nothing cheaper, nothing more threadbare, nothing more sold-out to standardization than the so-called "white" skin, stupidest idea in history if it weren't one of the deadliest. From this point of view you might even say that the craftsmen got what was coming to them, hoisted on their own well-crafted petards, if they'd only broken from their male-gender privileges and their white-skin privileges and allied themselves with the women workers and the black workers and the darker-skinned workers overseas under the yoke of nascent U.S. imperialism but no they had to go and be a craft aristocracy crafting weapons for imperialism to put down their darker-skinned brothers and sisters at home and abroad from the coolies breaking their backs on the railroads out West to the toilers of Haiti and the Philippines before going home to a hot supper and warm wifey bed. The white molders had to go and put their faith in the U.S. government to hear their white voices and adjudicate their white male demands, big mistake, even though the special Congressional committee ruled against the installation of the Taylor system or at least elements of the Taylor system in federal manufactories Taylor and his system of so-called Scientific Management really won the day, the legislation passed in Congress was toothless legislation meant only to keep out a few elements of a system which everyone who was anyone knew was the wave of the future, they even staged a war known in the history books as "World War I" in order to speed up the process of mechanization and rationalization and integrate the workers into the process more quickly and efficiently while distracting them with war-jingo and patriotic bunting, war just another means by which capitalism institutes worker-disabling technological "advances," it is just another form of capitalist speed-up but one which tries to prettify the carnage by draping it in a flag, everybody on board under the flag, the class war by other means. And under the flag they all got on board the liberals like "people's lawyer" and later Supreme Court Justice Louis Brandeis and also Ida Tarbell the muckraking "trust-buster" journalist and even the labor leaders (so-called) of the AFL along with the bosses to help ensure that Taylorism was extended to every possible occupation in every branch of the economy, including of course Henry Ford who was busy integrating Taylorism into his production lines although he denied it, Ford denied the direct influence of Taylor and claimed he came up with the idea of the production line on his own, if he was influenced by anything it was by what he had observed in the Chicago slaughterhouses with their killing queues in which the livestock were disassembled into deadstock, the light bulb went on over Ford's head just flip the queues into reverse and you can assemble instead of disassemble which is why even today between the slaughterhouse and the industrial factory you can see the family resemblance, the slaughterhouse and the industrial factory kissing cousins or even kissing siblings, a cross-eyed hillbilly family resemblance brought out with particular expressiveness a few years down the line in the Taylorized Nazi death camps. And all done in the name of efficiency of course, from death camp to Ford factory the great battle-standard of efficiency, efficiency which means doing more with less in this case meant more and more managers and bureaucrats and specialists, funny paradox, an explosion of managers and specialists in all fields of the social factory including social workers and psychologists and teachers and doctors and academics and book reviewers, irony of history, layer upon layer of softcops to police the workers in their Terrorized I mean Taylorized workplaces and their Taylorized homes, courtesy of the Taylor System of Scientific Management helping to bring us the lowest possible prices hey presto the new professional-managerial class. What used to be in the brains of the craftsmen and expressed by the rule of thumb was transferred by degrees to the big Planning Room where the new professional-managerial class held their scientific juju coven, from the brains of the craftsmen into the notes of the stopwatch men and thence to the Planning Room which grew into the Big Brain of the professional-managerial General Staff under the battle-standard of Efficiency, such was the grand design of Taylor not efficiency but war, Taylor was a general in a war, it is the class war and it is a permanent war and there are no civilians there are only combatants and among the combatants you are either a friendly or you are a foe. The rule of thumb was replaced by the rule of Science and Efficiency which was really the juju-rule of war-managers, the craftsmen's thumbs were cut off and made into slide rules and stopwatches and job cards for the managers and every job that was not a professional-managerial job was reduced to something which could be performed with few skills and vestigial thumb-stumps or no skills and no thumbs, the workers were turned into thumbless employees and consumers, employees on the job and consumers off the job or rather consumption everyone's second job, the imperative to consume and consume, this insatiable hunger to buy and consume some portion of the product of our labor which is really the quenchless hunger for a substitute object for the lost thumb, from the humvee and the flat-screen TV to the iPod and the Blackberry this search for the bygone thumb, replacement objects to suck as fetishes and pacifiers, the workers reduced to sheer thumb-sucking orality which my witty spellcheck insists on correcting to "morality," the Arsenal where the rule-of-thumb once prevailed now a shopping mall where the great-grandchildren of the rule-of-thumb craftsmen come in search of replacement objects for their bygone thumbs, haunted by a vestigial memory like the flesh-eating zombies in George Romero's movie *Dawn of the Dead*, which is set in a shopping mall. And speaking of movies did you know that the whole film industry got its start out of Taylorism and time-and-motion studies, little-known fact, cinema which is based on the speeding up of separate still photographs to produce the illusion of motion came only after the use of still photography to break down

the motions of working people at their jobs, part of the overall effort to use technology and surveillance to disassemble
the work process and therefore also the worker, Etienne
Marey in France and Eadweard Muybridge in the U.S. taking stop-motion photo images of the movements of men
and beasts in order to study them and make them amenable
to ever greater and more precise measures of scientific juju-
control suddenly discovered that flipping through a stack of
photos with the managerial opposing thumb produced in
the images the illusion of motion, in the same way that our
hero in the B. Dalton's Bookseller flips through the pages of
Claire Messud's acclaimed literary novel *The Emperor's
Children* ("Ambitious, glorious, and gutsy," *Elle*) Marey and
Muybridge realized that you could produce a simulation of
motion, and that when you calibrated the precise speed and
feed of these images the motion went from fragmented and
herky-jerk to seamless and fluid and as-if-real, and thus out
of the impulse to control workers and extend the domain of
knowledge and science (i.e. managerial power) cinema was
born. Cue dramatic theme music. And a great plan was conceived by the professional-managerial General Staff in the
big Planning Room: Using the very same means by which
they disassembled the work process and the workers and
took away their lives they would give them back a simulacrum of their lives, they would dazzle and distract them with
ghost lives and fantasy lives by running the frames forward
at the precisely-calibrated time and motion of the simulation of life even though it was really just pictures in motion,
or motion pictures. A special sub-branch of the Planning
Room operation was created for managing the consciousness of the workers through moving images projected into
the brains of the workers, with a special sub-group of managers called producers and directors, one of whom named
D.W. Griffith was put in charge of directing the moving pic-

ture called *Birth of a Nation* with its figure of the heroic
Klansman, a moving picture to celebrate being white and
American and take everyone's mind off the fact whilst chat-
tel slavery had supposedly been eliminated there was still
this booming business of wage slavery. And *Birth of a
Nation* even given a special screening at the White House
under Woodrow Wilson, the racist scumbag president
whose cabinet included William Bauchop Wilson as his first
labor secretary, W. Bauchop Wilson the former organizer of
coal miners and then the chairman of the special Congressional Taylor hearings where he had pretended to take the
workers' side was now the President's Secretary of Labor in
order to oversee the Taylorized exploitation of the very
workers he had earlier pretended to defend, and Samuel
Gompers invited too, Gompers the former cigar-roller and
later president of the American Federation of Labor who
had testified against the Taylor method at the hearings was
now a cigar-chomping labor-broker and champion of the
Taylor method, all sitting down with Woodrow Wilson to
preview *Birth of a Nation* and sign-off the secret plan to
give workers back simulations of lives in the form of fantasy
motion pictures celebrating the birth of their white American nationhood. Meanwhile work at the Watertown
Arsenal on the banks of the Charles River went on and the
river in the Arsenal's shadow ran on, through all the historical mutations of the Arsenal this river flowing at its own
sweet will, the time and motion of the river different from
the time and motion of the factory on its banks, the time
and motion of the river going in curls and loops and
meanders, like time which does not go in a straight line but
has eddies and contraflows this river's true name is the
Meander, this looping meandering river named after King
Charles I by the settlers who came and changed the names
of everything in the years before their descendants changed

the names of the tools in the workshop on its banks, this river known as the Quinobequin by those who peopled its shores before the settlers drove them away and as it waters still whisper today: Quinobequin the Meandering One. The ascription might be apocryphal but then sometimes it is the apocrypha that spells the secret identity, there is the linear official story and there is the meandering apocryphal story and there is linear time and there is meandering time and it was meandering time until the settlers came with their Protestant work ethic and stopwatches and new names for things including the river, different times different histories different strata and all still here, brimming beneath our hero's feet and looping in our hero's mind this collective unconscious of lives in labor and labor in lives, time out of time or all times together, ancient, dusky rivers with time past and time present and time future and all kinds of other literary associations flowing by along with the rest of the detritus of civilization, always flow and always strata and always histories, sedimented, layered, each place, its her-stories and theirstories. If you were to write a truly "real-istic" novel it would have to include these histories of lives in labor and labor in lives, each novel would have to be an endless *roman fleuve* of these loops and strata, each novel a failure because it could not possibly encompass it all, each novel necessarily a fragment and a failure, to be the writer of honestly "realistic" novels it would be necessary to fail, the only integrity again and again to start and to fail, each novel a failure and a botch and the measure of its success its degree of failure, its pitch of failure and abdication of authority, but the publishers won't print such novels, novels must participate in the alienation of their time and endorse and reproduce the alienation of their time or else they won't be bought and they won't be sold, the marketplace the non-place where commodities are cleansed of all traces of work, for a commodity to be a successful commodity and especially the commodity called "literary fiction" it must efface history and efface labor, every trace. Our hero stands in the B. Dalton's Bookseller in the Arsenal Mall in Watertown Massachusetts flipping through a copy of Claire Messud's *The Emperor's Children* ("Riveting," *Atlantic Monthly*), on principle of course despising B. Dalton's and all the rest of the metastasizing chain-bookstore phenomenon it is sheer accident that finds him standing in this lowly B. Dalton's chain outlet in the Arsenal Mall he makes a point of patronizing independent bookstores and purchasing his books at independent bookstores, although truth to tell he has been spotted on occasion in the Borders Books in the swanky Atrium Mall in Chestnut Hill, his snout alternately over a book and over the plastic lid of a cappuccino, more than one occasion, in the upscale Borders Books in the upscale Atrium Mall it is possible to put aside one's principles and indulge in the pleasures of the browse, the caffeinated pleasures of the literary browse, to overlook the crassness of the whole chain-bookstore phenomenon which the décor in Borders attempts to dissimulate anyway so it's rather to participate in the dissimulation, you can always indulge your outrage and indignation later for example in your car driving out of the Atrium Mall parking lot oh those despicable chain-booksellers grrrrrr! A cancer! It's much easier to bracket your principles briefly with a nice foamy cappuccino and a comfy chair and a carpeted floor underfoot and classical music wafting through the air but at a B. Dalton's where there's no cappuccino no comfy chairs no classical music and linoleum instead of carpet one's principles tend to come to the fore. Our hero stands in the B. Dalton's Bookseller in the Arsenal Mall in Watertown Massachusetts nosing spitefully through Claire Messud's acclaimed literary bestseller *The Emperor's Children* a gentrified literary soap-opera in a downscale mall, a mall with a B. Dalton's instead of a Borders, he has come to the mall this afternoon to shop for clothes but the task of trying on clothes in the dressing rooms where he's always certain he'll be suspected of shoplifting and therefore spied-on by hidden cameras as he reveals his hairy flabby gut and dirty underwear in order to wedge himself into the too-tight clothes he's over-optimistically plucked from the racks is so humiliating that he needs to calm himself in a bookstore between forays, to calm and to balm his nerves in a book-browse even if only a cappuccino-less downscale B. Dalton's book-browse, not a nice bookstore at this mall and not very nice clothing stores either, Gap Outlet Marshalls Old Navy wouldn't catch Claire Messud motoring over from Somerville to buy her vestments at Old Navy but we have caught our hero here, he has intentionally selected this downscale mall to shop for pants because he feels guilty spending his wife's money so he has decided to express a little class solidarity with working people everywhere by returning to his downscale roots, instead of shopping on Newbury Street where the professional-managerial class purchase their vestments he will head to the dying down-scale mall where the thumbless great-granddaughters of the Arsenal artisans peddle vestments mass-produced according to Taylorist principles by their class sisters in Asian and Latin American sweatshops. He has come in search of a pair of what his downscale and probably adoptive mom and pop used to call "dress pants," slacks or khaki trousers something ironically enough middle-class-looking because he has been summoned to jury duty and he's a little paranoid about it, he has only faded raggedy black jeans and even more faded raggedy blue jeans the only ones that fit since he stopped working and started putting on pounds and he imagines a uniformed officer of the court or even a judge issuing a fine and sending him home for showing up in such disrespectful attire, like the famous John Houseman scene in *The Paper Chase* except a court of law instead of a law school, in the faded raggedy black jeans he's wearing now or in his even more raggedy-assed blue jeans with the permanent greenish hue of grime worked into the fabric he is sure to be singled out and made an example of, probably wouldn't even get past the security station inside the front entrance, he will come in for an extra-close inspection possibly questions even interrogation *You can't come in here looking like that, with those ratty jeans and that big Arab nose and looking at the judge with those beady eyes, shifty and beady and that weird green color, special Al-Qaeda x-ray contact lenses transmitting everything back to one of Osama's lieutenants or even Osama himself for their big terror-bombing of the Boston courthouse . . .* so he'll wear his one button-down shirt that still fits and a new pair of slacks or khakis with pleats and a belt a new belt and hold his head down to foreshorten his nose or no that'll look suspicious but if he holds his head too far up he'll look arrogant and haughty and they'll feel called upon to take him down a few pegs he'll just have to brazen out the nose but it will be easier to brazen out the nose if the rest of the costume represents compliance and conformity, he's already gone to SuperCuts to scale back the kinky hair and of course he'll shave himself so aggressively that morning that his face will be florid with razor burn but then he'll appear flushed, won't he, like he's nervous about something, can't help it he's got sensitive skin practically breaks out in a rash from even the shadow of a razor passing over his cheek so he doesn't shave every day but then he's got that heavy five o'clock shadow by noon dark enough to make Richard Nixon look like a peachy-cheeked princess next to him, even with the new slacks he'll have yet this terrible dilemma to face, whether to shave that morning and show up with the suspicious red blush or shave the day before and show up with the suspicious stubble. He'll probably go with shaving that morning, even scrape extra hard so they'll see the abrasions and the nicks with bits of bloodstained toilet paper stuck on and understand that his blush or flush is from shaving instead of nerves about any sinister mission of Al-Qaeda reconnaissance. He's been at this stupid mall for two hours already going in circles over whether to buy a stupid pair of polyester slacks or a stupid pair of pleated cotton Dockers for jury duty but his B. Dalton's book-browse spite-break has cleared his head and allowed him to recognize that the mall would be an ideal setting for one of his anti-stories about In-Between places, that the mall too was a place where people went around in circles and never got out, place out of place and time out of time, a movement that is a stasis, suspended, a suspense, it's an ideal place, could even weave in material from its history as an armaments factory and the controversy over Taylor's time-and-motion studies the infamous stopwatch how promising is that for material, golden opportunity for his larger plan to blow up so-called "literary fiction" from inside out, an ideal candidate for his projected set of subversive texts starring In-Between places such as rest stops and baggage-claim terminals, this mall practically begging to be worked up into one of his genre-busting anti-stories and maybe this anti-story he would even finish, would figure out how to finish or rather to anti-finish (closure bad) and then go back over the whole mass or mess of sketches fragments and notes and pull them together (or rather anti-pull etc.) and finally be able to justify his existence as the groundbreaking writer his wife is temporarily subsidizing rather than the lazy-assed almost middle-aged ABD dropout he suspects she sometimes mistakes him for. He's been restored by the pleasures

of his spiteful browse and he's ready for action, he has con-
firmed the superiority of his talent and vision vis-a-vis
Claire Messud's pathetic work of philistine middle-brow
commercial trash masquerading as literature *The
Emperor's Children* ("Laughable!" *The Little Wayfarer
Plain Dealer*), the thought crosses his mind that he ought to
break the book's spine before putting it back on the shelf
where the other copies of the same title await their sister's
return but he decides that this would be childish, or churlish, or both childish and churlish, or rather consciously he
decides that it would be childish and churlish whereas uncon-
sciously it is his respect even veneration for book-objects
which stays his hand, a respect even for bad book-objects so
long as they're book-objects and which if they're bestselling
book-objects he envies as well as respects, mitigating
against his vandalistic impulse this fetishistic respect laced
with envy and admixed of course also with his fear of surveillance, let's not forget that, his certainty rather that from
behind the scenes old B. Dalton or even Simon himself has
been reading over his shoulder and will suddenly pop out to
exclaim, *You break it, you buy it – and at ten percent off
because it's one of our Nice-Price Monthly Titles!!!* Thus
our hero returns *The Emperor's Children* to the shelf
without breaking its spine, but then dismayed by his gut-
lessness he takes the face-out copies and turns them so that
only the spines (unbroken) are visible, a compromise, take
that, and guiltily nods to the cashier or excuse me sales
associate as he passes the counter on his way out, the bored
sales associate who hasn't given him a second thought since
twenty minutes ago when she had sized him up as a book-
sniffing nut, one of those strange lone men who drifted into
the store in the afternoon sometimes to sniff books before
drifting out again, our book-sniffing hero feels his guilty
coward's smile rebound off the sales-associate's expression-

less mask and return home as a rictus of chagrin. But Christ does he ever have to pee, has had to pee for some time now and fortunately he knows right where the restrooms are because it's going to be his third trip this afternoon, second floor behind the food court he makes his way to the escalator and escalates to the east end of the second-floor concourse, this is going to look suspicious multiple visits to the can if Simon's keeping track and you can bet your bottom dollar Simon is keeping track, control room somewhere with a wall of screens like NORAD hey look it's that Arab-looking customer lurking around the restrooms again, our hero stops to buy a soda at the Burger King hasn't spent any money yet but it will appease Simon if he patronizes the vendors, before his third and definitively suspicious visit to the men's room he buys a prophylactic Burger King soda in the food court which is made up to look like the old Boston Garden, with a broad open-girder ceiling and the girders painted tan and aqua like in the old Garden and a huge sign that says "Boston Garden Memories" (his is wetting his pants at the Celtics game his ostensible dad had taken him to), and of course the original Boston Garden scoreboard suspended over the tables, the centerpiece and main attraction and the size and heft of a stuffed mastodon, four TV monitors at each of its corners playing NESN for the few diners with their cold Sbarro pizza slices or trays of congealing Master Wok chow mein. He wants to take notes on it all for his anticipated anti-story, if he had brought his little Moleskine™ writer's notebook he would take detailed notes, a real writer would always have her notebook with her so what does that make him, as he heads into the restrooms he makes a mental note for a third time of the large plaque listing Simon's ten commandments for proper mall comportment including Thou shalt not wear improper dress gang regalia or Arab noses and Thou shalt not take pictures without Simon's permission, a visual culture worried about people making visual representations they haven't anticipated someone old-school enough to want a written representation but it would look suspicious nonetheless, Plan B in the event of photography's interdiction, Arab-looking guy spotted in the food court scribbling detailed notes it can only mean one thing, after 9-11 shopping malls frequently cited as tempting targets for mad bombers and other malefactors but what self-respecting suicide bomber would choose a mall as pathetic as this one give him a medal for putting it out of its misery. He could come back another time with his notebook or else after he buys his new pants he could look for a place to buy a small notebook and a pen if there happened to be any antique stores in the mall, kill two birds with one stone but of course he's not interested in killing anything no just a figure of speech he hastens to send out pacific vibes just in case reading minds is part of Simon's overall surveillance program here, reading minds in order to bring you the lowest possible prices, surveilling him and trying to read his mind while he shakes off the last drops of pee. Not that a wet spot would be that obvious on his black jeans one nice thing about black jeans although his are pretty faded but as he makes his way out of the restroom and back onto the concourse he almost spills his soda over his crotch double-checking the zipper on his raggedy-ass faded black jeans oh shit see he's already busted here comes a security guard. Simon prefers to work behind the scenes but Simon has eyes and ears on the floor as well, the guard appears in the white skin and the white shirt with the badge on the shoulder that are worn to distinguish the guards of the private security firm from the brown skins and plum-colored smocks of the private cleaning firm. The security guard is heading right towards our hero whose anxious vibes on his highly-suspicious third trip to the can have no doubt blipped the radar screens in the NORAD-like security center, but right as our hero braces himself for questions a black woman pushing a large double stroller intercepts the security guard, cuts in front of the security guard with her large double stroller and stops the security guard with a question of her own. He is saved, saved by the black woman with the question and the double-barreled stroller, some kind of message there or allegory maybe. In a quiet polite Haitian-accented voice the black woman with the double stroller asks the security guard her question which is where she might find the elevators to return to the ground floor, in a polite almost apologetic Haitian lilt the black woman asks her question, our hero can hear the question as he passes and he can see the black questioner and white questionee out of the corner of his eye because he doesn't want to be caught staring, this little tableau of the black woman questioning and the white security guard looking her skeptically up and down and then demonstratively back and forth from her to the double stroller before issuing the snide official riposte, *Well, how did you get up here in the first place?* And the instant the white guard says this he flicks a glance at our hero and catches our hero's eye, the corner of the white guard's eye fleetingly catches and snags the corner of our hero's eye, not a look of suspicion or interrogation anymore but a look of complicity, over in an instant as our hero moves on this look of their sudden complicity as two white males supposedly sharing the same amused disgusted appraisal, *Can you believe the stupidity of these negroes?* Yes, our hero whose skin is darker than the security guard's skin but much much lighter than the Haitian woman's has been granted a reprieve in the form of enlistment into the White Brotherhood, courtesy of the security guard's flickering look of racial solidarity our hero has only to nod to sign up. But fortunately our hero passed by without nodding, did he not. Didn't he? Not nod. He did not nod, no. No? Maybe his head moved a little, involuntarily moved, motion imperceptible and assuredly involuntary, when you're walking it is simply impossible for your head not to move, to bob or to sway, however involuntary and barely perceptible this bobbing or swaying which is most certainly not nodding. He did not nod but maybe he blinked, that's the problem with the language of looks the slightest twitch or blink can be a masonic affirmation or construed as such, blink once if yes twice if no he blinked once didn't he? Did he just sign up, sell out? If he did it was not intentional, assuredly not intentional but the doubt remains, among the endless possibilities of betrayal the possibilities of self betrayal, an impulse, an instant. He takes a seat at one of the food-court tables and over a long draw on his soda straw watches as the security guard walks away in one direction and the black woman pushes her double-barreled stroller off in an another, three molecules in the strange chemistry of race (five if you count the contents of the stroller) having met in brief problematic combination before going their separate ways. His sympathies are all with the black woman of course but he can't help being relieved she took the bullet for him, figure of speech, no real bullets, nothing to be proud of but need he be ashamed? There'd been no real compliance or enlistment, had there? Or if there had been a tiny semblance of such it was surely an ironic performance on our hero's part, a blink or a nod of enlistment "in quotes," as it were, rebounding back at the white guard's smug mug, an act of resistance in the form of a witheringly ironic (if subtle) postmodern "performance" of compliance. If our hero were to write a story about the coming of Taylor and Taylorism to the Watertown Arsenal it would surely be the story of an ironic performance misconstrued, epically misconstrued, for such was the secret of Frederick Winslow Taylor himself, the secret saga told here for the first time in the form of our hero's self-exculpatory musings. For it is painfully obvious to anyone looking at the historical record with anything like a little psychological acuity but especially a little acuity about the psychology of the artist that Taylor was nothing other than a performance artist before his time, *avant la lettre* as it were, a dramatic artist who had thrown himself into an elaborate lifetime parody of a so-called "scientific" efficiency expert, with campy side-allusions along the way to the great American tradition of hucksterism from the roadside revival preachers in their little tents to P.T. "there's a sucker born every minute" Barnum in his big tent (see Melville's *The Confidence-Man* a big secret influence on Taylor). Taylor didn't even really like industry and technology and in fact he despised industry and technology and the corruption of so-called science in their service, it is a little-known fact that as a youth Taylor's reading had included the works of John Ruskin, *Sesame and Lilies* and *Unto This Last* and so forth, Taylor read Ruskin and he worshipped Ruskin but he kept it to himself, Ruskin's *Sesame and Lilies* and Whitman's *Leaves of Grass* and Thoreau's *Walden* and the novels of the little-read and less-regarded Melville were his sacred books and he was going to spoof industry and technology by putting on the performance of an obsessed inhuman Ahab committed to the "rational" application of science and efficiency (so-called) to absolutely every aspect of human existence, aspects he would multiply by breaking down every human action into sub-actions and sub-sub-actions and applying the efficiency-ruler ruthlessly to them all, without ever breaking character he was going to produce a parodic charade of this ruthless relentlessness or relentless ruthlessness which was a cruelly real force of history in the form of capitalism. It is a well-known fact from the biographical record that on his mother's side Taylor was descended from New England Abolitionist and Transcendentalist stock, the ideals of abolitionism and transcendentalism and Quakerism were the atmosphere he breathed in his childhood the very milk he imbibed at his mother's breast yet it is never questioned why he turned his back on these ideals and made himself the servant of their negations, it is a question which has not been asked let alone answered, until now that is, the question asked and the riddle unriddled: Taylor did not, forsake the faith that is, secretly did not. It is a well-known fact from the biographical record that throughout his life Taylor suffered from insomnia or rather supposedly suffered from insomnia self-reportedly suffered from sleeplessness and that as the years passed this purported sleeplessness grew worse and worse but what he was really doing was begging forgiveness of the moon, now it can be told, out into the garden of his Boxly estate he would slip in his nightshirt and lie in the grass to beg forgiveness of the moon and absolution of the moon-silvered leaves of grass, on his back the moon and on his stomach the grass, blade by blade forgive me forgive me, each blade, Frederick Winslow Taylor's nocturnal apologies for his diurnal performance in which he never once broke character, he apologized to the half moon and quarter moon and moon crescent and moon full and to the lush grass and sparse grass and grass buried in three feet of snow, nothing but his nightshirt, to the organic rhythms of nature at night he apologized for the mechanical grind of work in the day, to the times and the motions of Nature he dedicated his Art but nobody knew because he never let on, a life's work indeed he never once broke character, Borat and Stephen Colbert mere amateurs measured by the Taylor standard, no wonder his wife was unhappy he saved all his mojo for the machines by day and the moon by night it all went into his Art but he apologized to the moon and begged of the grass its absolution, he loved nature and he was committed to nature but most of all an artist he was committed to Art, to his performance and to the perfection of his performance, perfection of the life and perfection of the work one and the same, to make this inhuman robot of himself insisting again and again on bringing out the implicit inhumanity of the machine and behind the machine and giving it vampiric life the relentless and inhuman logic of Capital itself, he let the logic of Capital inhabit him, he effaced with supreme negative capability his own ego and made himself servant of the logic of Capital the better to parody the logic of Capital, Capital's rational irrationalism, in his person and his deeds down to the last detail to spoof and to vamp and to otherwise parody Capital's irrational rationalism hence his chief props the stopwatch and the slide rule, the stopwatch to represent empty quantitative time which was supplanting the qualitative time of nature and the slide rule to represent empty quantitative space which was supplanting the qualitative space of nature, the time and motion of Capital transforming qualitative use-value into empty quantitative exchange-value to bring us the lowest possible prices and cheapen life itself, Taylor with his stopwatch and slide rule like Blake's Urizen with his draughtsman's compasses leaning out of the heavens, bad Nobodaddy himself, Taylor furiously gesticulating in jerky mechanical movements like a libido-less demiurge of engineering with his slide rule and his stopwatch he was a prop comedian, not even naturalistic acting it was presentation of character not dramatization of character it was positively Brechtian, more precisely it was an art of ironic over-commitment, what the philosopher Slavoj Zizek would later formulate about *Neue Slowenische Kunst* and the art-music group Laibach, "*more* x *than* x *itself*," the revelation and the disclosure of totalitarian logics through the performance of a straight-faced identification so seamless and airtight it can only be parody, turning into its opposite and bringing out that ideology's obscene logic, one hundred years before Zizek and Laibach it was Taylor discovering and perfecting this obscene art of performative over-identification. Heralded as a visionary and a man before his time and he was but not in the way everyone thought, everybody fell for the act and totally missed the irony, you can fool some of the people some of the time but what happens when you fool all the people all the time? Never had to swear anyone to secrecy because even among his own family and closest collaborators they fell for it lock stock and barrel, lonely artist perfecting his craft, everyone thought his craft was "scientific management" but his craft was really a craft of performance of grand subversive parody which unfortunately wasn't subverting anything other than working people everywhere, Capital's endless powers of cooptation, at first he thought folks would catch on surely sooner or later they had to catch on but no matter how late it got they never caught on, hence his nightshirt apologies to the moon and the grass he had to atone somehow, after all what was he supposed to do get up on a soapbox before the Congressional committee to unmask himself and deliver an edifying speech about the "real meaning" of the performance which everybody had failed to figure out for themselves? Everybody knows that soapboxing is bad art, his text would be "message-y" and the critics would pan it, he would live in ignominy for spoiling his great work with a speechifying "message." No, better to leave his performance to posterity, pristine for posterity, for the ages, great artists always misunderstood in their own time but admittedly not often in this particular way, misunderstood because taken at face value, Swift's modest proposal taken seriously by this or that witless wanker but come on, eat children? Please. Time every motion? Please. And yet everywhere they fell for it, gobbled it up, couldn't get enough of it and the strain was killing him, should he ruin his art his lifetime's work this grand edifice for the sake of nature including human nature whose enslavement his art was accelerating rather than thwarting, moral dilemma or is it an aesthetic dilemma which should be put first, Art or Nature? Irresolvable contradiction it burst his brain as irresolvable contradictions have a tendency to do he died of a stroke. Several decades later his monument: a battleship named after him, the S.S. Frederick Winslow Taylor what a sick irony is that, sick epitaph, death-dealing warship manufactured by his art and bearing his name. Maybe Taylor's own book makes a more suitable epitaph, read against the grain *Principles of Scientific Management* turns out to be a kind of parody, a genre-busting spoof of a scientific study in the form of an anti-novel, with episodes "in scene" including dialogue and setting, for example the famous episode of Taylor and the pig-iron handler "Schmidt," based on the real-life Henry Noll who could load and unload the greatest quantity of pig-iron in the least amount of time an astonishing forty-seven tons in one day thus busting the rates for grateful pig-iron handlers everywhere, a scene of temptation in which Taylor seduces Noll-Schmidt by appealing to his vanity and cupidity, Taylor speaking Standard English and Schmidt assigned a ridiculous campy Pennsylvania-Dutch accent who could have fallen for that but they all did: TAYLOR: *Schmidt, are you a high-priced man?* SCHMIDT: *Vell, I don't know vat you mean.* TAYLOR [twirling mustache]: *Oh yes, my good fellow, you do* . . . Schmidt the loyal worker-figure like an earlier version of Boxer from George Orwell's political allegory *Animal Farm*, Boxer the simple and trusting workhorse intoning his mantra "I will try to work harder" and he does he works harder and harder until he can't work anymore then it's off to the knackers to boil him down for hide and glue. Our little wayfarer who has fared his way to this table in the food court beneath the old Boston Garden scoreboard in the Watertown Arsenal Mall where he slurps the dregs of his soda through a straw this slurping hero of ours had misunderstood *Animal Farm* when he read it for his junior-high English class, he read it in one breathless sitting and by the last page it was already his bible book the first in a series of venerated bible books but he loved it because he misunderstood it, rather drastically misunderstood it. When they finished the book or had pretended to finish the book or the Cliff's Notes of the book or whatever except for our hero who had somehow managed to read all 97 pages in the allotted three weeks the teacher asked the class, Can anyone tell us the message of the book? And the next thing you know our hero found his own hand in the air, he the shy boy who never raised his hand never volunteered always safest keep a low profile had raised his hand and the teacher surprised at seeing the hand up of the boy who never raised his hand called on him, and he said stuttering at first he replied that the m-m-message of the b-book was that the animals at the farm would just have to try harder n-next time, since things had gone back to the way they'd been under Farmer Jones or even worse with those pigs in charge walking around on two legs they would just have to try again, if at first you don't succeed try try again, right, like the Little Train That Could well this would just have to be the Little Animal Farm That Could, not stuttering anymore and his voice not quavering hey this class participation stuff's not so bad after all when you've got something to say, out tumble the words and they are the words he means and he's excited, sudden fluency, inspiration, he says those animals would just have to try to take over the farm again, they have to rise up once again but this time along with getting rid of the humans they would have to get rid of the pigs, you need to get rid of the humans but then you still have to kill the pigs, out it came just like that, *The message of the book is KILL THE PIGS!!!* His parents were contacted and a conference with the school psychologist arranged. This was well before Columbine but they had some very forward-thinking teachers and administrators at this school visionaries even got to spot the evildoers early nip them in the bud counseling and a course of lithium indicated smart kid but quiet a loner adjustment problems. Auspicious start of a promising career. His favorite book as a teenager and the one responsible for making him into a radical maladjusted word-nut was his favorite because he had misread it and misinterpreted it, didn't get the orthodox meaning but made up a heterodox one instead, it was the apocryphal heretical interpretation that shaped his mind and misshaped his mind, this book which clearly teaches that any and all efforts at radical collective self-organization lead always and everywhere to butchery and tyranny because of our fallen and brutish natures and that one way or another we're always going to have bosses over us because it's nature, human nature, by what sinister kink in his own brutish nature did our hero manage to screw up and extract the exact opposite meaning, wrest sick optimism from salutary pessimism, as if this book were just pointing out pitfalls to be avoided the next time we rose up to Kill the Pigs, because to his misshapen mind there would always be a next time and maybe next time because of this book we'd have a better idea which Pigs to Kill. And maybe it's just because of the mild buzz from the soda on his otherwise empty stomach that our hero in the food court of the Watertown Arsenal Mall now feels that there might be hope after all, the modern world has to be more than just a Taylorized conveyor-belt stuffing mass-produced trash into the open maws of mindless thumbless mall-zombies because he possesses this example from his own life this living example of a text conveyed to him by his Taylorized education which he'd digested in his own way, turned to his own account, whose prescribed and orthodox meanings he had subverted and continues to subvert, maybe such opportunities for subversive appropriation are available to us everywhere, cracks in the armor of the big machine, fissures, gaps, opportunities to be seized, maybe every text of pessimism and despair can yield up such subtexts of wild subversion, each type its antitype, shreds of heretical apocrypha, perhaps even here, yea here, in this food court in the Watertown Arsenal Mall where a hundred years ago the molders and machinists rose up against the Taylor method but because they had only been defending their AFL craft-privileges and their white dick privileges they had failed, maybe their grandchildren their great-great grandchildren would get it right one day because there's always this heretical subtext and antitype lurking somewhere, for every 1911 Watertown Arsenal strike there's a 1912 Lawrence Bread and Roses strike, the textile mills of Lawrence, Massachusetts a few miles to the north of Watertown where the immigrant women workers were savagely exploited became the scene of the great Bread and Roses strike, organized with the help of the IWW who didn't discriminate against race or sex but tried to bring all workers into the One Big Union, Bread and Roses the road not taken, always a road not taken, always another branch in the river of time, never know when these white proles and black proles and brown proles stuffing Cinnabons into their mouths out of cardboard containers and licking their fingers might rise up in a body and sugar-rush next door into the Foot Locker and Lady Foot Locker to grab the heaviest boots off the racks shouting *Kick the*

Bosses in the Ass, Power to the Working Class! Here's our hero like Winston Smith at the end of Orwell's *1984* clutching the slender straw that our hope lies in the proles, the proles . . . Maybe after all it's not the books our hero read as a grown-up the Joyce and Woolf or the Beckett and Bernhard but the things they'd made him misread in school like *Animal Farm* and *1984* and *Lord of the Flies* and the things he read on his own in the same years like *Lord of the Rings* and all those superhero comics that form the bedrock of his sensibility, and one day he'll join some doughty fellowship armed with AK-47s and clad in balaclavas and kafiyas (which my reactionary Zionist spellcheck insists on correcting to "mafias") and venture into the Taylorized sweatshops and shopping malls of Mordor to bring down Sauron or Simon or whoever and melt his evil ring of power back down to the bad penny it was to begin with. Maybe one day – but in the meantime he's got one of those Cinnabons for himself. Hot from the cardboard box he's stuffing it into his mouth and licking his fingers and humming "The Internationale" – *Arise, ye prisoners of starvation* – the words in his head and the tune in his throat because of course you can't sing "The Internationale" with half a Cinnabon in your mouth, on his feet because he's too sugar-rushed to sit still which he mistakes for being too full of revolutionary ardor to sit still – *Arise, ye wretched of the earth* – with a mass of warm gummy Cinnabon wedged between his tonsils like a small deer in the gullet of an anaconda he wishes he had some of that soda left but he doesn't so he chases the first half of the Cinnabon with the second half of the Cinnabon, the cardboard container and the napkin sticking to his fingers – *For justice thunders condemnation* – he licks his sticky fingers and gets a piece of napkin in his mouth which mixes with the second sweet warm gummy gob of Cinnabon – *A better world's in birth!* Heading west along the second-storey concourse out of the food court towards the anchor stores Filene's Basement and Marshalls – *We have been naught, we shall be all* – he stops to lean on the railing where the concourse overlooks the ground-floor main plaza and the up-escalator bringing shoppers to the food court and the original Boston Garden scoreboard – *De dum, de dum, la la la laaa* – and with a wetted tongue and sticky napkin shreds he tries to clean the frosting off the stubble around his snout – *So comrades come rally* – and then he'll head into Filene's Basement to keep shopping for his jury-duty disguise, or rather because licking is providing insufficient moisture to clean the sticky off his face – *This is the time and place* – he'll have to turn around for a slam-dunk suspicious fourth trip to the men's room – *The International working class* – and because he has to pee again – *unites the human race!* Our hero is just about to turn around and head back for a very suspicious but unavoidable fourth trip to the men's room when he sees a figure on the ground-floor main plaza walking towards the up-escalator, a familiar figure, our hero sees and spies and descries and almost cries out, That's him! The heartbeat in our hero's breast and the free indirect discourse in his head both speed up, for it is indeed he, unmistakably he whom our hero has seen before – and more than seen. Tall but otherwise average build and average looks, suspiciously average looks, thinning brown hair bland nondescript face just descript enough for a positive ID, unmistakably descript in his deceptive nondescriptness, it's that Jim Wood character again, for the third or is this the fourth time enter Jim Wood, actor, shape-shifter— charlatan! Three strikes and you're out, pal. Or four, whatever. Don't think just act turn the tables get the upper hand, no second thoughts when this Jim Wood gets to the top of the escalator just pounce, like that sign over there in the Foot Locker window says Just Do

It, even if you've got Cinnabon all over your face. Our hero closes to the top of the escalator and posts himself between the rubber handrails to cut off escape routes unless of course it is Jim Wood coming after him and he's hurling himself at his feet who cares seize the initiative for once in your life, be not he who is acted upon but he who acts, thinning crown of Jim Wood coming up the escalator and then the bland eyes seeming unsurprised and the bland smile as if for an old acquaintance, college chums or something – *What? You here? Long time no see!* – Christ this guy's good, already in character and prepared with his lines doesn't matter don't think seize, seize the initiative! Our hero takes a final step forward to block the actor's path and raises one sticky hand not to shake but to block and admonish and our hero speaks, on the second-floor concourse of the Watertown Arsenal Mall this cliffhanging chapter conclusion of our hero speaking: *Jim Wood*, he says, *You are under arrest.* ("Sheer Genius!" *The Boston Globe*)

The Little Wayfarer

et's get one thing straight: our hero overestimates how much he resembles a person of Semitic origin, a person of Jewish or Arabic descent and on balance just a hair more like the latter than the former. OK, OK, we admit we can see it, but come on, little hero, it's not as much of a slam-dunk as all that! Once upon a time it would have been called his crochet or his hobby horse, and in another time and place his *idée fixe*, but we can now with the absolute precision of scientific terminology identify it as that type of psychological obsession known as "facial dysmorphia." Maybe you've heard of its limelight-hogging cousin among the physiomorphic pathologies, "body dysmorphia" – you know, anorectic high-school girls seeing fatties in the mirror, or at the other end of the spectrum their coronary-case dads over the hecatombs of their backyard barbecues imagining they could still slip into their JV jerseys just as easily as they're going to suck the marrow out of two or three slabs of ribs. Well, facial dysmorphia is the same for just the face, distorting one's perception of one's own visage, most typically in the direction of the nonstandard or undesirable – but aren't those always the same thing? And in our hero's case, moreover, and indeed most deplorably, it's a condition that's conditioned (because conditions are conditioned by prior conditions just as they condition subsequent conditions, such that everything, and not only thick, lustrous hair, is subject to conditioning) by the worst racial stereotypes: hooked schnoz, pendulous slavering lips, shady skin and kinked profuse hair as the setting for fanatical acquisitive eyes – the features of the menacing cartoon yids you'll remember from Nazi propaganda back in the day, or, come to think of it, the features of the menacing cartoon jihadis in the Danish newspaper, *Jyllands-Posten*, in September 2005, just pry off the yarmulke and pop on a turban and the scary Jew who was going to destroy European civilization in the 1930s and the scary Arab who is going to destroy European and more importantly American civilization in the near future if we don't do something about it are basically the same dude. And somehow our poor hero has internalized this caricature, such that when for example he sees the reflection of his slightly largish nose and so forth in the display window of the Victoria's Secret in the Arsenal Mall in Watertown, Massachusetts obtruding into whatever ass-game he was right then imagining with the mannequin in the frost-blue camisole it might as well be the cartoon ghost of Yassir Arafat that parents in West Bank settlements frighten their children with coming to join in the ass-fun. He remembers seeing Arafat on TV when he was a kid and thinking he was going to grow up to look like that instead of like his dad who, although a second-generation Portuguese-American, had been told on more than one occasion that he resembled Desi Arnaz, a Cuban. So how did this condition get started? But "how" is a proverbial tough nut, and cracking it might turn out to require a volume of its own – lest you think this is all just a *jeu d'esprit*, or, worse yet, a digression, when it is in fact something essential to every forward-moving narrative: a nutcracker – so let's ease into our investigation with something simpler, like when? It started when our third-person hero started going through puberty, around eleven twelve thirteen (for a boy his voice cracked early), in junior high, that baptismal font of the adult world's indignities, a tricky time for most and no cake-walk for our little wayfarer. Around this time he started to suspect that he'd been adopted, his other *idée fixe* or more properly obsession, our hero is a creature of double-barreled obsessions, one just isn't enough for him, he has to go for the obsessional double-whammy, you see how they work together, tag-team, in tandem, a comedy duo or buddy flick if not Siamese twins, around junior-high age he started to think he was some kind of orphan and most likely an Arab orphan, a dusty urchin from the winding byways of a souk, snatching a tangerine or two in the instant the muezzin's call distracts the shopkeeper and retiring after his furtive meal for a nap in the shade of a camel, it sure beats having to suit up for PE. Now it's not so weird for kids at that age to have intrusive thoughts that they could've been adopted and even for a while to entertain such intruders rather than dismiss them as the bogeys and will-o'-the-wisps they so patently are, in most cases anyway, ninety-nine point nine, you get the idea, literalizations of their incipient sense of difference, their otherness, other even to themselves, which strikes them quite properly as alien and strange before it devolves, alas, into the hyper-trophy of fatuous narcissism that characterizes the success-fully socialized grownup. This adoption business should have been nothing more than what the experts scientifically term "a phase," which, in the optimal scheme of things, one "goes through," but our hero for some reason made up his mind to get stuck there, remanded, detained, ever to eddy around and back, fondling his face in the mirror while he fingered the same sticky questions: Question one did he look different from his mom and dad, his brothers and sisters? Sure, a little. But there was a story for this, spit and image of a long-dead relative, happens like that once in a while, different branch of the bloodline, father's father's folk, stayed behind in the village, there's even proof of a sort, warped sepia-toned photograph, blurred figure in a hat, maybe it's just credible, they said a fishing village and he could make out a boat. Funny kid! Don't worry your head so much! What an imagination! (Next week came the school field trip to the mock-up of the Mayflower docked in the silt of Plymouth harbor where slight rockings imperceptible to everyone else managed to render our little hero seasick in spite of the fact that all Portuguese are natural sailors.) Question two did his parents treat him different from his brothers and sisters no they did not, not different, or at least not worse, and in fact a little better, maybe a tad too solicitously, suspiciously with solicitousness? Isn't the typical pattern to be strict with the first, relax with the middles, and mollycoddle the last? Only here it's been reversed, the firstborn coddled . . . still it's been known to happen, e.g., James among the Joyce sibs, perfectly credible alternate explanations and scenarios. And yet our hero persists, or rather *it* persists, like a pebble in his mental shoe, this suspicion he's adopted, I mean that he's *been* adopted, he stays stuck in that phase or it sticks to him, maybe because it called up reinforcements, its supplement or its supple, unshakeable complement: not only adopted, but Arab. Now plenty of kids growing up in Duxbury, Massachusetts, go through the phase where they think they're adopted, and even, considering Duxbury, praying they're adopted, but not many go through a phase where they think they're Arabs. In Dearborn, Michigan, maybe, but not Duxbury, Mass. And why Arab and not Jew, at least he'd met some actual Jews growing up, first girl he'd kissed, Anita Trachtenberg, lived right down the street, whereas he couldn't say that he'd ever really met an Arab – or as he put it to himself, *another* Arab – until college, where the few Arab students at first pegged him for a Hillel House habitué. Could his fixation have anything to do with having watched all those reruns of *Jonny Quest*, his favorite cartoon when he was a boy? You remember *Jonny Quest*, don't you? In the show, Jonny and his dad, Dr. Benton Quest, travel the world in jetpacks and hovercraft searching for adventures among hostile natives. There's no Mrs. Quest, she died some time back, instead they're accompanied on their adventures by an, er, a male companion, "Race" Bannon, a sort of intelligence agent and bodyguard figure who's also supposed be a tutor for young Jonny and his dusky-skinned, turban-wearing sidekick, Hadji – *ah ha!* – yes, Hadji, who just happens to have been *adopted* by Dr. Quest! But before we get all carried away let's not forget Jonny's little dog, with the adorable folded ear and the patch of black fur around his eyes, Bandit. The subtext, in case you have to have it spelled out for you, is that Dr. Quest is fucking Race Bannon, Race Bannon is fucking Jonny, Jonny is fucking Hadji, and Hadji gets to fuck Bandit. Whether or not Bandit fucked Dr. Quest so that everyone on the show got to be Lucky Pierre is disputed inside our semiotics team, although clearly all five of them regularly fucked the natives. The cartoon was part of a larger plan to homosocialize boys for careers in the military battling Third World insurgencies in the larger geopolitical context of the Cold War. According to this plan, boys growing up in Duxbury, Mass, and watching syndicated re-runs of *Jonny Quest* over their Saturday-morning cereal would identify with the eponymous hero, with his blindingly white skin and his little quiff of blond hair. But not our hero – he couldn't even watch cartoons right! He always fantasized that he was Hadji, his spontaneous identification was with the dark-skinned boy in the turban with the Arab-sounding name, maybe one day just like Hadji he would get to be friends with a boy like Jonny and even be adopted into the family of a boy like Jonny . . . Of course Hadji wasn't always the second fiddle, he had a few chops of his own, exotic and Oriental powers like ESP and hypnosis, in the opening credits there's always this shot of Hadji charming a snake, Hadji with one end of a flute in his mouth and his fingers playing up and down the shaft of the flute, which makes the snake come out of the basket, a tumescent hooded cobra rising up out of a big round basket, OK just about the gayest thing you could imagine, you can't make this stuff up, and our hero too a little spellbound by it, we've got to admit, in the end we've got to admit that it probably says more about his well his um his er his at times *fluid* sexuality than about his ethnic identifications, in the final analysis (although this analysis is interminable) our hero's identification with the Hadji character on *Jonny Quest* tells us more about his sexual fantasies than his ethnic origins. And anyway wasn't Hadji supposed to be Indian? Although with that name and turban he could've been an Indian Muslim, or a Sikh. We're grasping at straws here, but what else could have planted that Arab seed? The packs of Camel cigarettes that his father smoked with their pyramids and minarets and palm trees? Seeing *Lawrence of Arabia* on TV? Maria Muldaur's pop hit "Midnight at the Oasis" which he enjoyed hearing on AM radio before he knew any better? It doesn't add up to much, does it, and what little it adds up to still points more to Castro Street than to Cairo. But maybe that's it, after all, maybe the Arab thing is just a blind for the queerer half of his character, a way of (mis)understanding his own identities, in which one exotic out-group stands in for another. Because, come to think of it, it was around the wonder years of junior high that our hero also picked up the following bit of sexual apocrypha, from among the sticky soiled counterfeit passed around between young boys in their bathroom gossip, although he long ago forgot it (but isn't memory strategic?), *Dude, did you know that if we were, like, growin' up in fuckin' Arabia or someplace like that, we'd have to like get buttfucked by an older dude before we ever*

had anything to do with bitches, see – this from the neighborhood ethnographer, an expert in such matters – *becuz of
the way that the bitches are all, like, kept separate until
you marry one, or they get three, that's like the trade-off,
you get to marry as many bitches as you can afford when
you grow up but when you're our age you have to get
fucked in the ass by an older dude, and suck him off and
everything, this hairy older dude who's like, you're
assigned to him. It's part of their fucking religion.* And how
do you think our hero reacted to this National Geographic
moment? *Whoa, dude! That is some sick shit!* Yeah, so sick
it gave him tummy butterflies and he couldn't wait to get
home that afternoon and lock himself in the bathroom. And
maybe that's all we've got here, orphan and Arab as overde-
termined figures for this fundamental ambivalence of his
character, or rather of his personality, comprised as it is of
multiple characters. Knotty boy! But fortunately we have
additional information, yes that's it additional information
has come into our hands, certain materials, in the form of a
file, a dossier, made up of certain documents, comprising a
record – spotty, admittedly, incomplete, in places possibly
apocryphal, yet suggestive. And to help you to contextualize
the contents of this dossier, to frame them as it were, or let's
just come out and say to completely prejudice your reception of them (thus evoking another meaning of "frame"),
please allow us to introduce them into evidence under the
heading of the following principle, which some regard as a
law: Just because you're paranoid doesn't mean they're not
out to get you. Because, you see, now that we've determined
that our hero's obsession with being an adopted Arab is
merely a product of his imagination with little causal connection to his family experience and social environment
beyond the hypothetical possibility that it evolved as a psychological displacement of his problematic bisexuality, we

must now bring you the following newsflash: He *was* adopted, and he *is* an Arab. It's true that he overestimates the extent to which he resembles a person of Semitic origin, a Jew or an Arab and on balance more like the latter than the former, but it's also true that he's an Arab. This is not a contradiction. We can safely affirm that his fears are completely irrational, because little in his actual surroundings could have credibly put meat on the bones of such a non sequitur, even one which, quite coincidentally, happens to be, in a narrowly empirical sense, true. He is an Arab. How it would alarm our hero to learn this! How quickly would his "I knew it!" be succeeded by "Oh shit!" He already spends too much time in bed, but now we would never be able to get him out from under it! And what then would his reaction be to learning that not only is he an Arab, but an Arab of that most suspect and outcaste tribe, a Palestinian! And not only a Palestinian – as if this weren't enough to tip him completely over the edge – but the blood kin of an infamous Palestinian terrorist! The one his followers called al-Hakim, the wise, but whom we know as the late George Habash, founder and leader of the Popular Front for the Liberation of Palestine! Wow! What a development! So now, let's let our hero hang for a while, leave him hanging on the cliff of his sudden confrontation with his shadowy double on the second-floor concourse of the Arsenal Mall in Watertown, Massachusetts, and turn our attention to this other story, this submerged or suppressed or possibly even apocryphal history, or more precisely backstory, usually in a story the backstory about the hero's lineage and life-up-to-now comes pretty early, early but not on the first page, first you're supposed to open with some action as a "hook" and then you're supposed to give some background, that's the way it usually goes, you start out with some action to "hook" your readers, and indeed you're told in every writing class in every MFA program in the world that you've got to give "the conflict" right away on the first page in order to "hook" the reader, buster, or agents and editors will simply toss your whole MS into the wastebasket for the Salvadoran cleaning crew to dispose of that night, or rather since these days we're all "green" they'll toss your MS into a special bin to be recycled that night by the subcontracted Guatemalan recycling crew, whatever, you get the idea, one way or the other if you don't have the "hook" of a dramatic "conflict" on the very first page of your work of "literary fiction" you are going to be shoved down the memory hole by the subcontracted help, it's *in media res* or bust, pal, Homer did it, Aristotle said it, and I believe it. But then after you've "hooked" your reader and they're there with their lip or cheek tugged out into a grotesque bleeding tent of flesh helplessly compelled to turn the page, unless of course you have them hooked by one of the eyes, you've really got your reader by the balls if you've got her by the eyes, spurting blood and tears and blobs of eye-jelly all over your finely-crafted sentences in the helpless compulsion to turn the page, then it's essential to keep them on the line by playing with them before you reel them in (don't worry we'll be cutting bait on this metaphor pretty soon), and you play with them by suddenly diverting the narrative into backstory, into exposition about the hero's past, so that all of the hero's actions and reactions in the unfolding intensifying conflict (the "rising action") make the hero psychologically coherent and "rounded" and most of all sympathetic, you can't be expected to sell a story if the main character's not sympathetic, your readers have to *care* about the hero and find the hero sympathetic, and to be sympathetic the hero has to have plausible psychological motivations and as we all know these are based on our past histories, our backgrounds, our backstories, according to the well-known literary principle of cause and effect, the appearance of temporal depth and the appearance of psychological depth go together and mutually reinforce each other and cause the effect of realism, people don't just go around doing shit for no reason that's not realistic, but if they don't do anything at all it won't be dramatic, if for example they just wander around in circles trapped inside various non-places such as airport baggage-claim terminals and highway rest-stops it wouldn't be dramatic, you've got to be realistic yet dramatic, even if real life is rarely dramatic and drama is rarely realistic you've got to find the balance, the middle way, the as it were golden mean, and for this balancing act to come off you've got to have backstory, see, like maybe a second page of backstory after a first page of "hook"-action, or if it's a novel a second chapter of backstory after a first chapter of "hook"-action but then you have to get right back to the action after the backstory, that's just the way it's done. And we confess that we've been a little dilatory getting there ourselves, here we are on page 166 and only now does it look like we might be getting a little action, maybe this thing can finally be teased into a conventional story after all, with a plot and so forth, and a crisis, and some kind of epiphany and closure and redemption at the end? Well, wait and see. I wouldn't jump the gun or anything. Maybe since you're still with us after so many dilatory pages we've got a pretty good idea that we can just keep finger-fucking you. Anyway right now we're going to talk about our hero's mother – his biological mother, that is – a Palestinian Arab and cousin of PFLP founder-leader George Habash. We're going to try to piece together a spotty, fragmentary record into something like a portrait, in the form of a narrative. We'll tell you what we know to be factually true (Aristotle's definition of history, i.e., the necessary) and what it is plausible to infer (Aristotle's definition of fiction, i.e., the probable, by which a lot of so-called histories turn out to be fiction), but so far we have to admit that it's little like trying to tune in a TV program on an old black-and-white set with a coat-hanger for antenna in some trailer park way out in the back of beyond, it's a pretty fuzzy picture and who knows it might just be a figure we're making up ourselves, Rorschach-like, out of patterns in the snow. Suffice it to say that it's a small figure, dark, on a long dusty road, glaringly bright, faring her way and not getting anywhere, or anywhere we can see. Yes, before our little wayfarer there was another little wayfarer, wending her winding way, our little wayfarer turns out to be the sequel, the Little Wayfarer II, and here we have the original, the Little Wayfarer I, though hard to make out, a figure always in retreat, maybe the only thing keeping her from disappearing completely that she makes so little progress, no progress at all, really, but turns in a vanishing eddy, vanishingly small but still there, this speck, this mite, at the limen, in the margin, makes you blink, might just be dust, after all it is just dust. On a dusty road, wending her way, backwards or forward it's all the same, she's always there, on that hot, footsore road, dry as dust, bone dry, always that glare, always the thirst— But no, we can only infer that her feet are sore, that the glare stabs her eyes, that she's famished from thirst, even a plausible inference is just guesswork, and if this makes us feel distant from her experience it has the effect of making her seem just as distant from it on the other side, as if "experience" were the median and she in exile from her own being, and maybe after all that is what she is feeling, or rather not-feeling, when we see her there, or that figure she makes – just numb, dumb, intransitive distance. And that's it, we could end it there, a kind of sad contradiction, of someone faring her way, exiled, unhoused, yet never getting anywhere, like someone treading water, except in this case dust, treading dust. It all depends on how you arrange your materials, and what screws you put to them. There's such a disjunction between the objective chronological record and what are called her subjective experiences, if she has them, which are entirely closed off from us apart from what is suggestive about this image, this trace, unless of course it is an abyss. We could at least make a start, however, by telling you about the town she was from, called Lydda, except that Lydda doesn't exist anymore, it's been erased, it has no more reality than a place out of myth or fable. But maybe that gives us a clue how to begin: Once upon a time, there was— Or wait, since we're doing this, let's do it right, in the manner of a Palestinian village storyteller: *There was, or there was not, in the oldness of time . . .* a town called Lydda, or al-Lyd, standing in the plains between Palestine's coastal lowlands and the hills of the interior, where for centuries the Christian and Muslim townspeople had lived together in peace, Christians had lived in Lydda since ancient times and Lydda even makes an appearance in the Christian's holy book, in the part called Acts 9:32-35: "*As Peter traveled about the country, he went to visit the saints in Lydda. There he found a man named Aeneas, a paralytic who had been bedridden for eight years. 'Aeneas', Peter said to him, 'Jesus Christ heals you. Get up and take care of your mat.' Immediately Aeneas got up. All those who lived in Lydda and Sharon saw him and turned to the Lord.*" And it's a funny coincidence that our hero (sorry for any confusion but we're talking now about the Little Wayfarer II) once puzzled over this very verse without knowing that his own biological family had long roots in Lydda, instead he puzzled over the name Aeneas and how he could be a paralytic here and an exiled wanderer in Virgil, he pondered the puzzle of being paralytic yet peripatetic, but most of all our hero was struck by Peter's injunction to Aeneas to "take care of his mat," a moment which helped crystallize his thinking about why Christianity was such a raw deal: "You're healed – now get up and make your bed!" And admittedly this piously pushy aspect of Christianity came to be resented from time to time by the Muslims themselves, in spite of their overall inclination to be neighborly their patience wore thin when it came to such pushy-pious things as Crusades, and in fact the largest mosque in Lydda the grand mosque al-Umari was built by the Sultan Rukn al-Din Baybars to thank Allah for helping him run those Crusaders out of town, but episodes such as this were exceptions to the peace-loving rule, and even though by the first Little Wayfarer's time Lydda had long been known as the "city of mosques" it had a well-attended Christian church too, among the numerous beautiful mosques and sharing a centrally-located square with the grand al-Umari Mosque itself there stood a church of the Christian Orthodox faith named after the revered dragon-slayer St. George, revered by the Muslims as well under the name Ghader or Khader, and which contained the holy martyr's tomb. And who knows maybe George Habash's parents had this saint in mind when they named their son, they were a Christian family with roots in Lydda going way back, like most Christians in Palestine at that time they were middle class and had produced their share of merchants and mayors, lawyers and priests, civil servants and judges, and with George in the medical program at the American University in Beirut they would soon have their doctor too, and even though George's parents had moved their family to Jaffa there were still plenty of the rest of the Habash clan back in Lydda, the ancestral home, where for example our little wayfarer was growing up, Little Wayfarer I the mother of Little Wayfarer II but still a young girl at this time, the fateful year 1948. She lived in Lydda but she dreamed of Jaffa, the previous year her father had taken her and her younger sisters to Jaffa on one of his trips to consult with his partners about his business which was buying bulbs and seeds from Syria and selling them to England and France and while he consulted with his partners the girls' nurse took them to see the local marvels the original chains that had bound Andromeda to the rock and the very bones of the Leviathan that swallowed Jonah, after which they met back up for tea with George's family only to learn that alas her handsome cousin had returned to Beirut that very morning. Then it was back to Lydda but to the new house not the old house, the new house among the other new houses in the Haqouret Al-Qura district with a new brass knocker on the door instead of an iron knocker and with four servants, one to cook one to clean one to mind the children and one to polish the brass knocker and answer its call, saying "*Mîn hada?*" and stalling the bill collectors and ushering guests into the mandara or in pleasant weather the courtyard where, bowing, his left hand over the breast of his immaculate blouse, he poured them steaming cups of coffee while her father asked after everyone's health. It was essential to keep up that hospitality for which the family as a whole was known and moreover in a house that communicated a proper sense of the family's standing even though at the time this meant living a tad beyond their means, her father seldom discussed such things with his wife let alone with his children but it is likely that our wayfarer had a sense that they were in some kind of straits, if not wolf-at-the-door (though he was to come) at least bill collectors, and after the guests had finished their coffee and said their goodbyes and were ushered by the servant back out past the brass knocker their place was taken in the new house by a familiar cloud of knit brows, dyspepsia, and whispers cut short that seemed not only to have followed them from the old house but to have thickened in transit. It was business that burdened her father, primarily the business of his business and secondarily this business of Palestine, because the two were related in some way our little wayfarer was never quite clear about, even though her father wasn't the best businessman (he should have been writing poems about flowers instead of trying to sell them, to tell you the truth), it wasn't entirely his fault that his ventures failed to thrive and hadn't been thriving since around the time that his third daughter (our little wayfarer) was born. Through no fault of her own she had been born the year before the start of the Uprising, the great Uprising against the British which hadn't gone all that great for the Palestinian people in general nor for her father's business in particular, but because nobody bothered explaining all this to our wayfarer it gave her instead, like a little account of gloom opened at her birth and added to every year, a regularly compounded sense that everyone had been better off before she showed up. Most of all "everyone" meant her mother, her mother was burdened too but her mother was burdened not with the business of the business nor with this business of Palestine but rather, as befit a mother and a mother's burdens, with the business of being a mother, let no one say that her parents neglected the burdens proper to what God and tradition had seen fit to portion out between the sons of Adam and the daughters of Eve. For years the mother had wanted to give her husband a son, or rather had wanted to give her husband's family a son, many sons, as many as the wives of her husband's brothers had been able to contribute, she contributed five daughters but never a son, or rather she contributed daughters and sons but the sons had a tendency to die, one dying a few months after he was born and one dying a few months before he was born, after which the doctor told her that she would probably never have another child and that, if she were interested in remaining the mother of the ones she already had, she probably shouldn't even try. She kept trying, however, and at some cost to her health she had two more children, two more daughters, making five daughters in all and making our little wayfarer, thirteen years old in 1948, the exact middle daughter. Unfortunately her middledom was not of the comfy, cushioned, crowded kind, but rather the lonely middledom of a decade all to herself: her two big sisters were five and seven years older (both married now and with homes of their own) and her two kid sisters were five and seven years younger, making a five-year gap on each side of our wayfarer. The gaps were where her dead brothers belonged. Coming in the long wake of the brother that had managed to draw breath for a few short months, our little wayfarer had been something of a disappointment, as you might imagine. She had a nurse to look after her, and her two big sisters would sometimes play with her like she was a doll, but in general her mother's verdict seemed to rub off on everyone else. Still, so far was the little wayfarer from bearing a grudge that she actually grew up wanting to care for her mother, she had been born with a strong impulse to care which the fact of not having very much of that particular behavior directed her way had strengthened rather than the reverse, and if the people around her seemed as grudging in receiving such childish ministrations as she was able to offer as they were in reciprocating, this served only to channel our little wayfarer's ambitions to the future and gave her a goal in life – she would grow up to be a nurse. It was no good trying to get some practice in the meantime, though: someone would always be shooing her away, for she was regarded throughout the family as a clumsy child, a child liable to smash delicate things, a reputation whose origin lay in the responsibility she had been vaguely and most unfairly assigned for having elbowed her adjacent siblings, the two doomed males, into oblivion. And her mother was not going to let anything like that happen again, not this time, because finally, finally – this was about a year and a half ago – had come the birth, at last, and stopping the mouths of all the naysayers, of a healthy son! There was cause for rejoicing in the new house in the Haqouret Al-Qura district, but cause for concern as well, and not only because of another nestling clamoring for its feed. This birth had exacted an awful price, as if most of the mother's already-diminished store of animal spirits had been imparted, in some last-ditch umbilical potlatch, to the newborn. More than anything her mother needed rest, but while all in the household stood ready, as usual, to accommodate her, she would not allow it to herself. Even though the infant appeared perfectly ruddy-cheeked and fattening up nicely thank you very much after his underweight premiere, his mother could not be persuaded of his health, and when his health was not in question then the salubriousness of his surroundings were: invisible dangers lurked everywhere, and some disaster, some catastrophe, would befall her little man if she relaxed for an instant the terrible vigil that only a mother, however weakened, could be trusted to keep. In these new circumstances our wayfarer, as you might imagine, saw less of her mother than ever, but by now she had finally reached the age when her thoughts were tending elsewhere anyway, outwards to the wide world, thinking for example more and more about how when she became a nurse she would be able to assist her uncle George in some clinic or hospital. Innocent thoughts: she was still too young to picture to herself a real romance and too modest about her chances to picture it with someone like her cousin. She only saw him a few times a year, at holidays and weddings, where he always cut such a fine figure (as even people outside the family said), a bit of playboy, it is true – you know what Beirut does to a young man – but serious when he wanted to be, hard-working and good-humored, and with something in his voice, even when he was just telling people about a sailing party or what it was like to play a game called tennis, that commanded his audience's attention. Out of all her relatives George was nicer to her than anyone, he always took special notice and sometimes even brought her a gift, a doll or when she was older a box whose treasure was to smell like the forest when you opened it, but his best gift of all was something he'd said last year at her sister's wedding, when most of the guests had gone home and it was just close kin left over and the conversation got around to the dreaded inevitable topic – marrying off the next daughter. After a brief painful silence one aunt was heard to remark that there was always the convent in Ramle, and although our wayfarer knew there was no shame in going into the convent in Ramle she hung her head anyway in something like shame and because she respected the sisters she had met from the convent in Ramle she felt ashamed of her shame, she couldn't concentrate on what anyone was saying after that because it was just then occurring to her that there was really no contradiction between being a nun and being a nurse and maybe the mother of God had it in mind for her to be both, but then she heard her cousin George speak, and unlike everybody else he was speaking *to* our little wayfarer as well as about her, he said that even though it would not be many years until she had to think about getting married, when the time came there would be no problem finding her a husband because not only was she a brave generous girl with a lovely sensitive soul but she had the most beautiful eyes of anyone in the family, indeed her eyes were the family's crown jewels – he said it in English first, "the crown ju-ells" – and when her aunts and uncles and cousins laughed he protested, No, I speak the truth, the Queen of England has nothing like them! And the little wayfarer looked down again but this time it was not shame that was making her blush, for while it was true that she had the plainest face of all her sisters and moreover sitting atop a short and sturdily cube-like form of the kind that would interest only a *fellah* who wanted a wife to harness to his plow it was also undeniable that hers were the most beautiful or at least the most striking and unusual eyes, and even though she knew that her cousin was exaggerating when he said they were like the skies on the morning of creation, the feathers of the peacocks in the gardens of the Alhambra, and the mother-of-pearl that the master craftsmen of Bethlehem have burnished to a peak of manifold iridescence (grazing a finger across the bracelet he had once given her and which she always made sure to wear in his presence), she also knew that he wasn't poking fun. When she returned to school she made a concerted assault on her studies, knowing there was a long road ahead if she wanted to be a nurse and that she would have to rein in her mind's tendency to wander. Such a mature little wayfarer! But not so mature that she did not get carried away, so to speak, by the events that unfolded so suddenly and strangely the very next year. Some nights she had the experience of falling asleep so quickly that it seemed like she went from waking life to dream life without any transition, now it was like that all the time. The winter term at the school for Christian girls where she was a day student was abruptly cut short when the classrooms and dormitory were requisitioned to become a hospital, and now here she was, practically already a nurse! It was part of the general mobilization of the whole town, volunteer committees were springing up everywhere and everyone was involved in one or another of the frantic activities. There were defense committees for each neighborhood, there was a committee of laborers to dig trenches and build barricades, and there was a merchants' committee that her father was part of (even though he was a wholesale trader and not a shopkeeper, as he pointed out, straightening the new fez he had purchased for the occasion) to collect the supplies that everyone would need and discourage hoarding (her family continued to hoard only because they were certain the neighbors were hoarding), and there was a committee to collect money and buy weapons that her oldest sister's husband was on and in the spirit of the times many of the women in the better-off districts such as the Haqouret Al-Qura district were persuaded to sell their jewelry to raise funds (unfortunately her mother's jewelry had long since been pawned, but secretly in Jaffa so that the neighbors wouldn't notice and get the wrong idea), and then even though there weren't all that many weapons yet there was training for the volunteer militia that her second-oldest sister's husband had joined, on the soccer pitch of the boy's school at the edge of town they could be seen going through their drills with their collection of old hunting rifles, shovels, and broomsticks. Best of all there was the medical committee which had taken over the little wayfarer's very own school to turn into a hospital and they needed volunteers for all kinds of things so she just kept turning up for class every morning until they gave her something to do, and now she was practically a nurse which so far meant mostly making and rolling bandages. But she tried to keep from smiling while she laundered the old linens and cut the long strips, because it was supposed to be a serious time, as she knew from overhearing the grown-ups. Almost as invisible to the servants as she was to her parents, it was easy enough to linger in the colonnade after dinner and listen to her father and his guests in the courtyard talking until late in the evening, the Christian men of Lydda she had known all her life, uncles and cousins and family friends sitting in their jackets and fezzes, smoking in the evening air and drinking coffee and arak, pausing with faintly patronizing respect when the muezzin's call drifted overhead and then going on, back and forth: "Let's not overreact! The Jews are not a warlike people, they're traders and merchants and professional men, like us—" "Except when they try to be *fellahin*, and farm!" "But you'll see – there'll be some haggling and then there will be a deal." "No, no, you don't know them now. Hitler has changed them." "You're right. The Haganah is stronger than we know, they have built it up in secret, with money from the rich Jews in America." "We'll be alright – the Higher Committee will get Farouk and Abdullah to send their armies." "Abdullah? Pah! The Hashemite hates the Mufti. I'll wager he already has a separate peace worked out with Ben Gurion." "But he's not such a fool as to let a prize like Lydda slip through his fingers!" "We've always been friends with the Jews who are our neighbors here, in Bet Shemen and Bir Yacov. God willing there won't be any defending necessary." It was always her father to make this last contribution, and so the little wayfarer would feel comforted. Even when the fighting got underway – at first just skirmishes on the roads, mostly – there were two articles of faith, that they would be safe in Lydda because it was on the right side of the line on that map the Europeans had drawn up, and if by chance there was any encroachment after the British withdrew then the armies of their brother Arabs would sweep in to protect them. It was a matter of honor, and if they let Palestine be taken they would never recover from the disgrace. It was this latter hope, however, that came to predominate as the weeks went by and those who had long maintained that the Jews simply wanted to drive them into the sea came to sound like sages and oracles. The women in the bazaar exchanged terrible stories that our little wayfarer heard on her way to roll bandages: "I've got a cousin in Haifa, you know, and she told me that most of the big families have already left – the al Hadis, the Nusseibehs – they're going to wait it out in Beirut and Damascus!" "It's the same all over, and not only the big shots. Where my brother lives, he went to pick up his pay envelope but it's in a Jewish neighborhood and when they saw him on the streets they beat him to within an inch of his life! All the policemen had left town!" "He's lucky to be alive. My niece's family, up in Acre, where she was staying with her husband's family – the Jews put typhoid in the wells. This is the truth!" "And what about Deir Ayyub, where my family is from? That village simply isn't there anymore! Not one stone on another stone!" "So? Closer to Jerusalem and it wasn't just the village, it was the villagers! Everyone! Women and children as well as the men, slaughtered like goats!" Then one among the speakers, her voice dropping, went on to tell about something else that had been done to the village women, something that the little wayfarer couldn't quite understand, or maybe she was just too far out of earshot by that time, for she found herself hurrying on. But one by one, as the days passed, she heard of their fall – Tiberias, Haifa, Safad, Beisan – cities and towns she had heard of since childhood, and countless villages besides, until the day that Jaffa fell and the horror-stories came firsthand because the rumors were replaced by refugees. The better-off from Jaffa were boarded with the better-off in Lydda, and this included her cousin George's family who were welcomed into the homes of their Lydda kin, but most of the refugees had to live like Bedouins, they filled the alleys and courtyards and bustans and finally the streets themselves and she had to thread her way through them on her way to the hospital, wherever there was a tree there was a family beneath it, more than one, crowded into makeshift tents, not only the families of dusty villagers but of shopkeepers, craftsmen, and clerks. In less than a week the food that the merchants' committee had managed to store was all gone and after that if it wasn't made in Lydda or grown in the region you couldn't get it for a prayer and if you could it was priced too high, and finally the only thing there was no shortage of was garbage, piling up in the streets and in drifts against walls, and as the days grew hotter the smell of human excrement was so thick in the air that the flies simply hung in it without beating their wings. One morning after it was discovered that the sanitation inspector had fled with his family, the Lydda national committee banned any more departures out of town and now the roadblocks at the end of the main thoroughfares had to check those leaving as well as those coming in, and many more were still coming in. It got so crowded that even people from the best homes were getting typhoid and dysentery, and it wasn't long after her cousin's family arrived from Jaffa that one of George's older sisters – she had six children of her own to worry about – was trying to hide the fact that she had a fever. Still there was no sign of George, he had sent word that he was leaving Beirut but there was no telling when he would make it to Lydda because the Jews now had them almost surrounded, occupying all the villages between Jaffa and Lydda and advancing on Ramle in the south and Abbasiyya in the north so that their only lifeline was the corridor into the eastern hills through which they still looked for Abdullah's armies to come and succor them. Every day there were sounds of fighting from the villages and the drone of airplanes overhead, black spots in the sky that buzzed like locusts, first they dropped leaflets telling the townspeople to flee and then bombs to back the words up. Every time a wall fell there was always a family of refugees for it to fall on, and one bomb even landed next

door to the hospital. Our little wayfarer was in the dispens-
ary when it hit, the earth and the very air around her shook
like that time she had stood close to a passing locomotive on
a dare and like then she succeeded in hiding her fear,
although as the hurt and dying filled up the wards she came
to realize that her chief emotion was not fear but frustration
she could not be of more service. There was only so much
she could do, or was allowed to do – she had started going
from bed to bed with a ladle and a jug of drinking water –
yet every day the suffering and the desperation multiplied.
Still there were moments that lifted the spirits of the
townspeople and their huddled guests: one morning it was
a troupe of Bedouins with rifles and splendid horses
cheered by the crowd as they passed through on their way
to help defend the airport, on another it was a corps of *haj-
janah* from the east, mounted on camels and singing, in the
evenings it was Lydda's own men in flatbed trucks rumbling
out of town to make night raids against the invader's posi-
tions, and one day the garrison out at the boy's school even
managed to shoot an airplane out of the sky. On each occasion everyone remarked that surely the tide was turning,
surely Glubb Pasha was right then issuing the order for the
Arab Legion to march out of Latrun to their rescue. And
while they didn't get rescued, in answer to their prayers (for
surely these were prayers) they finally got a few weeks of
peace and calm, apparently a truce of some kind had been
reached, whereupon everyone let out a sigh of relief except
our little wayfarer who held her breath because she was still
waiting for cousin George. Then the truce ended and the
shelling began. This time it seemed to come from every direction at once, as if the Jewish army's artillery and mortars
were drawn up into the town's own orchards and fields. In
the courtyard of the new house in the Haqouret Al-Qura
district the little wayfarer could hear the whistling in the sky

and feel the thuds underfoot, distant at first but growing closer, until finally a servant had to drag her back inside, the last servant to remain with their family, saying that the invaders would be in the town any minute and now only Allah could save them, the servant raised her kerchiefed brow to the sky and implored *Ya rub Ibhamma*, but as far as our little wayfarer was concerned it seemed strange to expect God's mercy to come from the same direction as all of the bombs, just as it was absurd to believe that you would be safer inside walls just because they muffled the sound of the explosions. She wanted to go to the hospital but instead she was forced to stay in the house, where both of her parents had gone completely insane. Her mother had had the heavy oak dining table carried into the nursery so that she could shelter the baby underneath it, but as she had to lie down she had dragged the cot under the table with them, which left just enough room for her to wedge herself, clutching her swaddled bundle, between the cot and the underside of the table. Anyone who wanted to ask her if she needed anything had to bend over and squint into the shadows, and when they heard her mother's answer they might realize they had been speaking to her feet. Meanwhile her father paced in the mandara, insisting that the attack on Lydda was the result of a misunderstanding, a terrible misunderstanding, they had always had a special relationship with the Jews in the region and if only the mayor and Dr. Lehman of Bet Shemen could sit down and talk they could work everything out, some kind of agreement could be reached, Dr. Lehman was the mukhtar of the Jews at Bet Shemen and a sensible man who would listen to reason, her father had had many reasonable conversations with him, and so on and so forth, stopping only for the explosions which made him seize up like a man in a fit, so that his fez would slip down the back of his head. The house was filled with

Jaffa relatives but none of them was paying any attention to her father, they were all worried instead about George's sister whose fever was making her weaker by the minute or so they had been told, George's sister and her six children were staying with another of our wayfarer's aunts on the other side of Lydda and in the house in the Haqouret Al-Qura district they were all waiting anxiously for another report while hoping not to be flattened by a bomb. It wasn't until the next morning, however, that one of our wayfarer's young cousins, a boy barely older than she was, appeared at their door in spite of the shelling which had resumed at first light with the news: George! He was home! He had had to go all the way around, through Amman, but now he was back! He had embraced his mother and examined his sister, and now he was on his way – our diminutive hero held her breath – to the hospital to get medicine! The little wayfarer watched as everyone cheered. They were talking as excitedly as if St. George himself had shown up to slay their dragon, so the little wayfarer tried to speak up and let them know that her cousin would most likely have to stay at the hospital, they had only two other doctors on staff and today there would be more needy patients than ever, and therefore someone should be sent after him to fetch back the medicine. One or two of her relatives glanced briefly in the little wayfarer's direction with puzzled expressions, as if a monkey on a leash in the bazaar had thrown lentils at their backs, and returned to the conversation. Nobody seemed to see the little wayfarer as she opened the door and slipped outside. As a rule nobody ever noticed her much, but now this fact gave her the unexpected confidence that she might also be beneath the notice of falling bombs and toppling bricks. Once outside the gate she made her way down a narrow walk between high whitewashed walls and cactus hedges, the sky overhead was smudged with smoke and dust but it wasn't until she came around the corner of the bathhouse that marked the start of the older neighborhoods that she began to see what all that thunder had wrought, the tumbled bricks and masonry smashed to dust, the splintered exposed timbers and furniture in sticks, the bedding in rags, and the blood. Two old women in their black *abbahs* wailed and clawed at stones too big for them to lift, while across the street a donkey, still harnessed to the remains of a cart, stood patiently next to the body of its driver. Further on a group of neighbors were trying to keep a fire from a collapsed cooking shed from spreading to their houses, and a family of refugees inside a shop whose metal shutter had been torn away stopped briefly to listen to the pop-pop-pop of distant gunfire before they returned to their foraging among the mostly-bare shelves. Our wayfarer trotted along in the direction of the gunfire, she saw where the facade of the house that stood next to the old khan had been sheared away, exposing the rooms of the upper storey with the furniture inside still intact and in place, it reminded her of an illustration in the children's encyclopedia at school, a cutaway of the interior of one of the great ocean liners that showed the staterooms and galleys and captain's quarters and the engines, but it was an old encyclopedia and the ship was at the bottom of the sea. As far as she could see there wasn't any rule to what got wrecked and what was spared, she ran through pockets of no damage and no people either, a street of shuttered shops and empty coffee houses, a vacant square with a small mosque on one side and the factory where the Rantisis made olive-oil soap on the other, while just around the corner the street might be as thronged as for a market day and just as noisy. But every common sight now wore a different aspect, the way they sometimes did on holy days, and in fact one of the imams could right then be seen hopping away in the direction of the mosque, holding up the hem of his vestments and skipping over the blood like a finely-dressed matron trying to avoid puddles. One of the dying called out to his retreating figure, but he didn't seem to hear. Admittedly, however, many times already the little wayfarer had had to stifle her own natural impulse to stop and help, she had resolved to fetch the medicine for George's sister so that George could stay at the hospital and tend to the wounded with his mind at ease on at least one score, but the repeated spectacle of so many deserving objects wore her down and she was finally brought up short by a small child who tottered into her path and plopped down onto his bottom in the dirt, his little face so blackened that it looked like the soles of his bare feet. Our wayfarer knelt and wetted a corner of her scarf with her spit and began wiping the child's eyes and nostrils and mouth, she asked his name and if he was hurt, but the child only thrust out his hand and demanded – a little weakly, it is true – bakshish, bakshish. Bakshish! – the world could end and this little beggar would still be at it. She planted a kiss on his dirty forehead and got to her feet, hurrying on her way, running now even though the chunks of plaster and shattered tiles hurt her feet through the thin soles of her slippers. She knew she was nearing the center of town, she passed the Telegraph and Postal Exchange and the bank where her granduncle had been chief clerk for many years, and from time to time she caught glimpses of the minaret of the grand mosque and the broad peaked roof of the church of St. George. That church was her North Star, because the hospital, once her girls' school, stood right next to it. Soon she came to one of the town's main squares, a flat expanse of gravel with a fountain in the middle of it – one more burst of energy would take her to the hospital. But there had been no shelling for many minutes now and the townspeople were starting to emerge from their houses, blinking among the refugees in the street and asking each other for news, and she had to thread her way through them. A hush came over the crowd, though, when they heard the sound of engines in the distance. Then a cry rose from the far side of the square, like a current relayed from person to person until it reached the little wayfarer's ears – a column of Jordanians had entered the city! From the east, Abdullah's men, at last! The cheers were loud but soon enough she could hear the engines again, and then feel the road shaking under her feet, and all eyes turned toward the other end of the square where one jeep after another tore into view through a cloud of dust and circled around the fountain, jeeps and also a kind of metal vehicle that the little wayfarer had never seen before, all loaded with men in tan uniforms who lifted their weapons into the air and squeezed off short bursts of gunfire while they whooped and chanted *Khallielseif yugoui! Khallielseif yugoui!* to the delight of the crowd. But our little wayfarer's attention was drawn to a man who stood in the front passenger-side of the jeep that had pulled up in front of her, a space of about twenty or so paces separated them and she could see that he rested one sunbrowned hand on the jeep's windshield and the other on the black holster at his hip, and that on his sun-browned head he wore a black patch over one of his eyes and a little smile on his lips, curious patch and curiouser smile. The jeeps had been stopped for less than a second, it seemed, when the man with the eye-patch cried out in a different voice, not a chanting voice, and a different language, not Arabic, causing the heart in the little wayfarer's breast to feel like it took several extra beats at once, but by then it was too late to tell the difference between the heartbeats and all the gunfire that broke loose, not shots in the air anymore because the guns were no longer pointing at the sky. Now she was able to notice how some of the guns spit little points of fire out of their muzzles as they swept back and forth, to the right and the left and then back, and then she noticed how the crowd on their side performed a kind of mirroring dance, some slumping forward and others spinning backwards against the walls of their homes, where the blood made patterns like lace. There was now such a pitch of screams and gunfire that it seemed to the little wayfarer like a kind of deafness. No one was spared, not women or children or old people, in places whole families were piled together like butcher's trash, and if someone started to move again after the bullets had passed, the bullets would come back and finish the job. Some tried to flee into their homes and shops but the soldiers fired through the doors and windows after them, others dashed out of their homes in fear and confusion and those whose faces were spared died with looks of surprise on them. One of the latter, a woman still in her housecoat, ran out with a bundle hugged to her chest, when she fell the bundle rolled to one side and the soldier made sure to shoot it as well, but only feathers came out and he grimaced while his fellows in the jeep laughed at him. Through it all the little wayfarer stood, in as perfect a stillness as she could muster, as if to breathe or to move by so much as a hair would attract the attention of a ravening beast. She was aided by the fact that there was no other impulse to suppress, no urge to flee or cry out or plead or pray, or even, any longer, to help. She had retreated to a great distance inside herself, and she felt that while death fattened itself everywhere around her she was enjoying a singular amnesty. For most of her life she had been invisible, and here was its secret compensation. But through it all another figure had stood as well, and again she grew conscious of his presence, before her in the jeep standing straight and still, one sun-browned hand on the windshield and the other resting on the black holster at his hip, his sun-browned head cocked slightly back and a smile on his lips, one eye covered by a black patch and the other eye looking right at the little way-farer. For most of her life she had been invisible, and while she hadn't complained she could not say she had much liked it, either. Ungrateful girl! And thick-skulled too, her mother was right, but at last she had learned her lesson: it was best never to be seen at all, to be small and unimpressive and ignored, to go at all times and in all places unregarded and incognito, was the greatest of boons. To be unseen was to have a little ground under your feet – very little, it is true – but to be seen was a trapdoor. To be unseen was to have almost nothing inside that you could call your own, but to be noticed, to be caught in this searchlight, was to be . . . turned inside-out. She was being seen. And not just by any pair of eyes but by the eye in charge, the eye behind the eyes, not the eyes you're seen by but the eye that's your horizon, the condition not only of your visibility but of your very being. In this eye, our little wayfarer knew, she was a mote, a speck, and a thing naked and bare, no longer human, and subject to the annihilation of a blink. The condition of her being was a condition of terror. Not terror the feeling, but terror the medium: for fish, water; for birds, the air; for the little wayfarer, terror. She shook like a newborn kid and wet poured out of her, everything inside her turned to wet and went flushing out of her down her legs, sopping her slippers and skirt, and this eye that saw everything and saw her world into being and could blink it away in an instant saw her there like an animal shaking and shitting and peeing. He smiled and seemed almost to nod, and called out again in the language that wasn't Arabic, and the engines revved and the tires churned and spat gravel and in a cloud of dust the jeeps with the soldiers moved on. After a while a few pigeons returned to the tall date palms at the corner of the square, seeking haven from some other part of the town where the bullets now flew. The dust had settled and a scrawny pair of dogs emerged from an alleyway to sniff and lap at the carrion. Was our little wayfarer still standing there? Was she still there when survivors from the homes and shops on the square ventured out again to retrieve the wounded and separate the bodies of their loved ones from the dead refugees, and raise to the skies their curses and laments? Or by this time was she faring her way again, but now heedless and numb, wandering as one bereft? We don't know, there's a gap in our records, maybe there's a gap in her consciousness, too. Our evidence is anecdotal, at best, and much of it comes from the most fractured and fragmentary testimony imaginable, acquired moreover in conditions that cast into an extremity of doubt its already uncertain veracity. Add to this the fact that between the bare bones of verifiable historical incident and the gristle of questionable testimony all we've been doing is spinning the connective tissues and integuments of the plausible (i.e., writing fiction), and you might reach the conclusion that when it comes to the moment-by-moment experiences of Little Wayfarer I, to say nothing of the thoughts and emotions, the dreams and sensations, that make up her interior life, our whole enterprise is hopelessly quixotic. Some might go further and argue that even our claims to plausibility are suspect, because clearly a few of the touches here – such as the whimsical symmetries of birth order among the little wayfarer and her siblings, or the conceit that she could stand in the midst of the Ninth Commando Battalion's blitzkrieg, and not twenty paces from the jeep of its leader, Moshe Dayan, and somehow escape unscathed – are nothing more than warmed-over flourishes of Rushdie-esque hysterical-realism on the part of some benighted subaltern on our reconstruction team. Don't worry, we'll hunt down the malefactor and give him a good dose of a critical emetic to flush it out of his system. And not all of our documentary evidence is uniformly flimsy, by the way, so for example while we don't know where the little wayfarer was for the rest of that day, we have it on good authority that she was not at the hospital even though a mere half mile further would have brought her to its gates, touched at certain hours of the day by the beneficent shadow of St. George's peaked roof. So close, and yet so etcetera! Wouldn't the quietly plucky wayfarer we've come to know and love in the manner one comes to know and to love a sympathetic character in an eminently marketable work of literary fiction have made a dash towards the gates of her old school, the gates of her dream to be a nurse and to serve at her handsome cousin's side? But alas, as far as we are able to discern – and in this one detail we have an unusually high degree of confidence – she did not. Clearly something had put a dent in her quiet gumption, maybe looking into the eye of History had something to do with it, looking into the eye of History and discovering there no trace of her story, not the slightest glimmer of acknowledgement whatsoever that she had a story or was even worth a story, even a story where somebody else got to be the hero and she was just a sidekick which would have been OK with our humble wayfarer, her story had gotten blown out from under her and thus she was a tad unsteady on her beaded slippers, which might be the simplest explanation for why it took a whole day for her to wander back to the Haqouret Al-Qura district so that it was dark by the time she slipped inside past the brass knocker and past all her sisters aunts uncles cousins without anyone noticing and into the nursery where she curled up on the floor under the cot where her mother clutched her swaddled brother beneath the heavy oak dining table that had had to be dragged into the room to protect them from the sky falling until her mother's voice told her she smelled like filth and should go sleep with the goats. Poor little wayfarer! Or what do you think – is her hard luck getting too senti-mental? You have to have a sympathetic main character but you have to be careful not to press too hard on that pathos-pedal or you'll lose the very sympathy you're trying so hard to get, it's sort of flooding the narrative engine with pathos, as you can learn in any creative writing or driver's ed. course. But believe it or not, far from pouring it on, we're actually soft-pedaling the pathos wherever possible. God's truth! We can't help it if our little wayfarer is a *schlimazel* figure, that's the traditional Yiddish term for it and as far as we know the best one, a *schlimazel*, a person who always ends up getting the soup spilled on them, and therefore the eternal counterpart of the *schlemiel*, who does the spilling. Because after all let's face it, some folks just get crapped on wherever they go, don't they? Is it really so unrealistic that some folks just end up getting crapped on, again and again and again and again? Suffice it to say that the little wayfarer spent the following day in the house, burdened down by all the pathos and crap, it wasn't until later that she and her family learned what went on in the town that next day, about how all the men detained in the Dahmash Mosque had been massacred, about how some of the women who lived near the town center had been gathered together and used as a human shield in the assault on the police station where the last of the city's volunteer militia were holding out, and where one of the little wayfarer's brothers-in-law met his end, nor did they learn until the next day that George's sister finally died of her fever, by the time George made it back from the hospital it was too late, they had to bury her in the garden while her six children looked on because there was no way of getting to the cemetery. No, the little wayfarer and her family had stayed in the house with their share of the Jaffa kin until the morning after that when they heard the knocking, the knocking of rifle butts instead of the brass knocker but that was understandable because the servant in the immaculate blouse her father had once upon a time employed to say "*Min hada*?" and usher guests into the mandara had long since fled back to his village, and the soldiers, three of them, had to let themselves in. They pointed their rifles and shouted most rudely, one of them in Arabic: "*Yala barah, yala barah! Ukhrojo! Yallah ala Abdallah!*" Get out! Leave! Go to Abdullah! And sure enough, all the roads except those that led east, to Jordan, were blocked off with barricades of furniture the soldiers had pulled out of the homes. But at the eastern edge of town even the roads were barred from them, instead the soldiers drove them like livestock through a small gate and onto the barren fields, not only our little wayfarer's family but all the other families too, family after family, some who could trace their roots in Lydda back to before the year 500 AD, until they made a fair field full of folk. The sun had risen over the Judean hills and shone into their eyes and they knew it was going to be a hot day, but they also knew what had happened at Deir Yassin and Ayn al-Zaytun and now even in their own Dahmash Mosque, so they figured they might not have long to worry about the heat. The accounts of that time tell us that a youth was heard to say, "This is the day of resurrection!" and an older voice to snap in reply, "This is hell." Which side of this question do you think the little way-farer came down on? She had always been a believing little wayfarer, do you think she crossed herself and commended her soul to the Blessed Virgin? Or had she already learned to curse God until her tongue was bitter in her own mouth, like an uncured olive? We don't know, it'll probably be another twenty-four to forty-eight hours before she learns the really crucial lessons, but all the other details here are a matter of record, nothing needs making up. It's a matter of record for example that soldiers spread a blanket on the ground and commanded the townspeople to surrender their valuables, wallets coins jewelry watches fountain pens wedding rings, although a writer of fiction might want to use a metaphorical expression such as "rained down" to evoke the tinkling of the items as they dropped onto the blanket and perhaps even to suggest a sort of ironic contrast with the arid desert on that July morning, and the writer of fiction might also want to make the list of soldier's booty less generic by embellishing it with an idiosyncratic item such as, say, someone's accordion with ivory keys, or an heirloom such as family photograph in a heavy silver frame, or a cherished keepsake like the mother-of-pearl bracelet that our little wayfarer's cousin had bought for her in Bethlehem and made a tribute to her eyes. What a poignant turn of the screw that would be! Whose side are we on here, anyway? But to get back to the objective facts, as we are determined to do, we who are on the side of objective facts, we know for a fact that some of the soldiers committed the grave insult of thrusting their hands into the robes of women suspected of holding items back, and rather forcibly removed some items from the fingers and wrists of men slow to remove them, and shot the young newlywed who refused to turn over the biscuit tin that contained the young couple's wedding money, so that his body fell at the feet of his shrieking bride. Then the soldiers fired volleys over everyone's heads and again ordered them east, to Ramallah, in the territory under the control of King Abdullah, whose army had failed to descend from the hills to defend their city of mosques. The fields were full of jagged stones and the sharp sun-hardened roots of harvested crops that tore at their feet, but the soldiers couldn't have the roads thronged with forty or fifty thousand pedestrians when it was needed for trucks. Soon the fields ended, however, and the climb into the desert hills began, under the hot sun, the spring flowers long gone and the bleached thorns tearing at their ankles, every time they made it to the top of one hill there was a higher one on the other side, and by late that afternoon if the little wayfarer had stopped to look in her wake she would have seen a winding black line threading over the hills until it merged with the distant haze. Maybe it would have reminded her of a line of ants, and just as a child pokes at a line of ants with a stick, so every once in a while a contingent of soldiers showed up in jeeps to fire shots over their heads or strafe them with bullets, or else a plane might drop a gasoline bomb or two, and the line would become disorganized into frantic particles and specks. These events often resulted in another mass shedding of the luggage items that the expelled townspeople had tried to bring with them, until the way became littered with a piecemeal testament that their old lives would not be accompanying them in their exodus over the desert: bundles of clothing and bedding or pots and pans that women had tired of balancing on their heads, in one place a sewing machine and in another a crate of carpenter's tools, and here and there loads of furniture dumped from donkey carts and wheelbarrows to make room for the ill and exhausted. Women like the little wayfarer's own mother carried their infants in slings on their backs and held their younger children by the hands, but otherwise everyone now held only whatever water and food they had had the foresight or luck to grab on their way out the door, a tin of sardines or jar of powdered milk, a bottle of cooking oil, some flatbread wrapped in a scarf, and a few might be seen driving a goat in front of them or gripping a chicken by the legs. From time to time they happened upon isolated plots of tillage or vegetable gardens in tiers along the slopes and helped themselves to whatever was there, a writer of fiction might use this opportunity to imagine for example a man who stoops to pick as many eggplants as he can while our little wayfarer looks on, he's picked too many eggplants and drops one and stooping to retrieve it drops another one, and retrieving that one drops still another, and so on and on, a comical figure except that he's weeping at the same time, and although he's not really crying about the eggplants it still looks ludicrous and sad, and many years later, after she's immigrated, in Chicago or Springfield perhaps, our little wayfarer might happen to see a clown doing something like that at a street fair or carnival and have a bad reaction to it, one of her patented bad reactions, because by that time she'd started having bad reactions to things, what you might call episodes, and seeing this clown becomes one of them, and from then on her memories of what she witnessed on the Lydda Death March, we might as well let you know that this nameless, terrible event was later called the Lydda Death March, from then on her memories of the death march became retrospectively peopled by clowns, first one clown with his eggplants and then another and another, until there's a march of clowns, men clowns in fezzes and tarbushes and kaffiyehs and women clowns in their thobs and embroidered qabbeh winding away into the horizon of her mind, schlepping along even when she's not thinking of them, from one darkness to another darkness through a space that is cruelly bright, an unending procession, lugubrious faces and comical paces. Her episodes have a tendency to work that way, later events rewriting earlier ones, which is one reason why this testimony can be so confusing and must be approached with such caution, one clown at a Springfield carnival was all it took and she's hurled back fifteen years into that heat, that dust, that infernal brightness, that tramp tramp tramp of the endless footfalls, sand burning, thorns tearing, terrible thirst, but it's all mixed up now, nonlinear, what happened first, what happened next, all out of order, jumbled together, dis-membered then re-membered, but a botch, a Franken-stein's millipede with eighty thousand legs and a clown's face. How they reached the well at Jimzu, so parched, but the soldiers had gotten there first and two of them stood pissing into it and laughing, and she didn't even turn away, our formerly so modest little wayfarer, nor any of the women there, they stared blankly and set off again, must have been the first day because by the second day piss or no piss they would've drunk from that well, when for example they tied a rope around the waist of a youth and lowered him into a well and dragged him back out and sucked at his clothes they would have kept sucking even if he'd peed him-self, but a soldier gave the little wayfarer a capful of water from his canteen. Then all of a sudden it was snow, that first winter in the camp in Ramallah, one of the coldest on record on that so-called Hill of God and finally one morning a blanket of snow between the tents when they were moved into the Friends Girls' School and given a corner of a classroom, her experience of classrooms being that they turned into different things like hospitals and hostels, the kindness of the Quakers couldn't keep her from wandering back out into the snow which she had never seen before, she put a little on her tongue and let it melt and swallowed, they found her out there with blue lips and chattering teeth and had to lead her inside again, just a capful but she had been very thirsty on that hot day. One minute it was a sewing machine and a tool box and furniture and pots and pans and pillows littering their path through the desert and the next minute it was bodies, body after body wrapped in shawls and left behind, old men and old women and children and finally just anybody, unwashed and unburied, after a while not even shawls to cover them, and unborn babies dropped from wombs before their time, never to be remembered by a grave let alone a name, she saw the jackals feasting and turned away. Then the chill and darkness of night and everyone huddled in the *wadis*, they tried to light a fire but they heard the planes and had to smother the coals in sand, and in the hot daytime the soldier gave her the capful of water. Sometimes the *fellahin* from the villages came down to give or to sell them food, raisins or melons or old bread, and once it was a cart loaded with a roasted camel, almost the entire carcass in massive charred quarters, it had been so long since she'd eaten anything that even that stinking meat from what had to have been their oldest and sickest beast smelled good, but so many dinars for the tiniest bite, who had money like that? The soldiers took all our money! Everyone started to grab and tear at the carcass even though they were mostly Muslims and it was Ramadan, you were allowed to break your fast if it meant your life as long as you made it up later, even our Christian little wayfarer knew that, and the man started screaming and his son tried to beat them with a stick but it didn't matter, everyone was too hungry to care about being beaten with a stick but they didn't want to get shot, it was the shooting that made every-one start to run and not the stick, it was Jewish cavalry on top of the ridge but in the scrum around the cart they hadn't heard the rumble of the hooves, everyone scrambled away in all directions and the *fellah* and his son seized the handles of their heavy cart and gave a great shove, and her mother who had been standing some meters away not even trying to grab a share of that stinking meat was struck in the hip, and she spun in a half circle and the baby spun out of her hands, not in the sling on his mother's back at that moment but in her hands, but now not in her hands, his mother fell one way and he fell the other, she fell on her side in the dirt and he fell under the steel-rimmed wheel of the heavy cart. By the time she is in Springfield the little wayfarer won't remember any longer what the insides of her little brother's skull had looked like, or rather she will remember only in the displaced form of not being able to eat pomegranates any longer or even to abide the sight of their ruby seeds. The next thing she knew she was off in search of her cousin George, this time she was faring her way against the current, faring west as the line moved east and searching the faces as they filed past, somewhere among these hundreds and thousands was her cousin George and maybe he could do something, something for, for, it was getting hard to think, for his sister's fever, no, something else, that's right, she felt dizzy and had a new strange sensation in her bowels, as if food hadn't agreed with her but she hadn't eaten any food, she staggered away from the line in the direction of some boulders on the side of the hill in case she had to squat, she didn't know how she could have to squat when she hadn't had anything to eat or to drink but still she felt like she might have to, and a little further on she saw the walls of an old ruined farmhouse an even better place to squat, not to mention the shade, how long since she had sat in shade. In the shade was the Jewish soldier with the canteen. Further down in the *wadi* there were trees and a few soldiers and horses resting. The little wayfarer and the soldier looked at each other and then he gave her the capful of water, and as she handed the cap back she realized he hadn't stopped looking at her, it was almost as if his gaze like a long finger had lifted her chin up so that he could have her eyes again, in her thirst she had forgotten the rule about staying invisible, better late than never she decided it was time to turn around and go back to her people. Then she felt his hands on her shoulders. Then she was back in the long line, this time walking in the same direction as everybody else, only now her knees and the palms of her hands were sore and flaked with drying blood, some of it from the sharp stones which had cut her but some of it from her thighs. Then all of a sudden it was snow, that first winter in the camp in Ramallah, one of the coldest on record on that so-called Hill of God and finally a blanket of snow between the tents the morning they were moved into the Friends Girls' School and given a corner of a classroom, but nobody stopped her from wandering out into the snow again, she put a little on her tongue and let it melt and swallowed, one of the Quakers found her out there with blue lips and chattering teeth and took her back inside. Let's get one thing straight: Our hero Little Wayfarer II the son of Little Wayfarer I was not conceived under the sign of such corny, ham-fisted irony as this rape by an Israeli soldier, there were a number of such rapes during the Nakba and no doubt some of them after the heavy-handed manner of history resulted in ironic conceptions but this isn't one of them, our Little Wayfarer I was only just then having her first period so she could hardly have been ovulating too, at first the soldier was alarmed to see so much blood and then he was disgusted, he didn't even finish his business instead he spat on the little wayfarer and because he knew a few words of Arabic let her know she was unclean and wiped himself off on her scarf and kicked her while she was still on her hands and knees so that she fell on her side in the little mound of his own squat which was the reason he had been up there in the shade of the ruined wall to begin with and not down in the shade of the trees in the *wadi* with the other soldiers of his unit, and anyway if you've been paying attention you will have realized that July 1948 was way too long ago for Little Wayfarer II to have been conceived if he was watching *Jonny Quest* re-runs as a little kid, in fact he was born in 1972 when his mother was 37, a little old to be having kids but not at all impossible, even considering her circumstances at the time, or maybe especially considering her circumstances at the time, which we'll get to, somehow, somehow we have to link up this young refugee of the Nakba in the camps at Ramallah in 1948 to a baby picked out at an orphanage in Plymouth, Massachusetts in the early '70s by a loving couple of Portuguese-American descent who mistakenly believe they're infertile, but it's tough to connect the dots between that Palestinian biological mother and this American son because after she departs from the camps her trail grows increasingly, well . . . dotty. Eccentric, you might say, in the strictly geometric sense. The dots go like this: Not too many weeks after their arrival in the camp at Ramallah they bury her mother and her father swallows poison and dies with black foam coming out of his mouth. After three years in the camp the younger of our wayfarer's two older sisters (the sister whose husband had been among the volunteer militia members killed back in Lydda) takes the little wayfarer's two younger sisters with her to Amman to live with one of their aunts, leaving the little wayfarer with her eldest sister and brother-in-law who have one surviving little toddler of their own. Her brother-in-law has relatives in the United States of America, in Chicago, southwest side, on 63rd Street with all the other Arabs, and after a few more years he is able to arrange visas, and one of those Chicago relatives a second cousin nobody knows what to do with, kid works in his father's *halal* butcher shop but it's clear he's never going to be anything more than a butcher's assistant not to mention the police have already had to have a couple of talks with him about strangling neighborhood cats but there's nothing like marriage to calm a kid down, a nice Arab girl if one could be found for a young man of such shall we say limited prospects. Welcome to America, little wayfarer! We have the records of her transit, her arrival in Chicago, and then— a gap. As far as we are able to determine, the marriage never takes place, and next time the little wayfarer pops onto our radar screen again it's a few years later, we find her living in a single-room occupancy hotel for women in Springfield, Massachusetts and working in a box factory. A box factory – we know, it sounds a little too allegorical or something, but somebody has to make them, don't they? Boxes, we mean. Her job was to feed the sheets of corrugated fiberboard into one of the gluing machines in her corner of the poorly-ventilated warehouse, the sheets of corrugated fiberboard that had been stamped out by the stamping machines, the sheets of corrugated fiberboard were stamped out by the sharp adjustable templates in the stamping machines and then glued by the gluing machines and then folded by the folding machines, all according to the most up-to-date principles of scientific management. But what happened back in Chicago? Did she take one look at that cross-eyed mouth-breather in his bloody apron and strike out on her own? Was this the return of the plucky, peripatetic little wayfarer we had grown to know and love in the way one grows to know and love a sympathetic character in a work of literary fiction? Well, bully for her, but aside from place-names and dates she's farther from us than ever. She doesn't marry, we know that much, she just works at that box factory, one year, another year, and still another. We know that she passes her citizenship test (English had always been her best subject back at her old school), and there's some suggestion of sporadic attendance at services at the Greek Orthodox church, but other than that all we have is some anecdotal evidence that she spent a lot of her little free time walking around the town, and around and around, so that for example someone working late at their desk in a storefront office might see passing in front of the window three or four times in the same evening a small figure made smaller by a slight forward hunch, in a coat and a scarf, who never meets anyone's eye. Occasionally perhaps on such perambulations she might happen on a street fair or a carnival where the sight of a sad-faced clown juggling purple balls might cause her to miss a week or so of work, or on a farmer's market where a smashed-open pomegranate might cause her to miss upwards of a month, but the scientific managers of the box factory always took her back because in all other respects she was a steady faithful hardworking and best of all uncomplaining little wayfarer who never asked for a raise, or even a window open. Yes, she knew how to fare her way under the radar, that one, a doughty little cube of a person and as likely to be overlooked as your average cardboard box, and maybe no further trace of her would have appeared in our files before her death certificate had it not been her misfortune to be a *schlimazel* as well, one of those on whom History must always be spilling its soup, History working through this or that proxy to scald her every now and then with a little soup and the proxy this time one of the scientific managers at the box factory who also happened to be the boss's nephew, the double-whammy of science and nepotism. This boss's nephew liked to have his way with the women at the factory and some of them went willingly and some of them did not and if truth be told he preferred those who did not, after which he had them fired, but for the longest time he had taken so little notice of our wayfarer that unless she had been standing in front of him he wouldn't have known who you were talking about, that is until late one night after the second shift when he was going up the stairs and she was coming down and he saw her eyes. Out came the stopwatch. A true disciple of the Taylor method, he recorded each of his assaults in the logbook he kept for tabulation and analysis, determined to be as efficient as possible, to reduce and indeed eliminate all extraneous movements, to calculate the One Best Way to hold down, to stifle, to pry apart, etc. This time however when the little wayfarer got back on her feet she reacted differently than she had with the Israeli soldier, that time it had been next to the wall of a ruined farmhouse but this time it was next to a stamping machine in a cardboard-box factory, a stamping machine which at a scientifically-calibrated speed and feed stamped lengths of corrugated fiberboard into the appropriate sizes and shapes by means of its razor-sharp adjustable template, at that moment set for their most popular seller, the 18-N. It wasn't long, however, before a consensus was reached among the arresting officers, the guards at the county jail, the chaplain, the public defender, the district attorney's office, the examining psychologists, and finally the presiding judge at the hearing itself (plus the bailiff and the stenographer), that not only was this particular little wayfarer not competent to stand trial but that she was hardly competent to wipe herself on the crapper, which is how she ended up in the Taunton State Hospital with a diagnosis of schizophrenia, catatonic type. A clever ruse on our wayfarer's part, or had she just taken to faring her way in other regions, deep inside herself, maybe even listening for the lisp of a little blastula working its way through its division and multiplication tables? We can disabuse you of that last notion, at least: this was 1966, and like we said Little Wayfarer II won't be born until 1972. Either it hadn't been the right time in the wayfarer's cycle or the boss's nephew was shooting blanks, and since none of his other numerous efficient predations was known ever to have resulted in a pregnancy, we suspect the latter. It wasn't long, however, before the little wayfarer was back on her feet, because her catatonia, if that's what it was – and due also no doubt to the salubriousness of the hospital's pleasant lawns glimpsed through the bars in the windows and the beneficent effects of the liberal doses of Librium, thorazine, medico-moral exhortation, and electroshock –

was of the sort that alternated between periods of stupor and periods of excitation. During the latter she could be found wandering the wards, shuffling her quiet way among the other women intent on obscure itineraries and pastimes of their own, including bobbing, gibbering, drooling, gnashing, masturbating, playing imaginary musical instruments, conversing with angels, and cringing in the presence of certain orderlies. Sometimes she got it into her funny head to follow the nurses and repeat their gestures as if she were a sister of such ministrations herself, but a week or two in one of the seclusion rooms usually helped put a stop to that. At intervals, however, the little wayfarer would grind to a halt, slowing by degrees over the course of a few days until she froze in her tracks, or in her seat in the dining room, a spoonful of watery applesauce on its way to her mouth, or wherever she might happen to be, as if she had gone into hibernation, to Hibernia or an internal Patagonia, who knows, stuck in her last pose so that if somebody didn't move her she wouldn't move at all, till the cows came home or her hip broke, the doctor said, as he ordered the orderlies to put her in bed. Fortunately in her limbs there was pliancy as well as rigor, you could put her in pretty much any pose you wanted and she would hold it, like a large doll or mannequin, for instance praying or giving the Hitler salute or with pistol-hands like a robber doing a stick-up or with her hands in the air like the person getting robbed, or on all fours like a dog, or with one knee up like a dog by a fire hydrant, or all fours in the air like a dog getting its tummy scratched, a little harmless fun, it's a hard dull job being an orderly and you have to take it where you can get it. In these phases of stupor she was unable to feed herself, they had to snake a plastic tube up her nose and down her throat and squeeze food-mix through the tube, and because she couldn't go to the bathroom by herself they kept her in diapers and hosed her off once in a while, they stripped off her diaper and stood her naked in the middle of her room with her hands in the air in the pose of a person being robbed or taking a dive straight up into the sky, they stood her on the grate in the middle of the concrete floor of her room and hosed her down and then put her back on the plastic sheet on the thin mattress. And spring turned to summer, and summer to fall, and fall to winter, and one year to the next, seasons of quietly wandering the wards and seasons of even more quietly wandering deep inside of herself, and it could have gone on that way forever, with no change except that each time she slipped into the depths it took her longer and longer to surface, nothing goes on forever, shadows lengthen. It was one morning early in the summer of 1972 and the little wayfarer had been in her deepest and longest shadow yet, since the end of the previous year in fact, and she was being stripped down for her hosing off when someone managed to notice that along with the bedsores and diaper-rash she was gaining weight, patients rarely gained weight when they were on the food-mix-through-the-sinuses diet yet here the little wayfarer was putting on weight, and moreover in the tell-tale distribution suggestive of gravidity, parturition, in a word – pups. The staff obstetrician estimated it was at six months, surely too late for them to take certain measures, there was a lengthy debate but the measures were not taken. Next they gave a thought to which of the orderlies or janitors had been the culprit, it was naturally assumed that it had to be one of the orderlies or cleaning staff and not one of the doctors or administrators, the idea of a full investigation was mooted but then they remembered about four or five months back that a particular orderly had been dismissed, a particular Negro orderly had been dismissed because of missing medications and other suspected crimes compounded by a general aura of afro-sporting insubordination and no doubt this additional heinousness wouldn't have been beyond him either, a bad apple nipped in the bud, due diligence, tight ship, pats on the back all round. Of course we have made our own investigation but we are unable to come to any definitive conclusion, the personnel records of the time reveal that among the orderly and janitorial staffs were men of Greek and Armenian and African descent and a Lebanese immigrant, and among the white-coats and suits were men of German and Scottish and Jewish descent, it might have been any one of these, who knows, too many candidates and too few clues, she might as well have been raped by the United Nations. They moved the little wayfarer into the infirmary and eased her off the meds, binding her to the bed-frame just in case, but she stayed in her stupor, her stupor and rigor she stoutly yet pliantly maintained, except for one thing, one minor detail, a new wrinkle so to speak, which had to do with her mouth: words started coming out of it: . . . *out . . . into this world* . . . Lots of them: . . . *into this world . . . tiny little thing . . . before its time . . . in a godfor–* . . . *what? . . . girl?* . . . Yes, for some reason the little wayfarer's mouth got going, our little wayfarer who for most of her life had been the quietest little wayfarer imaginable, such that at times she had been taken for a mute and indeed might as well have been a mute, as if the only way she had left to fare was the way of words her mouth got going and wouldn't stop, for long spells sometimes hours at time, from our so long silent wayfarer a sudden logorrhea, a torrent of words, wild and whirling, in a staccato rat-a-tattat as if there could never be enough time . . . *walking all her days . . . day after day . . . a few steps then stop . . . stare into space . . . then on . . . drifting around* . . . But what the speed gave in urgency the disassociated tone took back, a tone mechanical and stripped of emotion save for a brief laugh or occasional scream, and even these sounded like someone rehearsing stage directions, viz., [*Brief laugh*], [*Screams*]. Mostly in Arabic but at times also heavily-accented English, at first the infirmary staff thought it was gibberish but the Lebanese mopping the floor nearby nodded and told them, *She speaks of someone receiving a bracelet from a cousin*, and then nodded again and told them, *She says it is snowing in the circus tent*, and when they asked what ribbon what circus he shrugged and mopped his way out of the ward and the little wayfarer's mouth kept on blabbing, sometimes all day and into the night, the wayfarer a disassociated shadow motionless on a narrow bed, everything still and dark except for her motor mouth lit by a beam of moonlight, in the darkness this halo of light around a ceaseless mouth, you could see it move and hear its quick whisper . . . *she did not know . . . what position she was in . . . imagine! . . . what position she was in! . . . whether standing . . . or sitting . . . but the brain– . . . what?* . . . The file which has come into our possession contains a set of notes on this final phase of her case, someone bothered to note down a few extended samples of her strange dictation at least when it was in English, or the Lebanese janitor could translate, a brief resurgence of interest in her case, a new symptom is always interesting and while schizophrenics often exhibit pressured speech and word salad it is hardly typical of catatonics in the slough of a stupor, make a note of that, so for a while some doctor or other transcribed samples of this strange dictation into her file, the words of the little wayfarer or rather the words of her mouth, as if her mouth were an autonomous thing, because the pronoun I never passed those lips, only ever the third person, only she, never I, only her, never me, the dismembered testament of some she and her, in fragments and shards, spat out . . . *what? . . . who? . . . . no! . . . she!* . . . which is why this testimony, if it can be called that, must be approached with the greatest of circumspection, as we have said, as we have maintained all along, don't say we didn't warn you, when we told you that additional information had come into our hands, certain materials, in the form of a file, a dossier, made up of certain documents, comprising a record, spotty, admittedly, incomplete, in places possibly apocryphal, yet suggestive, or when we alerted you to the fact that our evidence was at best anecdotal, and what's more all mixed up, nonlinear, what happened first, what happened next, all out of order, jumbled together, dismembered then re-membered, but a botch, and acquired moreover in conditions that cast into an extremity of doubt its already questionable veracity, well that's what we meant, this is what we were talking about, we've already lavished much more attention on this case than any of those doctors back at the Taunton State Hospital, and anyway whichever one of them had been recording the little wayfarer's words or rather the words of her mouth soon enough lost interest and who can blame him, because the words didn't add up, the words failed to go anywhere, the words failed to produce a satisfying narrative and instead showed every indication of just repeating themselves, of going around and around and then back, and around and back, like a tape loop, the doctors lost interest in the case and frankly so have we, we've done what we can in the way of narrative backstory and now it's time to return to the dramatic conflict, to our hero hanging on the cliff of his encounter with the shape-shifting Jim Wood at the top of the up-escalator to the second-floor concourse of the Arsenal Mall in Watertown, Massachusetts, or rather since a little time has passed since then at a table in the food court on the second-floor concourse of the Arsenal Mall in Watertown, Massachusetts. We've connected all the dots except for the last two or three, two or three remaining dots in the form of a few curt addenda at the end of the little wayfarer's file, jotted down by the duty nurse and trailing off like an ellipsis . . . For example the addendum dated July, 1972, which tells us that the patient's babbling upset the other patients in the ward, something had to be done, they couldn't put her back on the heavy meds yet so they put a gag in her mouth instead, the mouth kept running but you couldn't really hear it anymore unless you were in the next bed and when the mouth chewed through one gag they put in another, after all it was just for a couple of months. The addendum dated September, 1972, which tells us that the infant was delivered by Caesarian section, a healthy if underweight baby boy, they cleaned him up and by the time the patient emerged from the anesthesia he had already been shipped off to the nearest orphanage, the Home for Little Wayfarers in Plymouth, Massachusetts. And the addendum of October, 1972, which tells us that the patient died, plus the word "infection" and a question mark. Thus Little Wayfarer the First.

One story never ends but another begins, the circle of life blah blah blah, it takes ten or eleven months but our hero Little Wayfarer the Second finally gets someone to sign the papers and take him home from the orphanage, this anxious little pilgrim who jumps at every noise and cries all the time finally has one quiet day in which he gives a plausible impression of a rosy-cheeked and complaisant cherub, in other words totally unlike his usual self, the staff exchange looks with each other like maybe they should say something to the nice-looking Portuguese-American couple but who knows it might be this kid's only break, a real solid-looking pair these two, dad with his own landscaping business they just want a family too, they said they wanted a little boy and of course right off they notice the baby with the eyes like mother of pearl, bright and strange as if before his birth they had gazed out on a faraway land, the Portuguese-American husband shifts uncomfortably and starts pointing to the other kids but it's too late because his Portuguese-American wife has already picked this one up and can't tear herself away, away from those eyes, and the staff all hold their breaths because they can see the kid winding up for one of his crying jags, but the wife just rocks him against her breast and gently shu-shu-shushes him and he quiets back down and even smiles a little, she's got one hand cupping his head and one hand cupping his little bottom and she feels his diaper getting warm with pee and she smiles to herself and presses him closer and rocks him and hums, and the husband speaks up saying Maybe those eyes are not good for a boy's eyes but his wife, looking into them and crossing her fingers under the warm damp diaper, says Don't worry, don't worry, his eyes will change.

Human Wishes
a play
by Samuel Beckett

CAST OF CHARACTERS:

JOHNSON *Poet, critic, compiler of dictionaries, man of faith, the Great Cham. But mortal meat for all that: a depressed dropsical doubter.*

HODGE *His cat.*

SCENE:

A stuffed chair and an ottoman in the middle of an other-wise dark, empty stage. JOHNSON *sits massively in the chair, one swathed swollen foot on the ottoman.* HODGE *is curled on the ottoman next to* JOHNSON's *foot.*

JOHNSON
An interesting proposition. A lost Beckett play? And you say
you have it?

HODGE
Not on me, obviously, just in case you're getting any ideas.
But— what?

JOHNSON
[*Moving fingers to* HODGE's *mouth.*] You've got something, smutch, on your whiskers there. Naughty kitty been
in the cream? When you so charmingly placed me under
arrest I thought we might be headed that way again. You're
insatiable.

HODGE
[*Licking, grooming whiskers.*] Ha ha. It's just Cinn– but
why do I need to tell you! Anyway yes the manuscript is in
my possession. It's hidden and only I know where it is.

JOHNSON
And how did this supposed lost Beckett play come to be in
your lucky possession? Why should I believe it's authentic?

HODGE
When I tell you the story you'll know it's the real thing, just
like I knew. But I won't show it to you until you agree to my
terms. And you have to – you owe me.

JOHNSON
Name these terms.

HODGE
We launch a production in which you play Johnson. I'll dir-

ect. We just have to find an actor for the other part.

JOHNSON
The other part being the cat. And the cat speaks. I'm just thinking aloud here but might not the absence of talking animals in Beckett's other plays mitigate against the authenticity of this one? Who ever heard of a Beckett play with a talking cat?

HODGE
Who ever heard of a talking cat without a Beckett play? But like I said it's an early play. His first, actually, predating *Eleuthéria,* which people usually think of as his first finished play, and of course predating *Godot.* Nobody questions the authenticity of *Eleuthéria* even though it calls for seventeen performers. Who ever heard of a Beckett play with seventeen performers? You could even say that *Human Wishes*, with only two speaking parts and no elaborate set, anticipates the mature Beckett better than *Eleuthéria.*

JOHNSON
Maybe I'll do it if you play the talking cat. You can be my little pussy.

HODGE
I haven't been in a play since the sixth grade, when I was a beaver in a production of *The Lion, the Witch and the Wardrobe*. The reviews were not good. My whole problem is that I can only be me, which is where you come in. You're obviously a shape-shifter. You'll be Johnson, someone else will play the cat, and I'll appear, or more precisely I'll not appear, in my recurring role as myself. And don't worry about any huge time commitment; I'm anticipating a very

short run, just one or two performances before the Beckett Estate swoops in with a court order and shuts us down. But not before we'll have created a sensation—

JOHNSON
The only sensation I owe you is a blowjob. I'm mostly a top, but I'll repay if I have to. Not now, but soon.

HODGE
I don't want your blowjob.

JOHNSON
Sure you don't. Deep in that closet, aren't you? Is this Beckett play by any chance a closet drama?

HODGE
Very witty, Algernon. But—

JOHNSON
Or maybe you're just a pure bottom. OK, I'll top you. You can blow me again. Or I can fuck you. Not now, but soon.

HODGE
No, listen: I was able to retrieve the photos from my digital camera, and the last one's of you in your uniform, flashing that badge. Impersonating a police officer is a crime. How's this for topping, by the way? I can expose you.

JOHNSON
If you can do it as well as you expose yourself . . . do you always go around flashing your tackle at strange men in public johns? And I am listening, but it's just too incredible that you've discovered some lost Beckett play. I'll have to see it. Maybe you've got it in your ratty jeans there?

HODGE
Cut that out. You won't see it until you agree. And "it" means the playscript.

JOHNSON
[*Sighs.*] Alright then, tell me this irresistibly compelling story of how "it" came into your possession. I'm in the mood for a story. Purr me a story, kitty.

HODGE
Once upon a time—

JOHNSON
Not there. [*He pats his lap.*] Here. Nice puss.

HODGE
[*Not budging.*] Do you want to hear it or don't you?

[JOHNSON *assumes an attitude of exaggerated attentiveness.*]

HODGE
I learned about the play in St. Petersburg, of all places. The manuscript itself turned out to be in Paris but it was in St. Pete that I made first contact. I was there with my wife, happily married and thoroughly straight—

JOHNSON
Bi-curious, at the very least, I'd say. Nothing wrong with that. Plenty of straight guys just want to suck some cock now and then.

HODGE
I'm bi-nothing, thanks.

JOHNSON
Oh but darling you have all the signs. My gaydar's never wrong. In fact, you're a classic specimen stuck in the In-Between— Ouch, hey, watch those claws, kitty. I'm not the pain slut of this pseudo-couple. Daddy hit a nerve?

HODGE
Anyway I was with my wife in St. Petersburg but she was busy with her laptop at an academic conference that day and I was just wandering around the city—

JOHNSON
Just cruising along—

HODGE
As it happens I was following girls. Flip back to page 54 if you don't believe me – irrefutably I was following girls. Those beautiful Russian girls.

JOHNSON
Your head it simply swirls.

HODGE
Technically I was lost, but I had the distinct sensation that I was on the trail of something, the sense of an open-ended quest and finally also of a destiny, a literary quest and a literary destiny, a crossroads where I was riddled a riddle—

JOHNSON
Riddle of the sphinx. It's been done.

HODGE
Well it wasn't a sphinx, was it? It was the bridge by the fateful Belinsky House, where the Nevsky Prospekt crosses the

Fontanka. The Four Horseman Bridge.

JOHNSON
Describe.

HODGE
Four bronze youths, horse-wranglers next to their steeds, stripped to the waist—

JOHNSON
Supple muscular youths, smooth-limbed yummy twinks, about to be wrangled by their well-hung horsies—

HODGE
I don't remember these horsies being especially well-hung. You're thinking of Peter the Great's steed, the equine half of the famous Bronze Horseman statue, in Decembrists' Square, a couple of miles from where I was.

JOHNSON
Describe.

HODGE
Great sagging imperial bollocks like two bowling balls and a member said to resemble the profile of Peter himself, in homage or mockery. But the Bronze Horseman had already been worked up for literature, so I had to—

JOHNSON
It's interesting, isn't it, how writers take these political monuments and enviously transform them into literary monuments to stand for them in the Republic of Letters. The tsar sits astride his horse, but Pushkin sits astride the tsar. [*Warming to his theme.*] And then Biely scrambles up

to piggy-back on old Pushkin . . . what a circus!

HODGE
But we digress.

JOHNSON
Yes, we do digress. We want just the right proportion of foreplay and forward drive as we move towards the narrative climax. Too much and we never get there, too little and the climax is [*searches for the word*] . . . flat.

HODGE
Or isn't it rather the nature of digression itself to reflect the power of discourse over the agency of the individual speaker? Just who is the horse here and who the rider?

JOHNSON
But yet we digress.

HODGE
The shadows lengthen on the food court.

JOHNSON
Let us tarry not.

HODGE
So I solve the riddle and cross the bridge – how's this for advancing the plot? – and there on the other side is the Russian taxi driver I'd been bumping into on and off all day, leaning in the crook of the passenger-side door and smoking a cigarette, for all the world like what took me so long. In his pretty good English he says he can take me wherever I want to go, hook me up with whatever I'm looking for. Turns out this guy is like one of those helper-figures

in fairy tales, whose narrative functions had been anatomized by Vladimir Propp almost a century ago in that palimpsestically literary city.

JOHNSON
Now you're just teasing me.

HODGE
We set off. He keeps calling me Pushkin until I tell him I'm more of a prose guy and after that he keeps calling me Fyodor Mikhailovich. We're driving around Petersburg on this White Night until I'm thoroughly lost, this street and that, statue of Pushkin here and statue of Dostoevsky there like after all he just wants to point out the literary landmarks, until I have to pee really bad. Even worse than I have to pee now in fact, and that's pretty bad.

JOHNSON
Can we at least finish the story before you go to the cat box?

HODGE
So finally I tell him look we have to stop somewhere so I can pee. Luckily in Petersburg in all the parks and squares there're these rows of port-a-johns, in every park this row of light blue or sometimes beige port-a-pottys like you might see at a construction site in the U.S., usually about four or five of them, and at the end of the row there's always an old babushka who takes the money, an old babushka demanding ten or twelve rubles or whatever. And while I'm digging through my small change this babushka on her little stool is babbling away, a babbling babushka, weird babble doesn't even sound Russian and punctuated with strange laughs, and finally I dig out the right coins and with her trembling claw she hands me the usual receipt, Russia still so bureau-

cratic that you have to get a receipt even to use the port-a-john, this little chit covered with tiny Cyrillic print just to take a pee and torn in the middle by her trembling claw so you can't use it again, officially torn, all the while keeping up her crazy babble, and all at once it comes to me, in one of those gestalt-switch thingies, everything refocuses so that I can see that this receipt is no ordinary receipt and that the babushka's babble actually makes some kind of sense: "*What? who? no! she! . . . words were coming—*" It was English, in her thick and rheumy Russian accent this babushka was babbling English, and the tiny print on the receipt was English too, the print so tiny and the White Night so grey I don't know how I could even make it out but there it was, the words on the chit were in English and the words she babbled were English words.

JOHNSON
You're doling out details in water-torture drops, a common literary technique to build suspense. Please as they say cut to the chase.

HODGE
You said you wanted to be told a story. A story uses common literary techniques such as for instance doling out details in order to build suspense.

JOHNSON
But it helps if the storyteller is, well, *good* at it. Yes?

HODGE
Look I'm not even into telling stories. As a writer I'm committed to an anti-story aesthetic, or rather anti-aesthetic, blowing up story and aesthetics from—

JOHNSON

Or just a blowing. The default setting of writers who can't tell stories. But we'll talk about that later in this chapter, or closet drama, or whatever it is or anti-is. For now just get to the cum shot.

HODGE

The punchline, if you please. It's that she's babbling lines from Beckett's dramaticule, *Not I*. You know, the one with just the mouth on stage. Written in English in the spring of 1972 and first performed in New York at the Lincoln Center's Forum Theater in September of that year – the day of my birth, by odd coincidence – the cast originally included the figure of an auditor cloaked in a djellaba who listens to the ramblings of the mouth and makes gestures of anguished helplessness or helpless anguish at key moments in the mouth's logorrhea. This figure was eliminated in later productions leaving just the mouth. Through the babushka's thick and rheumy Russian accent I recognized lines from this Beckett dramaticule – "*then rush out stop the first she saw . . . nearest lavatory . . . start pouring it out . . . steady stream . . . mad stuff . . . half the vowels wrong . . .*" – like a permanent playback loop in the unemotive staccato-style delivery favored by Beckett himself. And so I spoke, a single word, a question: "Beckett?" And for the first time the babushka stopped her babble and looked at me, snapped me with a look and held my gaze. As if she too, like the taxi driver, had been waiting for me all along. "Help an old woman up," she said in her thick and rheumy Russian accent and ushered me into the nearest of the port-a-johns. And now I really have to go to the john myself.

[HODGE *hops onto the floor, stretches, sniffs at a leg of*

the ottoman, and saunters off stage-left. In the interval
JOHNSON *removes pen and notebook from his waist-coat pocket, one of those little "writer's" notebooks that advertise themselves as the kind used by Hemingway et al., and begins writing.*]

JOHNSON
Let observation with extensive view, behold mankind, from China to Peru . . . no— [*scratches something out*], *survey* mankind, from China to Peru . . .

[HODGE *returns, hops up onto ottoman and settles into place*; JOHNSON *tucks notebook and pen into his waistcoat.*]

JOHNSON
You have a fondness – no, a positive fetish – for stories involving bathrooms, don't you? If you're really so worried about original topoi you should remember that once Joyce took us into the jakes with Bloom that was the beginning and the end of that subject for literature.

HODGE
What about Pynchon? Slothrop's hallucinatory dive down the sewer after his mouth harp?

JOHNSON
Cartoonish pyrotechnics from a writer who cannot create character and therefore can't write real novels. But, pick your precursor, the point is the same.

HODGE
[*Sighs.*] We are all of us latecomers.

JOHNSON
And as it's not getting any earlier perhaps you'll pick up where your saga left off?

HODGE
Inside the humid stench of the port-a-jakes the babushka started her babbling again and I had to attend closely because the acoustics were as shitty as everything else in there. To compound confusion, she never stopped referring to herself in the third person, even reverting at intervals to the *Not I* script, which was obviously something of an obsession with her. But at length I was able to piece it all together—

JOHNSON
At great length.

HODGE
Well then let's get through a biggish chunk of it now without any – ahem – interruptions, shall we? Here is what the old woman had to relate: During World War 2 she'd been a Soviet agent, working in the French Resistance under the Nazi occupation. She was young and beautiful, of course, and everything was in black and white – think Garbo in *Ninotchka*. The glamour of cigarette smoke in moonlight is simply impossible to achieve any other way. Beckett, as we know, was also active in the Resistance, a member of the Paris-based cell that went by the code name "Gloria." His job was as a sort of intelligence hub: Resistance agents brought information on Nazi and collaborationist activities from around the occupied zone to Beckett in Paris, usually in dribs and drabs, this bit and that, building suspense I suppose. Beckett would consolidate this intelligence and translate it into English, typing it all out on sheets of paper

which he would then clandestinely transfer to the cell's photographer, known to Beckett only as Jimmy the Greek, who reduced the pages to microfilm. Next it was up to courier-agents to spirit the microfilms, typically disguised as cigarette rolling-papers, into the hands of British intelligence. More than a few didn't make it, of course, but instead went up in smoke, having been used to roll actual cigarettes. We'll never know the final number but it must have been terribly high – wartime rationing made it inevitable, I suppose. Anyway Beckett acquitted himself of his part in this almost Tayloresque sequence of specialized tasks with "quiet courage," as the ready-made phrase goes, escaping with "just the clothes on his back" and "only seconds to spare" when his flat was finally raided by the Gestapo. But what do you suppose became of Beckett's own writings that he had had to leave behind in that sudden escape? That secret was known to only one person in the world, but she didn't share it for over half a century – until she told *me*. Or rather babbled it out in that St. Petersburg port-a-potty for me to piece back together. This babushka, this old Russian crone, once upon a time a beautiful black-and-white Soviet agent working and smoking in the French Resistance, she knew because Beckett had told her. As a member of the "Gloria" cell she brought Beckett information from time to time, but she had also been assigned to cultivate the writer's more intimate company in the hopes of gleaning additional intelligence that she could channel back to her Comintern handlers. Beckett, for his part, was not immune to her charms, and since he and his partner, Suzanne Deschevaux-Dumesnil, had an "open" relationship – which usually means open at one end, in this case Beckett's – he and the beautiful Soviet agent became lovers. And in their pillow-talk moments, veiled in the smoke of post-coital cigarettes gauzily iridescent in the moonlight through the window, the normally reticent writer opened up and told the Russian what the lover in her, if not the secret agent, was eager to learn – about his writing. He told her that along with the sheets of typed-up intelligence that he regularly handed over to Jimmy the Greek, one day he had taken his own manuscripts to be mircofilmed, the better to conceal them from the Gestapo should his flat be raided. Unlike the other tiny sheets, these Beckett took back and tucked inside a little tin pastille case that he hid underneath a floorboard of his flat in the Rue des Favorites. Chief among these manuscripts was a drama, his first, based on the life of Samuel Johnson and entitled *Human Wishes*, after the latter's famous satiric poem, "The Vanity of Human Wishes."

[*Pause.*]

JOHNSON
Ah— I have a feeling that here I'm supposed to express incredulity that someone we associate so strongly with twentieth-century modernism should have concerned himself to that extent with the representative of such, mmmm, let's say a stuffy classicism?

HODGE
That'll do, yes. I'll admit it might strike us as odd that Beckett, with his later commitment to an aesthetic of failure and his interest in socially marginal types – bums, cripples, people who live in jars – should at one time have wanted to write a play about a figure as canonical as Johnson, that epitome of literary authority. Or such at least is the image of Johnson that we've inherited from Boswell, the disciple who enthroned the poet-critic as an all-wise, definitive father figure. In Beckett's own life there had been such a figure, of course: Joyce. How do you write after Joyce? Was

Beckett doomed just to play Boswell to another encyclopedic Great Cham? So Beckett combed through the biographical record and found a different version of Johnson – a Johnson not of authority but of impotence, not of settled wisdom but of doubt. This was the Johnson of the poet-critic's last years, of the dilatory and unconfessed love for Mrs. Thrale who, widowed at last, crushed him by running off with that Italian music teacher, Gabriel Piozzi—

JOHNSON
Pozzo?

HODGE
Piozzi. Which betrayal resulted in his – Johnson's that is – endgame: a depressive collapse, ill and alone in his study with no one but his cat to talk to, gripped by metaphysical terror, on the brink of madness, contemplating his impending death and the possibility of utter annihilation – a gaping, grinning void; darkness, dust! *This* Johnson became for Beckett the enabling, rather than disabling, precursor – you could say that writing *Human Wishes* was Beckett's attempt to write his way out of the impasse of literary authority. Much in the way that Joyce, come to think of it, deployed his speculations about Shakespeare and *Hamlet* as a lever to free his own creative psyche from the weight of literary forefathers. It's in these terms that Beckett's choice of Johnson as the topic for his first play finally makes sense – as does his attitude towards the fate of the manuscript once he had completed it. Beckett's biographers tell us that he abandoned the play unfinished, and only a short scene officially exists, the fragment published in the collection of Beckett's odds and ends, *Disjecta*. But what the scholars don't know, because Beckett never told them, is that the *Disjecta* fragment is from an earlier draft of the play, a full draft of which

he subsequently completed, at the end of the indigent 1930s. He was proud of the completed drama at the time, but then the war and the occupation came and suddenly he had other priorities, everyone had other priorities. The manuscript of *Human Wishes* went into a bottom drawer while Beckett started his work for the French Resistance, after which, as I've already related, a microformed copy went into that pastille case under the floorboards. Beckett wanted someone else, a third party, to be apprised of the play's secret whereabouts in case he was picked up by the Gestapo, so he told his lover, the Soviet agent. He told her exactly where it was hidden in his Rue des Favorites flat and she memorized it – how many floorboards out from the wall and how many over from the window, then pry up the board and there it should be, safe in its little pastille case. The babushka taught me the steps that Beckett had taught her, this many into the flat itself and that many out from the wall and so many over from the window, floorboard by floorboard and step by step, in the same rigid and exacting instructions for the movement of actors that Beckett favored in his own directorial approach, a Beckettian softshoe shuffle which was difficult, as you might imagine, to dance out in the confines of that port-a-john.

[*Pause.*]

JOHNSON
I take it this is my cue to ask how she knew it would still be there, that Beckett hadn't removed it at some point . . .

HODGE
Because decades later, in the 1970s, she ran into Beckett again. He was in Berlin to direct a performance of *Not I*, as it happens, and she was there working undercover as some

sort of cultural attaché. They went to his hotel room for one of those for-old-time's-sake screws and over their pillow-talk cigarettes, waxing reminiscent as the moonlight through the curtains waned, she asked him what had become of his Johnson play, and he told her that as far as he knew it was still under the floorboards in the Rue des Favorites – he and Suzanne had since moved to an apartment on the Rue Saint-Jacques. He'd only taken it out once, not long after his return to Paris after the war, and had looked over the microform pages with a magnifying glass, but he decided that it should remain suppressed. *Seulement un exercice, et un exorcisme*, he concluded. Rather than destroy it, however – as some kind of private joke, or whim, or test of fate, who knows? – he'd put it back in the pastille case under the floorboard, and he hadn't taken it with him when he moved. *Let it lie there*, he told her, *let it remain, at rest*. After he put it away, however, he noticed that he'd left out one of the tiny microformed sheets – it was on the desk by the open window, one corner pinned by the magnifying glass where it fluttered like a butterfly's wing – and this he folded into his wallet, as either a souvenir or an emergency fag paper should the need arise, considering the post-war rationing situation . . . Anyway he'd forgotten it until that night in the Berlin hotel room, when he showed it to the Russian agent and let her keep it, because suddenly it seemed to possess more significance for her than for him. And over a quarter-century later, in her babbling babushka-hood, this is what she gave me in lieu of a receipt for my trip to the loo, a single torn microfilmed page of Samuel Beckett's lost apocryphal play, *Human Wishes*. I was the one she had long been waiting for, and this was my ticket to literary immortality. The rest I could find at number 6 Rue des Favorites, that is if the building were still there and the original floorboards hadn't been torn up in some fit of yuppie remodeling, and if I could even get inside . . . well, as you can see there were still a lot of ifs. But as unlikely as it all seemed, I felt a weird confidence because, as luck or fate would have it, my wife that very morning had revised our itinerary so that instead of returning to the United States the next day we would be stopping in Paris for a week for her to meet with her neural imaging collaborators at the École Polytechnique.

JOHNSON
Imagine that.

HODGE
So while my wife and her laptop met with her Parisian collaborators and their laptops, I conducted a little research of my own, reconnoitering Beckett's old address. I was hoping maybe it had been turned into one of those house museums, in which case getting in wouldn't be a problem but the staff and security cameras would. But what I found was just a modest, nondescript apartment building with nary a commemorative plaque in sight. I waited and finally slipped into the lobby behind a friendly North African who'd been buzzed in. When he saw me punch the number on the elevator console he murmured sympathetically, *Ah, le prêteur sur gages . . .* This was true: The apartment, as I was to learn firsthand soon enough, was now inhabited by a greedy old pawnbroker who lived there with her retarded younger sister. I didn't have anything to pawn the first time so I had to act like I'd forgotten it and run out to an antique store; I returned with an old silver pocketwatch that had a globe engraved on the back. While the old woman was stowing away my pledge and counting out the money from the locked chest in the other room, I was busy performing the little soft-shoe shuffle I had learned from the babbling

babushka – so many floorboards out from the wall, so many in from the window . . . fortunately the floorboards looked like the originals, no linoleum or carpeting or anything. At one point the old woman stuck her head back into the room and caught me dancing around, but she just thought I had to pee really bad, which in fact I did. "We're not a pissoir, you know!" she grumbled. Anyway I found the spot on the floor, the very spot, and my heart pounded while I stood on it.

JOHNSON
So – call me nuts but I think I see where this is heading – you killed the old pawnbroker and her sister with an axe, and robbed them.

HODGE
No, see, I didn't want to go in that direction. It was heading that way, I admit, especially since I'd brought a small crowbar with me, which could have served in place of an axe. Once a narrative gets started it's got a certain tidal pull – to change it takes a mind like the moon. It's a real feat of concentration, but I managed it. I did it by shifting literary allusions – to *The Aspern Papers*, in fact, the Henry James novella.

JOHNSON
[*Nodding.*] In order to snatch a famous dead writer's papers from an older woman, the narrator finds that he must charm a younger. But, in James's story, a niece instead of a sister, and not . . . mentally challenged.

HODGE
I returned the next day with my crowbar and a box of chocolate-covered cherries and watched until I saw the old

woman go out with a string bag to do her shopping, then I
went up to pay court to the younger sister – younger being
a very relative term here. Like Miss Tita in *The Aspern
Papers*, the pawnbroker's sister was ensconced, or one
might even say embalmed, in a long virginity, but unlike
Miss Tita my virgin also drooled quite a bit. Between that
and my bad French there wasn't much for us to talk about,
so I took to popping bon-bons into her mouth, and when the
box was empty I made my move, wiping the spittle off her
chin and giving it a little kiss, and then a nibble, tasting the
cherry cordial from the—

JOHNSON
Ugh. Now *I* don't like the direction of the story. You said
James, but where's the restraint? I would rather you had
returned with an axe.

HODGE
And when the dear old girl was in her post-coital stupor I
did the deed. Beneath—

JOHNSON
Hold up there a minute, darling. If I'm following you correctly, you'd just finished doing a deed. And while so far this
has all been incredible enough to have the ring of truth, are
you really asking me to believe that such an unlikely gigolo
as yourself *got it up* for this drooling grey-pubed virgin? I
know I just asked for authorial restraint but now I feel I
must insist on one or two key details.

HODGE
[*Pause.*] I told you I had a small crowbar with me. [*Pause.*] It
was all a bit of a tussle anyway and besides, she couldn't have
known the difference. [*Pause.*] It was warm from my pocket.

JOHNSON
[*Approvingly.*] And then wet for the floorboards.

HODGE
Well, there's not a lot more to relate. My wife and I were scheduled to leave France the next day. Naturally I was in max vigilance mode after I had the microfilm with me and at several points thought that my plans would be thwarted. The first was when we were bumped from our Air France flight and interned in this strange *Zone Hôtelière* next to the tarmac of the Charles de Gaulle Airport where I expected at any moment to be set upon and searched by the gendarmerie. And then again in the baggage-claim area at Logan Airport, right when it seemed like only the interminable wait for our luggage items stood between me and Mission Accomplished – suddenly this customs official and her sniffer dog show up and take an interest in my bag. Naturally I thought I was completely busted. But it turned out that the only contraband the dog was interested in was an apple I had with me. I didn't know they trained dogs to sniff out fruit.

JOHNSON
Yes, he certainly sniffed you out. But except for the charming detail of the fruit-sniffing pooch I'm finding this part of the story incredibly boring, and therefore difficult to believe. In subsequent retellings I urge you to leave these two hardly credible episodes out. But in the main you have won my confidence: I fully believe that due to a psychic Russian taxi driver, a babbling babushka, and a drooling French virgin – and your own writerly underhandedness, of course – you have come into the possession of a lost Samuel Beckett play. I congratulate you. But so what? By the time the Beckett Estate shuts down your performance you'll be well on your way to becoming a footnote in revised editions of

that eminence's biography. That's the literary immortality
you're so excited about? Big wow.

HODGE

But it won't just be the production by itself – what I'm envi-
sioning is a full-spectrum cultural provocation. We're going
to go viral with it! We'll seed the ground with cryptic, suggestive communiqués beforehand, heralding an impending
Event of seismic proportions, without, of course, saying
exactly what it's going to be. Then, on opening night, right
as the curtain rises on the world premiere of *Human Wishes*
– I know a gallery where they might let us use the space –
we'll also be uploading the text of the play in html and pdf
and e-book formats on a special homepage that we'll have
set up, with Twitter feed and a blog, and pages on all the
social networking sites. And not just text but video too –
we'll record the dress rehearsal and put it on YouTube, or
we'll live-cam opening night . . . It'll be absolutely
impossible to stop it spreading! The court orders will be too
late, the play will be in too many peoples' hands. And that's
when we issue the manifesto! We'll have done a complete
end-run around intellectual property rights and struck a
blow for open-sourcing and the artistic commons!
Thumbed our noses at the guardians of culture, the people
who want to make museum pieces or academic bailiwicks or
commodities out of everything! We'll have thrown one
mighty sharp elbow into the collective solar plexus of the
gatekeepers, including all the editors who claim to be looking for "new voices" but only publish their MFA cronies and
writers who already have gaudy CVs. Because by that time
everyone will be asking: Who are these provocateurs of art?
There'll be an immediate interest in our own work – they'll
be beating down the doors! It's a *platform*, see? You can't
get lift-off these days if you don't have a platform! We'll

have made it onto the map! I've toiled in obscurity long enough! And so have you, I can tell. You're a provincial just like me, right? We're neither of us to the manor or is it the manner born – see, I don't even know which, even that's a sign I'm from the wrong side of the tracks. No manor-manners. The stra–

JOHNSON
[*Wearily.*] N-E-R, for your information. Although these days more honor'd in the breach than the observance.

HODGE
–the strategy for people like us, with low-to-no cultural and symbolic capital, is to go avant-garde and pick a fight with the mainstream, right? We have to stage a provocation to get on the map, and then people will start paying attention to our own stuff, to my writing and your . . . acting.

JOHNSON
[*Waving, as if bothered by gnats.*] The acting's just a sideline, a rehearsal, if you will. I'm after bigger game. And when I get on the map it's going to be square in the middle, the main stream, and not in any piddling avant-nothing tidal pool, let me assure you. That's all been done. Your precious avant-garde is *arrière-garde* – it is just *sooo* last century. These days it's the mainstream or it's nothing, hadn't you heard? I might be a top, but there's one big queen I give it up for, and her name is TINA – *There Is No Alternative*. You should make her acquaintance. More, you should make a point of letting Her Majesty fuck you every day. She'll run that mainstream right up your ass like a twenty-lane superhighway and take you right to the top. Want to know how I'm going to get there?

HODGE
Do tell.

JOHNSON
[*Unfolds newspaper photograph from waistcoat pocket.*]
Know who this is?

HODGE
[*Glancing.*] Looks familiar.

JOHNSON
Look closer.

HODGE
[*Sniffing the edge of the paper.*] Looks like you actually.

JOHNSON
It's not, but it will be. That's the literary critic, James Wood,
of the *New Yorker*.

HODGE
Um, OK, so you happen to look uncannily like a well-known
. . . journalist. Congratulations?

JOHNSON
Aren't you paying any attention here at all? That brilliant
literary critic you're belittling as a mere "journalist" is going
to be *me*. I'm going to replace him. It's not just *a* destiny –
it's *my* destiny. He and I already share the same name, and
without any plastic surgery at all we look almost exactly
alike. All I've got to do is lose a little more hair! That, and a
lot more of my instinctive libidinal *panache*. I've been planning this for years now. Not just planning – rehearsing.
Because the physical resemblance is just a serendipitous

icing on the cake, most of this is going to be accomplished with *acting*. I'm a wizard at disappearing into a role, you know – well, of course you do; in one of them I had you positively hornswoggled . . .

HODGE
[*Clearing his throat.*] You—

JOHNSON
It's a talent I've always had, from the start. My mother likes to tell the story about the time she thought wild dogs had gotten into my bedroom. One afternoon she heard what sounded like ravening dogs tearing me apart in my room – mad barkings, shrieks, the rending of limbs – but when she ran in there wasn't a pooch in sight, just me in my crib in my little diapers, laughing my head off at my precocious joke! Everyone figures I must have picked it up from hearing the neighbor's cat getting torn apart outside my window a few nights before – they'd had it de-clawed and it'd gotten outside, the poor defenseless puss . . .

[HODGE, *alarmed, consults his paws.*]

JOHNSON
Anyway, from there the next stop was mocking my relatives at family gatherings – holidays and funerals and so forth – including a dead-on send-up of mom telling that wild dogs story for the umpteenth. Not only did they think I was hysterically funny, they were terrified of me! A heady cocktail for someone whose testes hadn't descended yet, I can tell you. So when it came time for my first appearance on the stage, I didn't have any patience for being a bit part, let alone an understudy – I went right for the starring role. It was a junior high production of *Hunchback of Notre Dame*, and I beat out all the fine-

arts tarts from our obnoxious drama clique for the prize: Quasimodo. But then the drama teacher hauls out this papier-maché hump I'm supposed to wear. Instinctively I'm affronted. Hadn't they just seen what I could do? I start lurching around the stage again, inspiring fear and pity with my combination of hulking, malformed strength and mongoloid innocence. Then for good measure I cycle through the other roles as well, showing I can do them all – Clopin, Gringoire, Phoebus, the evil Frollo, and finally – Esmeralda! Cries of recognition and astonishment, louder and louder, accompany each turn! I'm running through the whole play, in double-time, triple-time, all of it, no costumes, no props! Finally I do Esmeralda and Quasimodo *both* – I grab myself around my waist and carry me up one of the backdrop pulleys! Careful, they cry, don't drop her! And when I plunge back down onto the stage, it's right onto that insulting papier-maché prosthetic! Pop – it explodes! Curtain! I take my bows to their frenzied hurrahs! Everyone is now my claque, even those miserable little drama-clique losers who'd been sniping and sniveling a moment before, they clap and whistle and cheer! From a clique, to a claque! Get it? [*Snaps his fingers.*] Clique-claque! Just like that! Clique-claque! And that, my friend, was only the beginning! [*He switches to English accent.*] Now with Wood it's like this, see, he sounds not quite a toff and not quite a twit, but a tincture of both, and *all* country parson. And gestures like a denatured engineer, like this—

HODGE
[*Trying to act unimpressed.*] That's not acting, that's impersonation. Like what's-his-name . . . Rich Little. That and a time machine will get you on Carson.

JOHNSON
Impersonation, like your understanding, is based on super-

ficial externals. What I'm talking about is getting inside, deep inside; sympathetic identification to the nth degree. And that's what makes my choice for my next and crowning performance so deliciously ironic, because James Wood's whole aesthetic – or *our* whole aesthetic – is founded on the idea of Negative Capability. The best novelists, we write, are always those who let the characters speak and act and think for themselves, freely and spontaneously, outside any preconceived straitjackets of authorial intention, exigencies of plot, or hamfisted applications of theme, so much so that at times these characters become surprising even to themselves, so fictively "real" are they! And only thus can they become humanly surprising to us as readers blah blah blah blah blah. That's the drill, the Negative Capability of the novelist and the corresponding "free, spontaneous human interiority" of the character, right? Wood's touchstone and gold standard, right?

HODGE
It most definitely is, and that's exactly the problem. That shopworn humanism is—

JOHNSON
Well, nobody has more Negative Capability than I do. Nobody. See where this is headed? I always disappear up the ass of whoever I'm depicting, but one day soon I'm going to disappear for good, my faggot Caliban up his literary Prospero, and leave not a goddamned wrack behind. It'll be the ultimate act of Negative Capability, and yet – and here's the really delicious part, the very pith and marrow of the irony – it will be accomplished by the greatest egotist, the completest narcissist ever to grind his boot heels onto the astonished face of the earth. Because that's me, too. I can make myself disappear into a seamless – not to mention

seemless – embodiment of an Other, and yet to me nobody exists *but* me. Got that? I combine in one person the grandest heights and depths of the Egotistical Sublime and the clammiest intimacies of Negative Capability, and this, my final act, will bring them together and synthesize them in the highest degree, as the utter consummation of *What I Am*. With the added benefit that he happens to be famous. Isn't this maybe the most perfect irony ever?

HODGE
Enjoy the irony now, because it's not a word with a high count in his critical lexicon. Too pomo.

JOHNSON
Just don't go calling what I do "impersonation," my feline friend. I'm no monkey – if I were I'd pull your tail. I'm an Artist! And this is making me a very horny Artist! [*Gestures at lap.*] Will you look at the tent I've got going here! I always make myself so horny! Nobody ever makes me as horny as me – I've given myself Wood! [*Laughs, looks around.*] They probably have security cameras in the men's room stalls here, don't they . . .

HODGE
Simon says no fornication in the restrooms.

JOHNSON
Simon who? He your steady boyfriend? Maybe we could hook up for a three-way – double-teaming *you*, I imagine. But right now we've got work to do. Even talent like mine is nothing without hard work, and I've been putting in the hours. I've studied him—and not just his words. I've attended his lectures, followed him around . . . more— I've met him, watched him eat in his own house!

HODGE

You know, it hadn't actually dawned on me till now that you're stark raving mad.

JOHNSON

It's the role of a lifetime, and I can pluck it off the silver platter destiny is holding under my nose just like the canapé that James Wood once plucked off mine. Listen up now and you just might learn something. This was back in 2001, and I'd been called in to work that evening for some kind of catered affair chez Wood in Somerville. I remember it very well because it also happened to be my thirtieth birthday and I was pretty depressed at how my career was not advancing at the same breakneck pace as the years. It was also only a few weeks after that whole World Trade Center thing and people were still going on and on about it in the most tiresome way imaginable, including that evening at the Wood reception. That was the context for my first encounter with my namesake, in fact – he was being upstaged in his own house by this so-called "tragedy," so he was trying to bring the conversation back around to where it belonged. "*Well, it just goes to show,*" I heard him say – I was just coming from the kitchen with a fresh tray of canapés – "*that whatever the novel gets up to, the 'culture' can always get up to something bigger!*" Then someone else interjected, "Uh oh, I think I hear next month's review coming!" and everybody laughed – nervous laughter I remember because of course Wood's remark had been in such breathtakingly bad taste. And Wood himself chuckled politely too, just to keep his voice in the mix, and he tried to go on, "*Well, Stendhal, you know—,*" but it was too late, everybody was going back to their boring little what-were-you-doing-when-the first-plane-etcetera stories. So I went over and lowered my dish of hors d'oeuvres in front of him and caught his eye, just to let him know that he and I were on the same wavelength. A little flash of conspiratorial knowledge passed between us – *yeah, everyone is supposed to be here to stroke your cock, and instead they're crying their crocodile tears over those people in the buildings, just to show off their hypocritical humanitarianism* . . .

HODGE
That's it exactly, because I've always thought that his warmed-over Christian-humanism was really just a blind for an imperialistic Will to Power—

JOHNSON
But then – all it took was a second – he couldn't stand it, couldn't stand that anyone knew this secret about him, maybe didn't even want to know it about himself. Come to think of it, it was a lot like one of those moments when you look into a married guy's eyes and it's clear as day that he's completely queer and trying to pass as straight, and in the next second the closet door in his eyes slams shut again and he's even pissed at *you* like you're to blame he just totally outed himself. So what Wood does is he snaps down hard on the canapé he's just picked up from my tray. He should have just popped the whole thing into his mouth but he was flustered so he chomps down right in the middle of that little slice of dried baguette, which explodes in a million pieces all over his shirt front, and already you can see the olive oil bleeding out from each tiny crumb. And he jumps to his feet and I expect him to start balling me out like it was my fault, but instead he starts – are you ready for this? – he starts *reviewing* the canapé. *There's too much oil – it makes the cracker slippery – there should've been more capers in the tapenade – to make the saltiness of the anchovies piquant and unforced – the point isn't to*

bludgeon diners with a single note of crudely unalloyed saltiness – and that sprig of dill, was that meant to be a Russian note?. . . He wasn't yelling or angry either – he'd got his sang-froid back – but instead it was all like I was supposed to be grateful for this helpful advice.

HODGE
Not to mention the temerity of someone from England reviewing food . . .

JOHNSON
Of course I was just serving the stuff, but somehow I found myself taking it personally, too. There was just something about him that was so . . . I was mesmerized. I was deeply annoyed, yet mesmerized. So when I got back to the kitchen I started doing this bitchy send-up of him and pretty soon I had the rest of the staff laughing their asses off, it was so dead on. *Omigod, you're him! you're him!*, they kept crying out between gasps. And then once I had them all rolling helplessly on the floor, even my boss, I just let them know, in the calmest, quietest, most English voice imaginable, that there needed to be more capers and less oil in the tapenade. And the minute I said that there was dead silence and every-one scurried to get back on task, and suddenly everything became clear to me. I had seen the future.

HODGE
Wow. That is really . . . I don't know what that is.

JOHNSON
I mean, I just *got* the whole James Wood phenomenon, why he's so successful over here. The thing about Americans is that they all want to be spanked by a Brit. It's like that TV show that was on a while back, the *Supernanny* – she shows

up and sets the kids in order by giving mom and dad the birch. Or before that it was what's her name on *The Weakest Link*, in that long black leather jacket like she was in the SS or something and those snarky put-downs, you know – "Hodge the Cat, you *are* the weakest link – goodbye!" Eeent! [*Laughs.*] Brits brought over to scold American permissiveness and sloppiness, that's all it is. And how could I leave out Simon Cowell! He's the avatar! Where's my head at today? That's the pop-culture version, but it makes sense there'd be a high-end version too. What is James Wood but a Simon Cowell for Americans who read?

HODGE
It's middlebrow kitsch trying to pass as "high-end," but otherwise you're right on. The fussy, priggish accent comes through even in the prose–

JOHNSON
But let's not go putting a very good marketing concept in an unnecessarily negative light! My main point was to show how my whole plan took root. Since then I've been back to the Wood house as any number of repairmen, delivery boys, what have you. I've even given him a couple of lifts to Logan Airport disguised as a variety of cabbies. And of course I've read every word he's written, tracked down all the *Guardian* columns and even earlier stuff, from the student literary mag at Eton. A lot of material, but he started young – a wunderkind.

HODGE
How I hate all wunderkind.

JOHNSON
And just think of it, only in his forties – I'm a bit younger

than him, but like any good actor I can play older – and already he's the most important literary critic in the United States. By the time he's – excuse me, by the time *I'm* fifty-five, I'm going to be the arbiter of all literature in the English language! By sixty-five, the Culture Tzar of all creation! Authors will have to approach the dais on their bellies, forbidden to look directly at me!

HODGE
I've got it now, you're not nuts exactly, but like one of those grandiloquent Marlovian overreachers.

JOHNSON
Yes! *"'And ride in triumph through Persepolis!' . . . Is it not passing brave to be a king, / And ride in triumph through Persepolis?"* Isn't that one of the finest moments in *Tamburlaine*? One of those moments, in that fledgling work, that attest to the great dramatist Marlowe would shortly, but briefly, become? And more, attesting as a kind of John the Baptist to the coming of a greater . . . to Shakespeare? Because what we see in this Marlowe passage is an early instance of the same self-forgetting of the character that would become the signature of Shakespeare's genius. Only ostensibly is Tamburlaine addressing, in all his Marlovian pomp and bluster, his lieutenants. Really it is Tamburlaine addressing himself, in a moment of unguarded spontaneity; he addresses himself and listens to himself, attending to the drift of his own speech as it pursues his dream to the very depths of his disheveled privacies. It's as if he is discovering a veritable empire as he speaks, but because he is so transfixed by the idea of external empire he doesn't realize that it's the empire of his own imagination that has ensnared him, and which in fact – the pathos of the tragedy, after all – is the only truly exhaustless one for mere mortals like

ourselves. But *we* realize it, we the audience or reader, that Tamburlaine, in speaking thus, is already fondling the "sole felicity" and "sweet fruition" of his "earthly crown," but has found it in the most unearthly and yet realistically earthy places of all, in the unknowable depths of his own human soul. [*Bows. Returns to his American accent.*] See? I can do it, can't I? Right off the top of my head, and it's pure Wood! Isn't that pure Wood?

HODGE
That's his shtick, alright. Neither gold nor silver, nor yet sounding brass. Just . . . Wood.

JOHNSON
Go ahead, give me another one.

HODGE
No, look, see, what you just said there, that James Wood patented humanist shtick, that's just more kitsch – it's kitsch-shtick! Say it three times real fast and you'll see!

JOHNSON
Look, my catty friend, there's a consensus now, at least among the people who count, that I am nothing less than the foremost literary critic of our times. The best. Cynthia Ozick has blurbed me to that effect. Not to mention Harold Bloom when we were still chums, the late Susan Sontag and Saul Bellow – the list goes on. And Adam Begley in the pages of the *Financial Times*. The *Financial Times*!

HODGE
Ad copy! *Caveat emptor.* That still doesn't mean that you—that he isn't a middlebrow philistine posing as a high-culture

aesthete, a book-reviewer posing as a serious literary critic!

JOHNSON
I don't—

HODGE
A real critic should have some brains and some breadth of reference, like Edmund Wilson at *The New Republic* before it became the cover-to-cover piece of neoliberal Zionist crap that Wood shilled for for over a decade! A real critic would be able to write about novels in the context of other literary genres – poetry, drama – as well broader cultural developments in the visual arts, music, and film! A real critic would undertake a dialogue with the important thinkers of her times – like with Zizek and Baidou and Agamben!

JOHNSON
You just sound like—

HODGE
A real critic would be discovering new writers and new trends in writing, not just passing judgment on whatever the publishing megaconglomerates choose to shovel onto the shelves of the big chain-booksellers!

JOHNSON
Oh please. At least he, I—

HODGE
In fact a *real* critic, these days, would exhibit some critical awareness of the whole commercial apparatus that brings "literature" to us in the first place! A real critic wouldn't participate in that mystification! But Wood is just so *narrow*! He—

JOHNSON

[*Outraged.*] Narrow? Ssssssst!

[HODGE *skedaddles off the ottoman and disappears underneath* JOHNSON's *chair.*]

JOHNSON

I'm not normally the hissing kind of queen but sometimes . . . [*Sighs.*] You protest too much, my friend: it is so obviously just the envy and *ressentiment* of the permanently marginalized. You know that never in a million years would a critic of my stature be reading, much less reviewing, the scribblings of a nonentity such as yourself, even if you did finally manage to get them published by some crappy little "independent" publisher, Null-Point Press or Margin House or Afterbirth Books or whatever. And if that doesn't work you can always start a, a – I can hardly bring myself to utter the unlovely word – a *blog*. Noun, verb – what mush. You could even do a little anti-me blog – wouldn't that be cute? You can blahhhhg. Uhh . . . [*Removes handkerchief from waistcoat and hawks something into it, inspects it, folds it away again.*] But narrow – that word I reject. I have length, width, breadth, depth, and girth. All those little fleas with their blogs say that I'm narrow, that's one of the clichés of the "blogosphere" – that I'm narrow, and that I'm nostalgic, that I want everyone to go back and write the nineteenth-century novel . . . well, to paraphrase Goebbels, when I hear the word "narrow," I reach for my gun. But in this case it's a shotgun, loaded with buckshot: my track-record of positive reviews for an array of unbelievably diverse authors! José Saramago, Ian McEwan, Saul Bellow, Graham Swift, Jeffrey Eugenides, Victor Pelevin, Jonathan Lethem, Kazuo Ishiguro, Geoff Dyer, Monica Ali, James Kelman, Marilynne Robinson, J.M. Coetzee, P.G. Wodehouse, Norman Rush, Michel Houellebecq, and W.G.

Sebald! What do all the writers on that list have in common but – me? And if I were so wedded to some strict diet of nineteenth-century realism, why would I have written so deliciously in favor of modernists such as Virginia Woolf, Henry Green, Knut Hamsun? Is Mann's *Magic Mountain*, which I have praised, a work of nineteenth-century realism or a work of twentieth-century modernism? Aren't the works of Bohumil Hrabal – and if anyone's reading Hrabal these days it's because of me – in the absurdist or magical-realist mode? And haven't you noticed that lately I name drop Beckett or Bernhard in almost every review – sometimes both! How's all this for "narrow," eh? And finally, to anyone who want to make out that I'm some kind of moralist, fuddy-duddy, fussbudget, schoolmistress, prude, prig, philistine, second-rater, non-entity, or prickly semi-hysterical compensator for my deep-seated sense of inferiority – listen up all of you – let me modestly assert that [*stands on his chair, makes megaphone of hands*], PROBABLY NO CRITIC OF CONTEMPORARY FICTION IS MORE DRAWN TO STYLE AND THE ENJOYMENT OF STYLE!!! [*Pause. Looks down.*] So . . . well . . . pretty impressive, eh? . . . [*Pause.*] Ahem! What are you doing down there, anyway? An especially tough bowel movement in the cat box? [*Stamps on chair.*] Are you even listening to me? [*Pause. Looks at the ottoman. Sighs. Lowers himself back down into chair and returns one foot to ottoman. Muses. Removes writer's notebook from waistcoat pocket and writes.*] I rejoice to concur with the common reader of the United States of America and with the republic for which it stands; for by the common sense of readers, uncorrupted by literary prejudices, under God, indivisible, after all the refinements of subtlety and the dogmatism of learning, with liberty and justice for all, must be finally decided all claim to poetical profit. Amen. Ka-ching!

[Enter HODGE, *cautiously, from beneath ottoman. He hops onto it next to* JOHNSON's *foot and begins grooming.]*

HODGE

Well – just for the sake of argument, mind you – how were you planning to replace the "real" James Wood?

JOHNSON

We'll work it out somehow, the details, you and me together. It's just got to be something that simultaneously gets rid of him and provides cover for any opening-night glitches and lapses on my part – not recognizing people I'm supposed to know, "forgetting" assignments and engagements, that kind of thing. I've got to have a reason for needing my memory refreshed, so to speak, on anything we haven't been able to pick up through our research. A car accident could be good, a roll-over alone on a highway somewhere up in the Berkshires – he likes to go out there every once in a while to get away. We carjack him coming out of his cabin, and I change into his hideous clothes. We drive the car out to some secluded hairpin turn and give it a little push over the brink, then I scramble down and crawl inside the wreckage. Oh, and you scramble down with me and give me a knock on the forehead or something, bloody me up a little – wouldn't you like that? A concussion, even!

HODGE

I would – but wouldn't that be cheating? Aren't you supposed to just *act* like you're all injured and covered in blood? And you can even play the wrecked car too and dazzle everybody.

JOHNSON

Ha ha ha ha ha. And then you scram and I wake up, alone,

in the wreck – in such pain, and oh so disoriented! I call 911 on his cellphone, or stumble back up to the highway, whatever, but it's done! Anything that I don't know after that can be chalked up to lingering amnesia from the bump on the head. Meanwhile you'd be in charge of the disposal.

HODGE
The— what?

JOHNSON
Well, what have you been thinking here? That I was going to tempt him into taking my place as a museum security guard, catering server, and community theater stud? And anyway this is going to be a huge upgrade for him, too! He gets to be younger! Gayer! And even more ambitious! He'll be exactly the same, only better!

HODGE
This, your plan, it's . . . dastardly. I never thought I'd have occasion to actually use that word but now I've met you and there's no other. You're a dastard.

JOHNSON
[*Accepting an Oscar.*] Thank you.

HODGE
But – just to continue the thought-experiment – what would be in it for me?

JOHNSON
Are you kidding me? Dunce – I'll discover you! Your little . . . writings or whatever. I'll promote you, puff your books, whatever it takes. I'm going to be the biggest critic in the world, and you'll be my number one find.

HODGE

But the kind of writing I'm interested in doing right now –
blowing "story" up from the inside – it's completely anti-
thetical to James Wood's conservative aesthetic. You've
read him, so you know his dismissive contempt for anything
experimental or avant-garde. The sudden turnabout would
give you away. You'd out yourself.

JOHNSON

Oh, please. You know I'll find a way to read your little stories that'll render them thoroughly house-trained, de-
clawed. Remember how I worked my magic on Saramago
and Bolaño, Lydia Davis and László Krasznahorkai? And
anyway, nothing can please many, and please long, but just
representations of general nature. As soon as you see that
you're being waved to the front of the line, you'll be churn-
ing out just representations of general nature in no time.

HODGE

Like his wife writes – like *The Emperor's Children*? Just an
hour ago I was down in the B. Dalton's reading that meretri-
cious piece of crap that's been so well reviewed. But that
brings up another little glitch in your plans, doesn't it: What
are you going to do about her? It's not just his tassel loafers
you're going to have to slip into.

JOHNSON

Well, they've been married for almost fifteen years now so it
couldn't be more than birthdays and anniversaries, and
that's probably pressing it. I did think about dumping her
and coming out as queer shortly after I made my move but
I don't want to end up in the "gay critics" ghetto. I'd have to
go [*shudders*] to the *Village Voice* instead the *New Yorker*.
[*Pause*.] Anyway she's a side issue, we'll figure it out some-

how. You've helped me figure out a lot already, let me tell you. I think you're becoming absolutely essential to the plan. Isn't that nice, to be needed?

HODGE
I haven't agreed to anything.

JOHNSON
But look at the wet dream you're being offered: the opportunity to satisfy the two biggest psychological motivations of writers – resentment and ambition – at the same time! What author could ask for more than that? Imagine, getting a career-making review from a critic you just killed!

HODGE
But I don't really want to kill him – physically, I mean. I wouldn't mind doing it figuratively, of course – critically, the ultimate bad review – but your plan is . . . [*Pause.*] It's weird, when you think about it: your plan is the sincerest form of flattery. The ultimate positive review turns out to be murder.

JOHNSON
That's where you're wrong, clever-boots. In its all-embracing wisdom American jurisprudence takes motive into account. Self defense, crimes of passion . . .

HODGE
Insanity . . .

JOHNSON
Call it what you want, but it won't be murder because it *can't* be murder. I'm him. I'm *more* him than he is! Put me in front of any jury and I'll make them feel it. I will compel them to see it as I do – that this was an act of love, and not

just any love but the highest, most sublime form of love that a human being can experience: the love that exists between a man and himself. That in his last moments he gazed into my eyes with a look of tender understanding, and assent. That when I crushed his windpipe, he came in his pants.

HODGE
Oh my god. My god!

JOHNSON
What? What? Was that last bit over the top? Too Burroughs?

HODGE
No, it's— I get it now, I see what's going on here! You think you're his *double*! His doppelgänger! What unbelievable . . . I'm speechless! It's too much!

JOHNSON
Well, so what? Overreacting a little, aren't you? Unless . . . oh wait, this is too cute! Were you thinking that *we're* the doubles? You and me – shadow selves? You're jealous!

HODGE
No, I— of course not. I just have to wonder what I'm doing here, that's all, if I'm nothing more than some kind of third wheel or afterthought or—

JOHNSON
Aw, don't be jealous, Hadji. Look, I can be your double, too.

HODGE
No, you can't. A character's double can't be someone else's double at the same time, it wrecks the whole idea. It's cheating. On the convention, I mean.

JOHNSON

Tsk tsk. Not very avant-garde now, are we? Do you want to push the envelope or don't you? Blow up the conventions from inside? Look, we'll double down on doubles, make it a kind of hall of mirrors thing, *mise en abyme*—

HODGE

No, I have to draw the line here. Either you're my double or you're his double. You can't be both. And if it's the latter I walk.

JOHNSON

Not to mention isn't the whole doubles thing in its classical form premised on the same depth-psychology model that you reject? The return of the repressed, all those exploded notions of human interiority? That's why I see us as more of a Beckettian pseudo-couple. Isn't that much better? And as far as my namesake goes, look, I won't be his double so much as his postmodern simulacrum. All surface. How would that be?

HODGE

[*Sniveling.*] I know, I know . . . I'm sorry, it's just – those old conventions, they've got a kind of gravity, you know, that's not always so easy to resist, let alone escape . . . sometimes I get so tired . . . and [*snivels harder*] it's just so *lonely*!

JOHNSON

There, there, Hadji . . . that's it . . . let it out . . .

HODGE

[*Keening.*] And I'm scared of jail! There are too many things that can go wrong! Besides I liked my plan. What's wrong with my plan? Why can't we just do my plan?

JOHNSON

It's a good plan – it can be our Plan B, OK? If we get sent to prison, we'll put on the Beckett play there. Beckett always goes over huge in prison. Plus all the sex we could want!

[HODGE *rises as if to leave.*]

JOHNSON

OK, wait – look, if it'll make you happy, we'll start on both projects simultaneously. You give me Beckett's Johnson and we'll set up a rehearsal schedule, and meanwhile you'll ride shotgun with me while we stalk and study the quarry a little more, his habits and movements and so forth. Eventually, whichever plan looks the most promising, we'll go with that one. Heck, I don't know, maybe we'll end up doing both! C'mon, pinkie swear.

[*They pinkie swear.*]

JOHNSON

Now is that better? You see I'm doing all I can here—

HODGE

[*Sniffling.*] And . . . doubles?

JOHNSON

Alright, alright, I'm your Secret Sharer already. Sheesh. I mean [*puts on accent*], I'm jolly well already James Wood himself, so no use being his double, right? What ho? Pip pip, old shoe?

HODGE

[*Drying eyes.*] I doubt he sounds like Bertie Wooster.

JOHNSON
You'd be surprised, Hadji.

[Blackout.]

Enemy Combatant

omeone must have dropped a dime on our hero, for without having done anything wrong he woke up one morning from uneasy dreams to find himself transformed in his bed into an enemy of the state. His wife was not next to him that morning but this in itself was not unusual, because it wasn't actually morning when he usually got up, unless you wanted to be technical about it and insist that 11:50 AM was still morning, by which time his wife would be already, like most people who worked for a living, at work, in a lecture hall full of students giving a PowerPoint presentation from her laptop, or in her office googling citations for an article she was drafting on her laptop, or at lunch munching a sandwich while reading a science blog on her laptop, or in her lab going over data with one of her grad students on her laptop, in one way or another simultaneously earning her and her spouse's daily bread, furthering by stubborn degrees the advance of science and laptops, and subsidizing – in theory anyway – the arts. Start again. For a long time he used to get up late. Sometimes he felt a kind of elevator-lurch and his eyes would snap open instantly, heart pounding, a ray of sun stabbing his face with such sudden brightness that his uncomprehending eyes marveled at their own tears. Other times he woke in fitful stages, slipping in and out of his dream and unable to tell right away the difference between the waking room and the dream rooms in which the shady business of his unconscious was being transacted, as if the painted backdrops of theater sets were being raised and lowered by pulleys from the heavens in a sequence that was always just about to allow him to name the play, but not quite. Out of zones of not-feeling his body would emerge piecemeal, an arm here and a leg there like a crime scene, but always inevitably filling in, fleshing out, and falling into place in that tentative revocable way his grubstaked corporeality had of meeting yet another day. But this morning something was wrong, it was as if he had emerged in an arrested somersault. This morning? Maybe it had been many ass-over-teakettle mornings, time only fell into place when space was there to meet it, but this was a trapdoor over a rabbit hole. It couldn't be his room at home, but it didn't make sense for him to be waking up anywhere else, so maybe it wasn't him, either. Lies. Start again. Where now? Who now? When now? Start again. All he could say for sure was that they had the wrong guy. But that's you in the picture, isn't it. Yes, that was him in the picture. And this name next to the picture, that's your name, isn't it. Yes, that was his name. And this is a real passport, isn't it. What do you mean, of course it's a real passport. Well then, we have the right guy. But if you really are a different guy, just tell us and we'll let you go. Just tell us your story and we'll let you off the hook. That was supposed to be a joke. There was a hook in the middle of the floor that he was chained to by his ankles and wrists. By that time he'd given up trying to hold the crouch position and was lying on his side. The puddle of urine on the concrete was creeping closer and closer to his cheekbone. Tell us a story. What story. Any story, as long as it's a true story. Tell us the true story of your life. Realistic. Yes, a true story is by definition a realistic story. Verisimilitude. Thick description. L'effet de réel. But what was happening to him was not at all realistic. The kick on the back of his skull abraded his cheek on the floor's rough surface. There was a Military Policeman standing behind him. At some signal from his questioners on the other side of the desk the MP would deliver blows. Again he told them his story. Such as it was. Noting first the main features, and proceeding thence to the finer points, filling in and fleshing out. Lies! We're going to take away one of your Comfort Items unless you cooperate. But he didn't have any Comfort Items for them to take away. Fine, then we'll take away one of your Basic Items. Your flip-flops, for instance. Now, do you want to change your story. He changed his story. He tried to tell them what they wanted to hear, a story in which he played the role of an evildoer. More lies. The MP kicked at his feet. The flip-flops flew off. His toes would be next. They showed him another photograph. Or rather, they handed the photograph to the MP. The MP bent down and held the photograph in front of his face and barked for him to look. The MP gave him a cuff on the back of his head to help him look. He had heard them fine the first time. He addressed himself to the image. He acknowledged that he was the man in the picture. Why was he dressed like a terrorist. He wasn't, he was dressed like a Bedouin. It was a costume party. Lies. No, truth. He was supposed to be Rudolph Valentino in *The Sheik*. Ah ha. Before you said a Bedouin. You can't even keep your story straight. Sigh. OK, OK, he was dressed like an Al-Qaeda in that picture. Another kick. And another. Another. The MP appeared to be freelancing. We want the truth, but you have to mean it. They continued asking him about clothes. That was the theme for the day. In the interrogation room the conversation had taken a sumptuary turn. They had started off asking him how he liked his three-piece suit. When the escort team brought him in and the MP pulled his hood off. How do you like wearing that three-piece suit. That was supposed to be a joke. It was a body-belt, handcuffs, and leg shackles. The MP hooked him by the suit to the hook in the floor. At first he had the strength to crouch, semi-upright. A figure frozen in the act of tying his shoe. Of adjusting his flip-flops. But now he was on his side. The flip-flops were a few feet away. His toes would be next. The MP bent down and fanned some pictures in front of him. There he was in his usual black duds. And black Converse All Stars with black sagging socks, what was that about. Didn't he have any self-respect. The MP stuck more pictures in front his face. He tried to focus. He wanted to know how they had gotten into his wife's laptop. They wanted to know why did he always wear black. What did he think he was saying with that. Did he know who else wore black. There was a TV on a rolling stand and they played him a video clip of men in black garb and balaclavas running through an obstacle course. The black-garbed men held rifles and leaped over barricades and rolled on the ground. They crossed hand-over-hand bars with rifles slung to their backs. He was one of those men. He had trained at that very camp. There he was in the group shot, listening to the imam. Impossible, he could never do hand-over-hand bars like that. He could not even do one pull-up. Many kicks. Next time it would be his teeth. There was a little blood in the piss puddle now. Blood puddle. Poodle. Shake him up, wake him up. They showed him his passport again. What kind of name is that. A Portuguese-American name. And what kind of face is that. Do you call that a Portuguese-American face. They showed him pictures of his mother, his father. Did he look like them. No he did not. Well then. He didn't want to argue with them. Maybe he was adopted. He had always believed that he was adopted. Lies. Your whole past is a paper trail. We know who you really are. Well in that case they should tell him. Because he really wanted to know. He'd been wondering all his life. He expected more blows but he was too tired to brace himself. Instead the MP stuck another picture in front of his face. Handsome, silver hair, mustache, sad intelligent eyes. Vaguely familiar, maybe an actor. Or wait, the man who owned the falafel stand near where he and his wife lived. That got laughs. Nice try. You're a terrible liar. You know who he is. Try to notice the family resemblance. Another picture. Huge honking schnoz. Through the slits of almost swollen-shut eyes the glimmer of alien irises. Shaved stubble scalp but the wiry brush of a pitch-black beard. He had no idea. The MP hit him in the face with the picture, the cold hard picture. A mirror. Take him back to his cell. The escort team marched into the room. They put the hood over his head. They put the blackout goggles over the hood. They unhooked him from the hook in the middle of the floor and pulled him to his feet. Don't get your piss on me you pissy-pants piece of shit. They had done that on purpose. They kept his head shaved but not his face so that his beard would grow and he would come to look like an Islamist. Like their idea of an Islamist. If they would just let him have a razor and a little soap he would shave. Or he would look however they wanted if they would let him go. Or just be a little nicer to him. He could see their side of things, after all. Stockholm Syndrome. Faster. In the three-piece suit he could only shuffle. Go faster. They pushed and he fell. They played hacky-sack with parts of him. He was a man of parts. Wake up. Get up. Stand up. *Stand up for your rights*. If he could just make it to the ocean he would swim to Jamaica. *Get up, sta—* Get the fuck up, Hadji. They hauled him back onto his feet. Without the flip-flops the gravel was sharp. Sometimes it seemed like a long way from the interrogation room to the cell, and from the cell to the interrogation room. Other times it seemed like a short way. On the same round trip, even – short out and long back, or vice versa. On all occasions it was circuitous. Right! Again right! They had made enough right turns he was sure they were heading back the way they had come. Then another turn and he would have to give up trying to keep track. It was hard to keep track of anything with all the noise. There was the sound of the generators that powered the fans during the day and the floodlights at night. There was Screamo rock music and country western ballads. There was the swaggering, jock-like bray of the soldiers, even the women soldiers had a swaggering, jock-like bray. It was evidently a stand-ard-issue bray. There was the recording of the muezzin's call drowned out in the next instant by the Star Spangled Banner. It was so hot and humid it was like being suffocated in a wet wool blanket. But then he remembered what being suffocated really felt like. When they had wrapped his head in a towel and held it in the bowl and flushed. He always knew he would end up in the toilet. Make him wake up. We're sorry is this boring you. No he was just tired. If he had stopped eating again they would use the tube just like last time. No he had just not gotten used to the schedule, being woken up every five minutes. Somehow he was back in the interrogation room. Maybe they had only taken him in a circle. Maybe he had only dreamed they were taking him back to his cell. When were they going to put him into one of the outdoor cages. That part of the camp was shit-canned in 2002, dumbfuck. Bad publicity. Too bad, he thought he might just be able to handle one of the cages on account of Ezra Pound. What thou lovest well remains. And maybe a breeze at night. Was his highness unhappy with the accom-modation. After all the trouble they had gone to. His cell built to such precise specifications. Designed with his mind in mind. They thought it would make him think of a pres-surized cabin. *The thought of a pressurized cabin caused him to experience anxiety*, see it says so right here, start of Chapter 2. There was nothing they didn't know about him. They thought it would make him think of a port-a-john.

Where he would be interred for life. Ha ha. In-turd. Get it. Oh yes they'd read every word he had ever written. Even his marginalia. His marginalia and his juvenilia. In other words, the collected works. Still, wasn't it thrilling. At last the recognition he deserved. Only apparently was he an utter nonentity. Outside he might be an utter nonentity but in the corridors of power he was a famous literary figure. Wasn't this all one big writer's wet dream. Too bad they were just yanking his chain. His biggest reader was actually a software program. Like Carnivore, only different. And don't expect a fan letter anytime soon. His stuff had the system crashing almost every hour out of sheer boredom. The programmers had to come up with a patch just to keep it going. Those jokers named it Red Bull. Seriously was there no end to his narcissism. Not to mention his pseudo-intellectuality. Here's one, carceral archipelago. Deep down he must have known how pretentious he was being when he spouted crap like carceral archipelago, didn't he. But just because you're a pretentious little pseudo-intellectual doesn't mean you might not end up in . . . the carceral archipelago. Laughter. In the meantime the MP had returned from his pee break. A kick for any misdemeanors in his absence. And a pinch in the neck for good measure. Just out of curiosity where did he think he was anyway. He named the carceral archipelago where he thought he was. Another round of laughs. What so all he had to do was hop the fence and he'd be hangin' wid his homies Fidel and Raul. So sorry to disappoint him. Hop the fence and it's sharks, Hadji, it's miles of Indian Ocean in all directions. He was in Diego Garcia, then. More laughs. They were just yanking his chain again. They were actually at a secret base in western Iraq and tomorrow they were going to shove him into a duffel bag in back of a jeep and drive him to Amman. Let Abdullah's Mukhabarat get the answers out of him. Real sweethearts, that crew. Or wait no they were in the secret camp in Poland. Or maybe they were on the moon. The point was that he was nowhere. He had no country and no name. He was off the grid. He was off the map. In the non-place for the non-people. A camp could be closed down. For purposes of publicity. But there would always be non-places for non-people. Always. Did he understand that. It was important for him to understand that. Because he was a non-person in a non-place. That was his choice. They hadn't made it for him. He had to be the uniformed soldier of a real state to be covered by the Geneva Convention. A real state. The Republic of Letters didn't count, asshole. But maybe he had one last chance. Every work of quality literary fiction includes a shot at redemption at the end. All he had to do to redeem himself was answer the questions. Why did they need him to answer questions when they knew everything already. He waited for the kick. Instead one of them spoke. The one who resembled the famous literary critic. They didn't need. They had no conception of need. He needed, not them. He was all need. In that case he needed for them to tell him what to say. He had tried to make stuff up but they didn't believe him. Maybe fiction just wasn't his thing. They should ghost write it for him and he would sign his name. He was not afraid to be a complete coward. He had no principles standing in the way of the most abject collaboration. They were afraid that wasn't how it worked, Hadji. Then tell him how it worked, even a little hint. Hadji should just say the first thing that popped into his head. Why were they calling him that. Maybe that was the very knot Hadji could undo for them. If he just relaxed the knot would practically come undone by itself. That pinch in the neck. Had they drugged him. They wouldn't do something like that, Hadji. Yes they would, did. And that wasn't his name. If it wasn't, now was the time to clear it up for them. All he had to do was answer their questions. He was in St. Petersburg last year, wasn't he. Why did he go to St. Petersburg. He'd told them about that already. All they had to do was flip back to the start of the third chapter. If he would be so kind as to refresh their memories himself. His wife was attending a science conference. Yes but what was he doing there, emphasis on he. Was it so strange that a husband and wife should travel together. But this husband and wife hardly even spoke to each other. Was it so strange that a husband and wife should hardly even speak to each other. Besides, he got anxious when he was separated from her for any length of time. She had blond hair and an open face. Everything seemed to go easier when she was by his side. That was hardly a convincing explanation. For a grown-up, that is. Now why did he go to St. Petersburg. To sight-see. OK then, while he was sight-seeing did he happen to meet a Chechen taxi driver by the name of Rasul Kusayev. Sight-seeing in scare quotes, taxi driver in scare quotes. He had taken a number of taxis, how was he to know. He knew the one they were talking about, he had taken a very long ride with Kusayev on his last evening there. And the ride just went in a circle until Kusayev dropped him off where he had picked him up, at the Anichkov Bridge. Oh that one, that driver was as Russian as they come. Yeah, right. What did he and the Chechen taxi driver talk about, emphasis on Chechen. The beautiful Russian girls, Pushkin, and Dostoevsky. The Russian girls Pushkin and Dostoevsky, is that some kind of code. No it was their drugs. Giving him much trouble pronunciating. Those beautiful Russian girls. His head it simply swirls. He should stop trying to game them. They had not given him anything. They had not given him much of anything. But the Chechen taxi driver had most definitely given him something. The name of a contact to meet in Paris. No, the driver was Russian and only stopped at a park for him to use a port-a-john. But from Russia he traveled to Paris, did he dispute that. No he did not. And when he was in Paris, he went to the Paris Mosque, didn't he. Didn't he. Did a cat have his tongue. He must tell them why he went to the Paris Mosque. It was in the guidebook, a legitimate tourist destination. Yes, for Muslims. Didn't he go to the Paris Mosque to meet a man in the tea garden. No, he did not. Yes, he did, he met Ismail Azzawi, an Iraqi national of Palestinian descent, in the tea garden of the Paris Mosque. How did he know Ismail Azzawi. He didn't know him, it was a coincidence, a chance encounter. He had met Azzawi already once that day, that morning, at the Institut du Monde Arabe. Is that where Kusayev had instructed him to make first contact with Azzawi. No, it was where he had gone to look at an art exhibition. The man they were calling Azzawi also happened to be there. Just happened to be there. As far as he knew, yes. To look at the art. Yes to look at the art. They had struck up a brief conversation about the paintings. That was all. Yes that was all. The whole thing could only be suspicious to people who never went to look at art. Oh that's right because everybody was a philistine but him. They had forgotten that they were complete phil-istines. And during this little art-chat he and Azzawi had arranged to meet later at the Paris Mosque. No they had bumped into each other at the mosque later that afternoon. By coincidence. Yes by coincidence. Lies. Their patience was not without limits. Unlike their power. Magniloquence. Why were they speaking like comic book super-villains. At a signal the MP gave him another pinch in the neck. Give it a moment to sink in. If he thought he was protecting Azzawi his loyalties were misplaced. Azzawi was in custody and had already informed on him. It had taken only minutes for Azzawi to give him up. Alacrity. Give that a moment to sink in. Now he was going to answer whatever they asked. For example, what did the words *Nothing odd will do long* mean to him. Nothing odd will do what exactly. What did that have to do with anything. It didn't, it was to test the dosage. Just ignore it. Now he was going to tell them what he and Azzawi had talked about. They talked about translation, the man they were calling Azzawi was a translator. They knew perfectly well what Azzawi was. They wanted to know what they talked about. About the things he translated. Sufi poetry. Art criticism. What else. Beckett. What Beckett. A few short prose pieces. A few of the later plays. For example. *Not I.* Make a note of that. Oh and *Catastrophe.* Now did he see how easy this was. What else did they talk about. About the prohibition on the representation of the human figure in Islamic visual art. How a lot of visual art from Muslim cultures transformed this prohibition into a play of motifs about calligraphy. Virtue out of necessity, but continue. How this has led some in those cultures to notions of the relationship of writing, absence, and silence that are only beginning to be appreciated in the so-called West. Oriental nihilism, but keep going. About the liberation that might ensue if, for a time, the human figure was dissolved into writing, letting "the human" decompose into the letters that spelled it out. Yes, that is the terrorist impulse behind so-called literary experimentalism. No, that is the secret promise of language, which is always Other. Never mind, we'll come back to it. We will always come back to it. What more did you talk about. About the illusion of a place of purity, where writing wouldn't always be a palimpsest. The dangerous illusion of a page without words for words without a page. And what's that code for. What is that a code for. They determined that he was cracking. But they also determined that he was fading. He was cracking and fading at the same time. They needed every available unit on alert. They had to gather close to hear his every word.

They surrounded his mouth with their ears. They knew for a fact he had given something to Azzawi to translate. They wanted to know what it was. He must tell them what he had given Azzawi to translate. Their earlobes tickled his broken lips. What had he asked Azzawi to translate. Tell them, tell them. Their earlobes felt his lips tremble. Their ears heard his whisper. Yes. Yes, he had. He had asked Azzawi to translate him into Arabic. Emphasis on him. He had given himself to Azzawi to translate. It was going to be an extraordinary rendition. Silence. No, there was laughter. He was laughing at them. They had the MP work him over for a while. They knew he couldn't feel it anymore but it was satisfying to watch. They brought in the Immediate Reaction Force team to irf him for a while. Then they gathered their mouths close around his broken ear. They knew he was still in there somewhere. They knew he could hear them. Deep-cover little sleeper-cell fuckshit that he was. They were going to tell him something. The one who resembled the famous literary critic had a special review just for him. Consider it a note slipped under the door. They were going to tell him that he was behind the curve. He wasn't as postmodern as he thought. He didn't stick to his own anti-humanist propaganda. He turned writers and critics into heroes and villains. What was that but a fantasy of human agency. They could tell him a thing or two about agency. There was no agency left but the Agency. And their covert program of promoting realist "literary fiction" was just a cover. The so-called Forces of Reaction were way the fuck ahead of him on all the important questions. They were sitting down with the Mossad and the IDF to work out how to fight the next war. The global intifada. Urban warfare to the nth degree. They were in a study group reading Deleuze and Guattari in one hand and *Finnegans Wake* in the other. They were learning to go through walls. They were going through the walls of occupied territories, townships, ciudades perdidas, shantytowns, colonias, barrios, inner-city 'hoods, precarios, squatters' camps, Hoovervilles, hobo jungles, favelas, banlieues, and rabbit warrens, not to mention artist studios, university lecture halls, anarchist infoshops, whatever. They were going through walls of stone, walls of timber, walls of stucco, walls of scrap metal, walls of cardboard and chickenwire, walls of mud, walls of thatch, walls of reinforced concrete, walls of cowshit, walls of plastic, walls of steel, walls of plexiglass, walls of lead, and walls of bone. It was all the same. They would take an incredibly serried and corrugated and labyrinthine three-dimensional environment and conceptualize it as a plane. They would theorize it as a plane, and then map out the strategy as if it were all one surface, going here and killing these guys, going there and killing those gals, and so forth. Then they would fold it up back up into its original three dimensions and, presto, a road map for going through fucking walls. But he shouldn't think they were talking about a real folded-up piece of paper with a bunch of Xs and arrows on it. That was just a primitive Newtonian metaphor for what was really a quantum operation. Not Xs and arrows but rhizomatic vectors. And what they had just described was only a single iteration, representing a single and so-to-speak unitary point of view for approaching the contested terrain. But they were up against multitude, a fucking hydra. So they exploded the unitary point of view by running a theoretically countless number of iterations. The original plane became a plateau in a conceptually metastasizing universe of further plateaus, each of which represented a further iteration from a different limited point of view. Then all it took was just a tilt of the axis, so to speak, and they could see it all again as one single plane, except this time it was more like . . . a mandala. Heady stuff, they were telling him. And once again all just a very figurative way of representing something that was beyond representation. Suffice it to say that in order to win they had to become more radically acephalous than the most leaderless and dispersed resistance. Hence the code name of the project: Here Comes Everybody. And he was invited. He had a part to play. Wasn't that exciting. Admittedly a small part. Even vanishingly small. Indeed it might consist only of vanishing. That would be up to him. But now it was time for him to get some sleep. Get some sleep, little sleeper cell. For once they were going to let him get some rest. He was going to need it. They had the escort team sweep him up and deposit him back in his cell. He was left alone for a long time. For what seemed like a long time. Out of zones of not-feeling his body emerged piecemeal, an arm here and a leg there, in some kind of arrested somersault. Maybe it had been many ass-over-teakettle nights, all he knew was that something was different. His wife was not next to him but this in itself was not unusual, at least not since he had woken up and found himself transformed in his bed into an enemy of the state. What was different was the quiet. No generators or Screamo or country western, no swaggering jock-like bray of the men soldiers and the women soldiers, no recording of the muezzin's call drowned out in the next instant by the Star Spangled Banner. If it weren't for the sound of his jagged breaths and whimpering he would have thought they had beaten him deaf. He crept to the door, put his ear to it. It moved. The door moved. They had forgotten to lock the door. He wobbled the half step back to the squat toilet in the corner of his cell and emptied his bladder in on and around it. On wet feet he returned the half step to the door. He took a deep breath and tried to calm the whimpering. He opened the door and stepped out. The food court was a mock-up of the old Boston Garden, with a broad high ceiling supported by fake girders painted tan and aqua just like in the old Garden. There was a sign saying "Boston Garden Memories" (his was wetting his pants at a Celtics game his ostensible dad had taken him to) surrounded by life-sized figures of Bill Russell and a bunch of white guys. The centerpiece was the original Boston Garden scoreboard, a black oblong the size and heft of a stuffed mastodon suspended over the tables with TV monitors playing NESN mounted on each of its corners. The diners didn't look up from their cold Sbarro pizza slices and trays of congealing Master Wok chow mein as he threaded his way towards the west side of the second-floor concourse and the anchor stores Marshall's and Filene's Basement, where the down escalator took him to the ground-floor main plaza and the revolving doors. Outside there was a system of looping driveways and parking lots. Signs informed drivers that trucks should go left, cars should go right. There was a concrete plaza with a restroom building and a snack kiosk. Inside the snack kiosk stood vending machines for sodas and coffee and salty and sweet snacks. In front of the vending machines a family was arguing. On the other side of the kiosk were a few picnic benches and an area of lawn with a few slender trees and shrubs in small circles of wood chips. From the main highway rose the susurrus of traffic, at times coughing to cacophony. Across the highway was another rest stop, the mirror image of this one. They floated on each side of the highway like two kidneys. He went to the restroom building and pushed open the door of the men's room. It was crowded inside but eventually he was able to insert himself into the front rank of passengers at one end of the carousel. There was a shudder and a jolt from somewhere underneath the central hump and the conveyor belt began moving, and the large interlocking metal plates which made up the surface of the carousel itself began moving. He ran his fingers over the whiskers on his upper lip and around his chin. He stroked the whiskers against the grain and felt stimulated and unwashed and under suspicion. The carousels were like the rotors of a giant electric shaver, he thought. All he would have to do was fall to his knees and place his breast on the rim of the carousel and lower his chin towards the large interlocking metal plates which made a shearing sound as they moved together and apart. He had an ambient sense of the people around him turning to look the other way and he turned to look, too. The woman in the blue and white uniform and the beagle-like dog were back, this time on his side of the carousel. He decided it would be better if he returned to the restroom. As he sighed himself into his pee and his bladder drained he noticed that the mounted gleaming urinal the plumbing fixtures and the wall tiles appeared to him like charmed items in a Cornell box. With the relief of peeing which he mistook for aesthetic experience although who's to say maybe it was, was that too, whatever it was it was a little bit of grace and a lighter step, so light in fact that instead of threading through weekend throngs up the stairs he transported himself instantly back up to the heart of the exhibition, from the bladder and bowels of the museum to its very heart, the room with the Soap Bubble Set and the Medici Slot Machines which he'd had to short shrift on the first go-round because of the annoying guard with the refulgent antennae, and instantly he remarked that his luck was holding out, it was a lucky day, he was lucky after all: the annoying guard was no longer there, either roving or at rest. Crowd of onlookers a little thinner too by lucky chance, now was his chance, he must address, address himself to the works! Not the plaques but the works! He noted the corks and chemist's bottles and Dutch clay pipes and liqueur glasses with blue marbles hung in them like planets and plastic lobsters lined up like ballerinas and the coiled springs out of clocks, he stole a glance at the new guard standing against the far wall and scribbling away in a little pocket notebook, quite a scribbler this guard, something familiar about him too, something familiar and maybe it was time to move on, down the stairs and out the exit and onto the sidewalk, but there was no way to shake it, that Artic chill knew the St. Petersburg streets better than he did and always thought five moves ahead, no way to tell which direction it would come at you next, you go one way it goes the other, you fake left cut right down Stolyarny Lane, cross the Kammeny Bridge at a running crouch, feint another left but turn right on Sadovaya Street, try to lose yourself in the crowd until you see the Griboedova Canal, then disappear into the darkest dankest courtyard you can find and pop out again through the back passage onto Srednaya Podyacheskaya Lane thinking you had just pulled off the perfect crime only to feel the chill tap on your shoulder of that super-adhesive hyperborean Porfiry Petrovich. No, nothing to do but sub- mit, one way or another the despotic Arctic was going to cop its feel, maybe it had even steered him to the Haymarket by its cunning ticklish byways, letting him think it was his doing, to arrive here in the Haymarket, this Haymarket today all market and no hay. And just as he was beginning to feel his breath, from the climb and perhaps a little from anticipation he surmounted the crest of the hill and roun- ded the curve and saw before him the chateau to which the French person had directed him, obviously and clearly this was the very chateau the French person had meant, the Château-Roissy Hotel on the driveway loop between the invidiously-appointed Suitehotel Roissy and the Kyriad Prestige Hotel Roissy-en-France, with the Novotel Roissy and the Millennium Hotel Roissy-Paris Charles de Gaulle on their respective sub-loops below and above them on the hillside. Shuttle-buses churned by in both directions on the tarmac loops. He returned to his room, passing the dour Ukranian housekeeper on the way. He stretched out on the small bed, put his left forearm over his eyes and listened to the sound of the tarmac-surf through the open treble-paned window. He felt the lamination in the chambers of his sinuses and in his gorge, his windpipe, and his lungs. He would never get out. Character was fate. Except that this was less a matter of character than of setting. It had been one cul-de-sac after another. Through a series of loops and figure-eights he had moved as if on tracks. His so-called "character" was nothing more than an effect, an epiphenomenon of these looping tracks. His internal monologue was a monorail. He had been hoisted on his own anti-story petard. On the other hand maybe his mistake had been to get mixed up in a plot. It had been no great shakes going around in circles but look where he was now. It was the same loop recapitulated on another level, where it tightened into leg shackles. He had exchanged a purgatorial vision for an infernal one. In another few minutes the escort team would hump back into his cell and dress him in his three-piece suit and take him to the interrogation room for more questioning. In another few hours, or weeks, or a whole geologic age, it didn't matter, this could end right here or go on for another thousand pages, a going on of going round and around, of riding the Moëbius monorail, of shuttling in the limen, of soft-shoe shuffle at the margin. Forever in the In-Between. Waiting to be taken out and read. This won't even be a proper novelistic conclusion because he hasn't gotten anywhere to speak of. A terminal non-starter. Might as well never have left the womb. And in a sense maybe he never has. But – hold on a minute here – the womb? This gives us an idea. Yes perhaps in reading out his interminable sentence we have stumbled on an out-clause. Maybe after all in this story or rather anti-story of loops we've discovered for our little hero – a loophole. It's not much and it's got some pretty severe downsides, but it's the only opening we can find and in the final analysis a pretty natural one for him to take. And so, courtesy of the serendipitously arbitrary agency of language itself in the form of the celebrated literary phenomenon of word association, it is time for our hero (drum roll please) to be born! And end again: He stretched out on the small bed, put his left forearm over his eyes and listened to the sound of the tarmac-surf through the open treble-paned window. He had accompanied his wife to a science conference at the University of Tel Aviv and now they were going home. They had checked out of their hotel early that morning and taken a taxi to the airport in plenty of time to be greeted by the smiling El Al counter person who told them that they had been bumped from their overbooked flight. Instead of being herded into the large metal tube of the El Al jet they had been herded into the smaller metal tube of the El Al shuttle-bus which shuttled them over a large number of looping roadways, unless it was rather a single roadway comprised of a large number of loops, going from one loop to another and from larger loops to smaller loops, and changing lanes within loops, until it had looped eventually into the driveway of the airport hotel where they were to spend the night. Now he was trying unsuccessfully to nap while his wife was downstairs in the lobby enjoying free wireless and a vending-machine cappuccino. On the other side of the treble-paned window was a development town called Lod on the edge of the metastasizing Tel Aviv conurbation. If you know Lod at all it's only because you've caught a glimpse of it from a taxi on the highway on your way to Tel Aviv, or from a train on your way to Jerusalem, or from the air, landing or taking off in an El Al Airlines flight into or out of Israel, because pretty much all Lod is known for these days is being the town where the Ben Gurion International Airport is located. The airport used to be called something else but in 1973 the name of the legendary first prime minister of the Israeli state, Daniel Ben Gurion, was bequeathed to its tarmacs and terminals, and now the town of Lod is pretty much surrounded by tarmac, the big tarmacs of airport with its three runways for local, international, and military flights plus enough spaces in their short- and long-term parking lots for 12,000 automobiles, and the smaller tarmacs of the roadways by which those automobiles arrive to look for parking or, having parked, depart. But these days nobody's really encouraged to tarry in Lod itself, among tourists that is, move along move along nothing to see here, hustled onto the bus for the holy sites of Jerusalem or the sun and surf of swinging Tel Aviv (that Club Med just a few kilometers from the world's most densely-populated ghetto, Gaza). However if you're not a tourist, if say you're a new Jewish immigrant into Israel then Lod might be just the town for you, because along with the Ben Gurion International Airport the city also hosts the Jewish Agency Absorption Center. This is the agency that handles the arrival of the *olim*, the Jewish immigrants to the State of Israel whose birthright is *aliyah*, which means the sacred right of return, to make *aliyah* as it is called and settle as a Jew among Jews in the great *Kibbutz Galuyot*, the diasporic melting pot, the great ingathering of international Jewry back to Eretz Israel, the sacred heimat that Jehovah promised would be restored to the people of the faith after the coming of the Messiah, in which case maybe they've jumped the gun a little bit because unless I missed it the Messiah still hasn't shown up but we'll ignore that for now, not important, minor detail, anyway as we were saying, anyone anywhere in the world who is Jewish enjoys this sacred Right of Return – that has quite a ring to it, doesn't it? – the sacred right guaranteed to anyone whose mom is Jewish, according to ancient Hebrew law you get to be a Jew if your mom's one. The Palestinians do not enjoy such a sacred birthright because they were driven out only a couple of decades ago whereas the Jews were driven out a couple of millennia ago, it's the way of the world that time hallows all things so the Palestinians won't be able to make their case until around the year 4000 and then only if they behave. This is in spite of the fact that, in terms of the actual blood flowing in their veins or as we would now say their genetic degrees of separation the Palestinians are more closely related to the ancient Israelites than are the Jews of the European diaspora, yes it's true there are fewer genetic degrees of separation between your average Palestinian and the ancient Hebrews of the days before the fall of the Second Temple than there are between say a German or an American Jew and those same ancient bygone Israelites, your average Palestinian mom is more Hebrew than your average Jewish mom but what the hell, why pick nits, split hairs, splice genes, even though come to think of it this makes a group like the late George Habash's Popular Front for the Liberation of Palestine less like a anti-Jewish terror outfit than like latter-day cousins of those heroic ancient Hebrews called the Zealots who had the chutzpah to try to stand their ground against the Roman imperialists and occupiers, maybe it would be better to compare the PFLP's audacious "Black September" hijacking campaign to the Zealot-led Great Revolt against the Roman occupation in years 66 to 73 AD, when the Zealots defended the Temple of Jerusalem with blood and honor and made their heroic last stand at Masada, and maybe George Habash and Leila Khaled should be acknowledged as the true descendants and heirs of Zealot military leaders like Eleazar ben Simon and Elazar ben Yair, maybe in terms of blood kinship and gene science we need to see the PFLP as more Israelite than the Israeli Defense Force and the Shin Bet but no that's quibbling, that's toying with ironies, that's playing gotcha games with what is merely empirically the case when the important thing is not what *is so* but what *must be so*, and what *must be so* is this great ingathering of Jewish people to Zion so that they can try to keep pace with these Arabs who breed like rabbits. And so the *olim* keep being shoveled in and processed in the Jewish Agency Absorption Center in Lod after they arrive at the Ben Gurion International Airport, but unfortunately after they're processed according to the techniques of scientific management some of them don't get that far in Israeli society, "get that far" functioning here as both a literal and a metaphorical expression. First the metaphorical sense, "not getting that far" in the sense of "up the ladder" of Israeli society, although to explain a metaphor with a metaphor might be a little like answering a question with a question. In Israeli society all Jews are equal but some Jews are more equal than others, the Ashkenazi Jews for example are more equal than the Sephardic Jews and the Sephardic Jews are more equal than the Mizrahi Jews, and within the class of Mizrahi Jews all are more equal than the Falash Mura the Jews from Ethiopia, there is absolutely nothing in Israel lower than an Ethiopian Jew, unless of course it is an Israeli Arab. Maybe instead of a ladder imagine a kind of totem pole of equals, a stack that's lighter at the top and darker at the bottom, you can see how it might be hard for some to move up. But we mean the expression "to not get far" in a literal sense, too, because there's a serendipitous correspondence between not getting very far up the Israeli totem-pole-of-equals and not getting out of Lod itself, after they're processed at the Jewish Agency Absorption Center a lot of the North African and Middle Eastern Jews, including a large number of the

Falashis who had been airlifted out of Ethiopia, tend to get not so much absorbed into Israeli society as bogged down in Lod, which because it's a total slum has a lot of poor Israeli Arabs and Bedouins living there too, it's about half poor Arabs and Bedouins and half poor lower-caste darker-hued Jews and they're all trapped in these drab decaying council-flat banlieues whose construction the Israeli government had once enthusiastically sponsored because they looked European instead of "Oriental," they bulldozed whole neighborhoods of Arab vernacular architecture and put up "Europeanized" council flats and when they needed room for more they built them on the abandoned vineyards and citrus and olive groves on the outskirts. After the expulsions of 1948 many of the houses of the residential neighbor-hoods were handed over wholesale to the new Jewish immigrants, whereas except for a few landmarks most of the old Arab town center was simply paved flat and built over. But so that the new inhabitants would have a place to come together and relax and chat about their lives of poverty and unemployment and discrimination and crime and drugs, the authorities made sure that a small section was left as an open space which they named Park Ha-Sha-lom – the Peace Park. And our hero is just about to arrive there, at the Park Ha-Shalom, because while we were giving you the lowdown on Lod he was tagging along by bus. Not one of the free shuttle-buses that circled from the airport hotels and car rental places and long-term parking lots to the terminals of the Ben Gurion International Airport and back, no, but a down-at-heels public bus that had rattled up to a single, bent signpost some thirty or forty yards down the sidewalk from the tinted plexiglass awning of the shuttle stop. The only other passengers, a trio of footsore Israeli-Arab hotel housekeepers heading home after their shift, sized him up as a Jewish tourist from the U.S. going into

Lod because he was either a congenital idiot or lost soul looking for narcotics. But all our hero really wanted to do was go for a walk, our peripatetic hero had gotten restless in that tiny prefab room and wanted to stretch his legs in the hours before he could present his meal voucher in the dining room, but around the hotel it was all tarmac and traffic so he thought he might as well catch a public bus instead of the airport shuttle and see if it took him somewhere different. Did it ever. Thrusting itself into the darkness of a culvert-like tunnel in the concrete buttress of an overpass, the bus emerged into harsh light and open bare fields on the other side of the airport's complex of tarmac loops and landscaped gradients. Our hero slid across the aisle to get out of the sun, pulled the window shut to block the diesel fumes, tried unsuccessfully to open the window again because it was too stuffy without the breeze, moved several more times in search of a seat that was both shaded and next to an operable window – a process complicated by the sun changing sides whenever the bus turned – at last plopping himself down in a pesso-optimistic attitude of outer resignation and inner resistance that the hotel housekeepers might have found familiar had they continued to pay any attention. After another turn the bus embarked on a long straight stretch with a wall topped by barbed wire on one side and an open irrigation ditch on the other. Our hero was on the ditch side and watched a boy poke a stick into water crudded with iridescent foam. The boy passed in an instant but the bus's distance from the billboard posted in the field beyond gave its cheerier images the illusion of moving at leisure: a colorful house and smiley-faced sun in the style of a child's crayon drawing, with Hebrew print cheerily informing those who could read it of new construction over in the exclusively-Jewish settler neighborhood of Hamat Elyashiv. With two or three seasick swayings the bus entered more densely populated streets, where the absence of sidewalks had the driver tooting his horn to scatter the small groups of women in headscarves and loose robes that seemed to brush the bus's sides as it rattled by. Out the scuffed window our hero saw shops that looked more like loading bays than retail facades – rolled-up aluminum service doors and stacks of boxes and crates, with a man in shirtsleeves sitting on a stool reading a paper and smoking, or two or three men together drinking tea and smoking. Looking up he saw the sagging crowns of untrimmed palms, television aerials and satellite dishes, stunted minarets and improvised rooftop add-ons, and the laundry-bedecked balconies of apartment blocks where every fixture and seam appeared in violation of some code or other, as if they remained standing only through an unspoken agreement not to notice that they were about to collapse. And even here where it was undeniably a neighborhood the rows of dwellings were dotted with the random ellipses of empty lots or piles of freshly-bulldozed rubble, as well as structures of uncertain status, that looked like rubble but turned out to be inhabited, or that looked intact but yawned their vacancy. The bus stopped and disgorged its passengers and took on new ones – the hotel maids had gotten off long ago – but each time our hero could still be found sweatily plastered to his seat. He had been waiting for a landmark of some kind, a site of historical or literary interest, or so at least he'd told himself because the alluring oasis of the hotel zone lingering in the back of his mind didn't jive so well with the author-adventurer book jacket image in the foreground. At last, however, our hero stumbled out across the street from a weedy, garbage-strewn lot that he had mistaken from inside the bus for a public park, but which in fact really was a public park (and a peace park, no less). He stood in a cloud of diesel exhaust, squinting from the afternoon sun in his eyes. When he pulled down the bill of his cap he saw that he had been squinting at a pair of youths who had been pacifically hanging out across the street, that is at least until this stranger had showed up and started squinting at them. While the youths inspected the stranger, the stranger inspected the puffy neon lettering of the Arabic and Hebrew graffiti on the wall next to him. While the youths rose from their bench in a leisurely fashion, the stranger looked at his feet and prodded at a syringe with his toe of his black Converse All Star. As the youths idly sauntered across the street, the stranger glanced at his watch in the manner of a person remembering an appointment, took a step first in one direction and then in the other in the manner of a person imitating a weathervane, and finally froze in the manner of a person in whom the impulse to flee is evenly matched with the impulse to play dead. By that time the shadows of the two youths and the solitary petrified stranger had intersected on the graffiti wall. The two teenagers were an Israeli Arab and an Mizrahi Jew who saw no reason not to be friends with each other because they both felt equally shat on, and at the moment they were additionally united in their unspoken intention to relieve the insane American tourist of his cap, watch, wallet, and whatever else he might happen to have on him. But when the stranger lifted his head and they saw his eyes the two friends paused. Those eyes, that our hero had inherited as the sole token of his birthright, the way some people possess only the key of the house from which their family had long ago been driven forth to wander in circles amid stones and thorns – when they saw his eyes the two friends paused, and the hands on the knives in the pockets relaxed. It would take another moment or two to place this stranger with the familiar eyes, but he was clearly someone they had met before, from the neighborhood somewhere, in a casual way, he'd probably just been out of town for a while, on a job or whatever. The young Israeli Arab was pretty sure that this was an old schoolmate of his uncle's who had been in the Ofer detention facility for the last couple of months, and the young Mizrahi Jew had him down for the dude from Ramle who used to drive a truck for his brother-in-law. Or wait, wasn't this his cousin's friend, from one of the Bedouin families they'd kicked out of Al-Mahata and forced to go live in that open sewer of Nevej Shalom? Or no, this was the guy the Nafar's didn't want marrying their daughter, because even though he'd graduated from the tech college in Beersheba he was determined to be a poet – *your words are so sweet*, the girl's mother had told him on the way to the door, *I'm surprised your mouth is not covered with ants*. Then again, you'd almost think it was Ali Abu Awaad's brother – what was his name? Yousef? – but of course he was dead. Whoever he was, the stranger nodded and shrugged his way between the two young friends, and they nodded and let him pass. Without speaking they lit new cigarettes from the pack they shared and watched his retreating figure get smaller and smaller down the pale dusty street of Lod, which once was named Lydda. He was last seen turning a corner near the old church of St. George.

$15

THE BLURBS GO HERE.
THEY LET THE READER
KNOW THAT THE NOVEL
HAS BEEN VETTED BY
INSTITUTIONAL
GATEKEEPERS. IF
SOMEBODY AT THE
DALLAS MORNING
NEWS FOUND IT
"A WHIRLWIND TOUR
DE FORCE," MAYBE
YOU WILL, TOO.

THE SYNOPSIS GOES
HERE. IT SHOULD
ANSWER BASIC
QUESTIONS ABOUT THE
NOVEL — WHO? WHAT?
WHEN? WHERE? WHY? —
IN A WAY THAT SUG-
GESTS WHAT LITERARY
GENRE IT CORRESPONDS
TO WHILE MAKING IT
SOUND AS MUCH LIKE
A MOVIE AS POSSIBLE.

THE AUTHOR BIO GOES
HERE. IT ATTESTS
TO THE WRITER'S
PROFESSIONAL
CREDENTIALS, STAMPS
THE NOVEL AS INTEL-
LECTUAL PROPERTY,
AND GENERALLY
REASSURES US THAT
THE DEATH OF THE
AUTHOR WAS JUST
AN ACADEMIC FAD.

ISBN 9780615577951

90000 >

9 780615 577951

SAY IT WITH STONES
SAYITWITHSTONES.COM

The Pitch of Failure / Until Next Time

> Literature doesn't fall from heavens, it comes to us thickly
> mediated, and those mediations are not merely "frames"
> or "contexts" but deeply braided into its very materials.
> Writing which is art – as distinct from "literary fiction" –
> is conscious of this and strains against it, against its own
> materials, and invites us to participate in that struggle,
> and its inevitable failure, and its inevitable next attempt.
>
> – Edmond Caldwell, press release for "A Dirty Bomb"

In *Human Wishes / Enemy Combatant*, Edmond Caldwell
offers us an astonishing text, one that is radical in content and
form, with a subversive mission running literally from cover to
cover, first word to last. Consider the volume's original 2012
back cover. Moving counterclockwise from top left to bottom
right, Caldwell's irreverent meta-critique commences in ALL
CAPS (see illustration opposite). *Critical Acclaim, Synopsis,
Author*: this book challenged prevailing commercial frames
for "the novel" even before the novel itself commences.

The book's double title, *Human Wishes / Enemy Combatant* similarly strains convention. How can a book have
two titles? What does it mean to call something two different names at once? *Human Wishes*? *Enemy Combatant*?
How do the two relate?

The second title is of recent mintage. Coined after the murderous blowback of 9-11-01, "Enemy Combatant" is the official
designation that enabled the U.S. government to claim legality
while detaining indefinitely those it deemed "threats to
national security", without offering them due process rights
asserted by the Geneva Conventions or the Constitution.

"Human Wishes", on the other hand, is less recent, referring to one of the great poems of Samuel Johnson, "The Vanity of Human Wishes." This mid-18th century English lyric
offers scathing tribute to the corruptive power of Money, that

"Wide-wasting Pest, that rages unconfined, / And crowds with Crimes the Record of Mankind." Caldwell found in Johnson a kindred critic of "the gen'ral Massacre of Gold":

> For Gold his Sword the Hireling Ruffian draws,
> For Gold the hireling Judge distorts the Laws;
> Wealth heaped on Wealth, nor Truth nor Safety buys,
> The Dangers gather as the Treasures Rise.

In Johnson's poem, the force of money all but guarantees a life of misery and obscurity for the true Scholar or Artist, who, at best, can hope to have their contributions recognized, once dead, often by the very foes who stomped on their life.

Edmond Caldwell was no stranger to Scholarship and Art sacrificed for Gold. His brilliant first novel, *The Chagall Position*, was rejected by all the Big House commercial publishers of fiction (some saw its genius but insisted the main character get a "sympathetic" makeover, something Edmond refused to do). Returning to college teaching in his last two years after art would not pay the bills (he had previously resigned a tenure-track position to focus on writing and raising his two sons), Edmond spent his last summer alive as a precarious adjunct at a public university beset by budget cuts, lacking assurance that he would still have work come Fall. Come September, they'd have to find someone else to teach Edmond's classes.

He died suddenly and tragically on July 31, 2017 – a devastating loss.

By Edmond's own admission, *Human Wishes / Enemy Combatant* aspired to be an anti-novel, a work that would "blow up so-called 'literary fiction' from the inside out". (138) The text pushes the form and content of the novel – home of the Bildungsroman and the Potboiler, of Developed Character and Narrative Action – to its limits, closely tracing embodied individual consciousness and experience through the fine grain of (increasingly privatized and state surveilled) "public" spaces, to the point that *individual agency* itself becomes a glaring fiction.

The book features a nameless protagonist who moves non-chronologically, through an apocryphal backstory, malingering in a series of *non-places*: highway rest stops, shopping mall bookstores, museum bathrooms, airport custom lines and baggage claim areas, hotels built solely to house those bumped from over-booked flights. In short, the kind of common areas that conventional "literary fiction" skips over to better move its protagonists towards the next plot point, but which millions of us regular folks spend our lives passing through (or trying to).

Alongside these "everyday" spaces, the book also explores the nightmarish *non-places* of CIA/NSA black sites, as well as the violently state-erased place of Lydda, Palestine (now the Israeli city of Lod), conjuring their absurd brutality in researched detail. These latter *non-places* differ from the quotidian tourist and consumer zones with which so much of the anti-novel is concerned. But the point is that these seemingly opposed realms are not so separate. In modern America the torture chambers and death squads are right next door, a state-sponsored specter that haunts and structures the hustle and bustle of everyday life. (Even shopping mall loudspeakers that once worried only of shoplifters, Caldwell reminds us, now police us all with the threat of threats to Our Way of Life.)

Further, these distinct realms shape one another. The violent displacement of the Palestinians emerges as the historical condition for the rootless wandering and perpetual insecurity which keeps our ("suspiciously Arab looking") protagonist from ever truly being at home in the world. Caldwell forces us to see these compartmentalized places as actually existing on the same Mobius strip of 21st century existence, pushing us to achieve a perspective that is adequate to this tangled global circuit.

Dominant literary conventions, in Caldwell's view, were inadequate for grasping the nature of this contemporary social reality. Thus, at a formal level, *HW / EC* takes aim at these conventions, disclosing not just their restrictive and pretentious artifice, but also their social complicity: Opening Hook & Backstory (164-5), Sympathetic Character (165), Realistic Yet Dramatic Story Plot (166), Narrative Closure and Cathartic Resolution (134), Deep Psychological Interiority & Epiphany (81). As Caldwell's protagonist reflects while studying a highway rest stop, "what was needed was *anti*-epiphany, which dissolves deconstructs and otherwise breaks down character into the ensemble of its constituents, in this case chiefly the constituents of the rest stop." (82) No mere backdrop, Setting becomes one of the novel's main characters.

Human Wishes / Enemy Combatant seeks to expose and uproot those ideologies which enable the myth of Individual Human Agency to live on despite the dawn of zombie capitalism, producing a mode of writing that takes seriously how contemporary social forces of domination make a mockery of individual freedom or autonomy, Environment determining Life more thoroughly than most of us like to admit. This unhappy revelation, that even our own "innermost thoughts" and beloved literary conventions are in bed with the military-industrial-surveillance state, might seem to court despair. But for a revolutionary communist like Edmond Caldwell – more Brecht than Beckett[1] – the point

---

[1] Edmond's final Facebook post shared Bertolt Brecht's essay, "Writing the Truth: Five Difficulties." At the time of his death, he had begun work on a new (anti-)novel tracing the apocryphal history of Samuel Beckett's life ... as a CIA agent.

of discerning the "thick mediations" and vulgar material determinations of social life and literature was not to reinforce prevailing fatalisms.

Edmond was no mere determinist. He was attuned to the exceptions to the rule as well, to those moments of rupture, those breakthrough Events when – whether through the vector of Love or Politics or Art – human beings could rise from deadwood delusions and become something ... *else*. Indeed, his outrageous, outstanding, still-unpublished first novel *The Chagall Position* provides us with a central character who is thrown back into vitality in both the realm of love and politics, after having lain dormant on both fronts – celibate and cynical – for over two decades. Set against the backdrop of rising Post-911 patriotism and the rise of the anti-immigrant Right in the American Southwest, the plot hinges on zombified high school Social Studies teacher Mr Browne, brought back to life by two events: a taboo-smashing love affair and a homeroom student rebellion catalyzed by a Latino youth who refuses to stand for the national anthem. Told in first-person retrospection, *The Chagall Position* is nonetheless a timely and radical book, deserving of renewed attention. It proves beyond doubt that Edmond Caldwell had mastered the form of realistic literary narrative that he would soon make it his task to detonate.[2]

Snapshots from "Time and Motion"

There may be no more profound example of Caldwell's

---

2 Let us also note that Edmond's struggle against the "literature establishment" was not confined to the novel. He could be found distributing his literary provocations in public places, by hand, stuffing photocopied polemics inside stacks of "One City One Story" Boston Book Festival booklets sponsored by State Street. He blogged and tweeted, but also spread leaflets in public transit stations, slid subversive bookmarks in the bestsellers at Borders Books, even wrote his own version of Jonathan Swift's "A Modest Proposal" to satirize what he saw as the slavish literary wing of the Boston gentrification establishment. And he performed it to their face: Edmond wrote *and walked* his talk.

explosive meshing of dystopian and utopian possibilities than his astonishing sixth section, "Time and Motion." The chapter is set in the Arsenal Mall, Watertown, Massachusetts, a mall built from brick buildings that were once part of the actual Watertown Arsenal: an empire-enabling arms factory that was also the site of the first recorded worker strike against the implementation of Frederick Winslow Taylor's system of Scientific Management.

Moving from the expansion of mall surveillance in the wake of 9-11 to the forced implementation of the original "Spy system" of Taylorism in 1911, the text explores the devolution of the Arsenal from a place where people once *actually made things*, to one where people now buy and sell things made elsewhere. Honoring the struggles of workers to defend the integrity of their craft, yet rejecting nostalgia – the early AFL's self-defeating racism, nationalism, sexism all come in for withering critique ("white dick privileges") – Caldwell offers a sweeping reflection on the transition from industrial class struggles of the early 20th century to the pervasive service labor and consumerism of the 21st – and what that means for literature.

His narrator lays out the stakes of the worker's defeated struggle in a single breathless sentence:

> The rule of thumb was replaced by the rule of Science and Efficiency which was really the juju-rule of war-managers, the craftsman's thumbs were cut off and made into slide rules and stopwatches and job cards for the managers and every job that was not a professional-managerial job was reduced to something that could be performed with few skills and vestigial thumb-stumps or no skills and no thumbs, the workers were turned into thumbless employees and consumers, employees on the job and consumers off the job or rather consumption everyone's second job, the imperative to consume and consume, this insatiable hunger to buy the quenchless hunger for a substitute object for the lost thumb, from the humvee and the flat-screen TV to the iPod and the Blackberry this

search for the bygone thumb, replacement objects to suck as fetishes and pacifiers, the workers reduced to sheer thumb-sucking orality, which my witty spellcheck insists on correcting to "morality", the Arsenal where the rule-of-thumb once prevailed now a shopping mall where the great-grandchildren of the rule-of-thumb craftsmen come in search of replacement objects for their bygone thumbs, haunted by a vestigial memory like the flesh-eating zombies in George Romero's movie *Dawn of the Dead*, which is set in a shopping mall. (131)

On the very next page, the text then moves to consider how the surveillance photography first pioneered by Taylor to expropriate worker know-how gets redeployed ... by the emergent film industry:

Using the very same means by which they disassembled the work-process and the workers and took away their lives they would give them back a simulacrum of their lives, they would dazzle and distract them with the ghost lives and fantasy lives by running the frames forward at the precisely-calibrated time and motion of the situation of life even though it was really just pictures in motion, or motion pictures. (132)

This reflection on film being repurposed to mask working-class alienation then prepares us for a stupendous meta-reflection on literary "realism" itself. Reminding us that the Charles River on whose banks the Watertown Arsenal Mall sits was once called the *Quinobequin*, or "Meandering One", by Native inhabitants, the narrator prompts us to reflect on the way reality is never reducible to a single fixed narrative – whatever the conquerors declare – but is rather composed of "different times different histories different strata and all still here, brimming beneath our hero's feet and looping in our hero's mind this collective unconscious of lives in labor and labor in lives."

This brings us to a powerful encapsulation of Caldwell's own impossible ambition as literary "realist". "If you were to write a truly 'realistic' novel," he writes:

> it would have to include these histories of lives in labor
> and labor in lives, each novel would have to be an
> endless *roman fleuve* of these loops and strata, each novel
> a failure because it could not possibly encompass it all,
> each novel necessarily a fragment and a failure, the only
> integrity again and again to start and to fail, each novel a
> failure and a botch and the measure of its success its
> degree of failure, its pitch of failure and abdication of
> authority ...

"But," he adds, pessimistically (no doubt drawing on the
experience around *The Chagall Position*):

> ... the publishers won't print such novels, novels must
> participate in the alienation of their time and endorse and
> reproduce the alienation of their time or else they won't be
> bought and they won't be sold, the marketplace the non-
> place where commodities are cleansed of all traces of
> work, for a commodity to be a successful commodity and
> especially the commodity called 'literary fiction' it must
> efface history and efface labor, every trace. (134)

Bear in mind that this entire searing "aside" takes place
as our nameless hero himself meanders, browsing a cliché-
ridden, "critically acclaimed" bestseller (Claire Messud's
The Emperor's Children) in a B. Dalton mall bookstore.
Contra such commodified "literary fiction" and the dictates
of its mystifying market-friendly "soft cops" (personified
absurdly throughout *HW / EC* by the recurrent specter of
New Yorker reviewer James Wood)[3], Caldwell offers a
meandering literary realism that refuses to efface the his-

---

3 In the margins of his personal copy of James Wood's *How Fiction
Works*, where Wood generalizes that "the reader is happy enough to efface
the labor of the writer in order to believe two further fictions: that the
narrator was somehow 'really there' [...] and that narrator is not really the
writer" (JW, 55), Edmond jotted the following: "for Wood it [literature]
should dissimulate, *not* draw attention to its procedures." On the next page,
Caldwell further mocked Wood's dictum regarding literature's
"disappearing style," jotting: "efface the labor – like a commodity."

tory and the intellectual and social labor that shapes the world, be it the idiosyncratic musings and gastro-intestinal perturbations of the "Little Wayfarer," or the systematic, collective pains of the toiling and expropriated masses whose thumbs and bones lie buried beneath the shining tile of the shopping mall floors.

But Caldwell manages still more. Against the tyranny of Taylorized work-life and literature, the text offers "heretical" reading as site of radical hope. Edmond brings the section home with his riotous reflection on his protagonist's youthful "misreading" of George Orwell's *Animal Farm*, a recollection which forms the basis for an important vision of literary resistance:

> His favorite book as a teenager and the one responsible for making him into a radical maladjusted word-nut was his favorite because he had misread it and misinterpreted it, didn't get the orthodox meaning but made up a heterodox one instead, it was the apocryphal heretical interpretation that shaped his mind and misshaped his mind, this book which clearly teaches that any and all efforts at radical collective self-organization lead always and everywhere to butchery and tyranny because of our fallen and brutish natures and that one way or another we're always going to have bosses over us because it's nature, human nature, by what sinister kink in his own brutish nature did our hero manage to screw up and extract the exact opposite meaning, wrest sick optimism from salutary pessimism, as if this book were just pointing out pitfalls to be avoided the next time we rose up and Kill the Pigs, because to his misshapen mind there would always be a next time and maybe next time because of this book we'd have a better idea which Pigs to Kill. (150)

The setting – a mall food court – laces the coming insurrection with irony; but revolutionary possibilities proliferate, despite the junk food:

> And maybe it's just because of the mild buzz from the soda on his otherwise empty stomach that our hero in the food

court of the Watertown Arsenal Mall now feels that there might be hope after all, the modern world has to be more than just a Taylorized conveyor-belt stuffing mass-produced trash into the open maws of mindless thumbless mall-zombies because he possesses this example from his own life this living example of a text conveyed to him by his Taylorized education which he'd digested in his own way, turned to his own account, whose prescribed and orthodox meaning he had subverted, maybe such opportunities for subversive appropriation are available to us everywhere, cracks in the armor of the big machine, fissures, gaps, opportunities to be seized, maybe every text of pessimism and despair can yield up subtexts of wild subversion [...] perhaps even here, yea here, in this food court in the Watertown Arsenal Mall where a hundred years ago the molders and machinists rose up against the Taylor method but because they had only been defending their AFL craft privileges and their white dick privileges they had failed, maybe their grandchildren their great-great-grandchildren would get it right one day [...] never know when the white proles and black proles and brown roles stuffing Cinnabons into their mouths out of cardboard containers and licking their fingers might rise up in a body and sugar-rush next door into Foot Locker and Lady Foot Locker to grab the heaviest boots off the racks shouting *Kick the Bosses in the Ass, Power to the Working Class!* (150-2)

For Edmond, the system, despite its *totalitaylorist* aspirations, would never be able to purge such "sinister kinks" so long as texts and readers subvert their teacher's managerial training. Just as capitalism's ceaseless revolutionizing would always produce contradiction and crisis: *there would always* be *a next time* to prepare for. And in that, there was hope.

But let's be clear: Not *hope* as a metaphysical savior that allows us to relax into a spectator's faith that things will turn out alright. Rather, Caldwellian hope is an injunction to scrutiny, to pay even more close attention to the texts of the world around us, in its never-ceasing circuit of people pressed to the rotors by the stolen monster thumbs of Capital. Such hope demands vigilance, study, and struggle to discern the cracks and gaps and fissures, so that we can be better prepared for the *next* revolutionary opportunity. Indeed, just about any chapter of *HW / EC* can be productively read as a box of tools to prod and sharpen a range of all-terrain subversive reading practices – always with an eye on *next time*.

*

The last time I saw Edmond was at his 56th birthday party, just weeks before his death. At the close of that intimate summer evening in Lynn Bennett's apartment, as if channeling his nameless protagonist at the end of "Time and Motion" (152-3), Edmond and I burst out singing the workers' "Internationale," our spirits buoyed by the sugary bliss not of mall soda and Cinnabons but scotch and Lynn's homemade chocolate raspberry tarts. Edmond and I did what we could with the red anthem there in that kitchen close to midnight, much to our beloved partners' amusement. No sooner had we finished the attempt than Edmond was planning for an improved reprise. *"Next time,"* he exclaimed, *"we'll blast the roof off the ruling class!"*

Next time.

Edmond passed me my personal copy of his neglected masterpiece, *Human Wishes / Enemy Combatant*, from the cluttered trunk of his parked car, following a poetry event at the Center for Marxist Education in Central Square, Cambridge, Massachusetts.[4] Since his passing, and the closing of Say It With Stones Press, some copies of this precious text have gratefully remained in circulation (thanks to the efforts

4 One of the organizers of that *Scrutiny* poetry series was Boyd Nielson. Together, we co-authored "Tribute to Edmond Caldwell" published in *Dispatches from the Poetry Wars*.

of Catherine Caldwell-Harris). But in recent years, for those without a connection to Edmond's close friends and family, the book has become difficult to obtain.

Thankfully now, with the thrilling republication of *Human Wishes / Enemy Combatant* by Grand Iota, the promise of Edmond's *next time* can be extended, in time and space, to all those who will be able to read this astonishing work for themselves.

Joseph G Ramsey
January 2022

Also available from grand**IOTA**

APROPOS JIMMY INKLING
Brian Marley
978-1-874400-73-8 318pp

WILD METRICS
Ken Edwards
978-1-874400-74-5 244pp

BRONTE WILDE
Fanny Howe
978-1-874400-75-2 158pp

THE GREY AREA
Ken Edwards
978-1-874400-76-9 328pp

PLAY, A NOVEL
Alan Singer
978-1-874400-77-6 268pp

THE SHENANIGANS
Brian Marley
978-1-874400-78-3 220pp

SEEKING AIR
Barbara Guest
978-1-874400-79-0 218pp

JOURNEYS ON A DIME: SELECTED STORIES
Toby Olson
978-1-874400-80-6 300pp

BONE
Philip Terry
978-1-874400-81-3 150pp

GREATER LONDON: A NOVEL
James Russell
978-1-874400-82-2 276pp

THE MAN WHO WOULD NOT BOW & OTHER STORIES
Askold Melnyczuk
978-1-874400-83-7 196pp

ROSS HALL
Andrew Key
978-1-874400-84-4 270pp

Production of this book has been made possible with the help of the following individuals and organisations who subscribed in advance:

Julia Aizuss
Joseph Albernaz
Alison's Poetry Commissions
Rees Arnott-Davies
Bethany Aylward
Thomas Beamont
David Bell
Jack Belloli
David Bierling
Charles D Blanton
Paul Bream
Andrew Brewerton
Ian Brinton
Jasper Brinton
Peter Brown
Eleanor Burch
Thomas Bury
Sean Canzone
Daniel Chedgzoy
Alice Christensen
Claire Crowther
Croydon Candles
David Currell
Daniel Daly
Kester Davies
Darragh Deighan-Gregory
Adam Dransfield
John Dunn
Hannah Ehrlinspiel
Andrew Elrod
Andrew Everitt
Allen Fisher/Spanner
Emily Fitzell
Val Fox
Donald Futers
Laura Gill
Jim Goar
Joey Goldman
Giles Goodland
Penny Grossi
Charles Hadfield

John Hall
Andrew Hamilton
LiHe Han
Daniel Hartley
Tom Hastings
Randolph Healy
Simon Horton
Kristoffer Jacobson
Richy & Gill Johnson
Laura Joyce
Christopher Kelly
James Key
Lindy Key
Danny King
Sharon Kivland
Scott Lavery
Monroe Lawrence
Katie Leacock
Johanna Linsley
Frances Madeson
Richard Makin
Michael Mann
Adriana Marshall
Ian Maxton
Tim MacGabhann
Clem McCulloch
Cameron McLachlan
Rod Mengham
Hollie Middleton
China Mieville
Jeremy Millar
Jenny Montgomery
Vijay Nair
Paul Nightingale
Jeremy Noel-Tod
Colm O'Brien
James O'Brien
Toby Olson
Catherine O'Sullivan
Flora Paterson
Sean Pemberton

Hestia Peppe
Willem Pije
Samuel Ramsey
Samuel Regan-Edwards
Will Rene
Asa Roast
Ethan Robinson
Mike Robinson
David Rose
Lou Rowan
Hannah Rowley
James Russell
Steven Seidenberg
Pablo Seoane
Kashif Sharma-Patel
Alan Singer
Valerie Soar
Sean Sokolov
Stryker Spurlock
Andrew Spragg
Joel Stagg
Kyle Stern
Daniel Straw
Alicia Suriel Melchor
Emma Townshend
Tom Veale
visual associations
Alex Rhys Wakefield
Melanie Walsh
Alex Walton
Wash & Dry Productions
Brendan White
Eley Williams
Tom Witcomb
Kate Wood
Patrick Wright
Edward Yates
Clare Young
Bryan Zubalsky
+ I anon

www.grandiota.co.uk

Lightning Source UK Ltd.
Milton Keynes UK
UKHW012111280122
397883UK00003B/244

9 781874 400851